HYMNs IN BLOOD

Advance Praise for *Hymns in Blood*

'Nanak Singh has long held a prominent place in the history of the Punjabi novel; the ink in his pen is propelled by Punjabiyat—that extraordinary shared identity, defying religion and binding this side to that, refusing to be severed by the border that now runs through Punjab. *Hymns in Blood* may be a work of fiction, but it is also a record of Singh's memory, his eyewitness account, a story inspired by people he knows and loves, a traumatic history that he has survived. And though it is a novel about the partitioning of land, it is equally about the significance of friendship and community, love and sacrifice. Sensitive and rich, it embodies the spirit of undivided Punjab, and seventy-five years on, serves not only as historical narrative, but also as a timely reminder of the consequences of manmade divisions. Navdeep Suri's translation of his grandfather's oeuvre celebrates the particular parlance and intentional cadence of the age that Nanak Singh wrote in and of.'

—**Aanchal Malhotra**, author of *Remnants of a Separation: A History of the Partition through Material Memory*

'Suri's translation of Singh's stunning classic is a breath of fresh air. In an era of great political upheaval, where violence, love, and steadfast loyalty co-exist, Singh captures the unbreakable bonds of an interfaith chosen family, and the power and grace of humanity. The world has never needed this luminous novel more.'

—**Anjali Enjeti**, author of *The Parted Earth*

'Heartbreaking and poignant, Nanak Singh's deeply felt novel, written in the immediate aftermath of the Partition of 1947 carries the raw stamp of an intensely felt and lived tragedy which broke apart not only two countries but also hearts, relationships, friendships, homes and trust. In these difficult times it serves as a stark reminder not only of what we have lost, but also what we lived through and what gave us hope.'

—**Urvashi Butalia**, author of *The Other Side of Silence: Voices from the Partition of India*

HYMNS IN BLOOD

NANAK SINGH

Translated from the Punjabi by

NAVDEEP SURI

HARPERPERENNIAL

An Imprint of HarperCollins Publishers

First published in English in India by Harper Perennial 2022
An imprint of HarperCollins *Publishers*
4th Floor, Tower A, Building No. 10, Phase II, DLF Cyber City,
Gurugram, Haryana – 122002
www.harpercollins.co.in

2 4 6 8 10 9 7 5 3 1

Copyright © Kulwant Singh Suri
First published in Punjabi as *Khoon de Sohile* in 1948
by Lok Sahitya Prakashan, Amritsar
This English translation © Navdeep Suri 2022

P-ISBN: 978-93-5489-742-9
E-ISBN: 978-93-5489-743-6

Typeset in 11.5/16 Adobe Jenson Pro at
Manipal Technologies Limited, Manipal

Printed and bound at
Thomson Press (India) Ltd

To my father
For that boundless love which touched so many hearts

Khoon ke sohile gaviai Nanak rat ka kungu pae ve laalo

*The paeans of blood are sung, O Nanak, and blood is
sprinkled in place of saffron*

—GURU GRANTH SAHIB [722]

Foreword

Nanak Singh

A S I START writing these lines today, I have this gnawing pain in my gut—a feeling of futility about everything that I have read or written since 1929. Everything's gone down the drain. My dreams of seeing this country stand tall and united have crumbled into dust. My eyes—yes, the same ones that had witnessed Hindus and Muslims and Sikhs sip from the same glass of water—are mute spectators to the carnage unfolding before us. They have seen brothers drink each other's blood. How I wish the good Lord had closed these eyes forever, spared them the trauma of having to see what they have seen!

One short year. That's all it took to bring our nation to this calamity. Who could have imagined it?

And surely, it is nothing but sheer mulishness on my part that I am using this book to bring Muslims and non-Muslims on the same page at a time when people consider it foolhardy to even mention both in the same sentence. I won't be surprised if some of my readers find this book swimming against the prevailing currents, but there is nothing that I can do about it. It feels like I am being compelled, that there is some strange and powerful force at work—a force that is driving me, driving my conscience and driving my pen to write this.

But what lies behind this compulsion of mine?

Maybe it was this picture imprinted in my eyes, one that will continue to shine bright till the day that the shadow of death arrives to cast a pall around it. An image of my beautiful and vibrant Punjab, which I have not just seen with my eyes but also experienced with my soul. Much of my childhood and youth were spent in a milieu where the Muslim and non-Muslim communities lived in complete harmony; where they didn't just live as peaceful neighbours but were ready to sacrifice their lives for their neighbours' sake; where every plate of food and glass of water was shared.

Pieces of that picture lie shattered around me today, and this novel is an attempt to show my readers some of those pieces. But this book isn't just a novel; it is a reflection of the ache in my heart, the scream from the very pits of my stomach, the wail from the depths of my soul. In writing this book, my pen has relied on the tears flowing from my eyes as much as it has on the ink from my inkpot.

Everyone around me speaks of the numbers. How many Sikhs have been massacred; how many Hindus have been killed; how many Muslims have been slaughtered. But for this unfortunate writer, the biggest casualty was humanity itself. How does it matter if the victim has the long hair of the Sikh, the shikha of the Hindu or the circumcision of the Muslim? The blood coursing through their veins is the same colour of red, the tears flowing from their eyes have the same salt. Try as I might, I haven't been able to discern any difference in the grief-stricken wails of a Hindu, a Sikh or a Muslim mother as she cradles the lifeless body of her son.

Ah! Which evil eye has cursed our blessed land to shatter the unity of our people into so many fragments? Who brought the embers of discord in our midst to unleash flames that haven't just devoured decades of peace and amity but also brought the fires of Hell to our very doorstep?

How did this happen and who was responsible? Was there a hidden force that caused this unprecedented destruction? There is no short or easy answer to these questions and I would request my readers to be patient and take the time to read these ten or twelve extra pages before I commence the novel itself.

Many of my countrymen would regard 1947 as an auspicious year, one that would usher in the long-awaited independence to India. But to me, this was an accursed year for our country. Our conception of an unbroken, undivided India that had evolved over centuries crumbled to dust before our very eyes. And the cause of this destruction wasn't some foreigner—we, our own people, were responsible.

Of course, the devil that is usually blamed for this catastrophe is the Angrez; his devious stratagem is often called the Two-Nation Theory, a poisonous seed that quietly germinated inside Mr Jinnah's brain before emerging in the form of the demand for 'Pakistan'.

Pakistan! Who would have thought this bizarre demand for Pakistan would end up breaking our country and dragging our society to such depths? Who knew that the blood flowing from the birth of Pakistan would turn our land crimson? Who would have imagined that my fellow Indians—brothers who had lived next to each other for generations—would lust for each other's blood? Who could have even dreamt that Indians—the same ones who remembered Iqbal's 'Saare Jahan se Accha', the ones who passionately sang the refrain 'Indians we are and India is our land'—those same Indians would unsheathe their swords and daggers to behead their brethren? Who would believe that the gods and angels of this ancient land would strip one another's daughters and sisters naked and dishonour them in public? That they would loot and burn tens of thousands of homes and leave their inhabitants to face the elements without a roof on their heads?

Ah! How I wish this accursed year of 1947 had never emerged, that our country had been spared the death and destruction that it wrought!

'India's become independent!' I hear these cries of celebration all around me. Yes, India is free from the clutches of the British. But did we care to think of the exorbitant price that we have paid for this independence? Let some of the statistics speak for themselves. Some four lakhs or maybe even five lakhs killed by knives and swords, bullets and bombs; around two crores rendered homeless and facing untold hardship as refugees in distant lands; seventy or eighty thousand girls and women abducted and vanished without a trace; around one and a half lakh men and women forced to change their religion; wealth and property to the tune of around two thousand crore rupees burnt or destroyed; and perhaps around five thousand crores rupees worth of silver, gold and jewels looted.

These are the barebone estimates of the price that we have paid for our country's independence. But beyond that, think of the intangibles! We have lost our invaluable sense of humanity, our territorial unity, our fraternal ties. Aren't these also a part of that price?

Maybe we should have risked everything in a direct confrontation with the mighty British empire. Like Stalingrad, it might have left half our population dead or wounded on the battlefield and reduced our cities to rubble. Maybe we would have lost the battle and maybe we would have died fighting and maybe we would have been left penniless. But we would have preserved our humanity and our sense of national identity. Where is the humanity of those sons of Mother India today when they display these ghastly garlands fashioned out of the mutilated breasts of women? Where did our sense of national unity take flight when the warm embrace between brothers became a sword at the neck, a knife in the back? We are raping our own sisters, setting fires to our homes with our own matches, breaking into our chests and trunks with our own hammers.

'The Angrez are brutal ... the British are malicious ... the British are satanic rulers who control us through a Divide and Rule policy...' We have been narrating these stories in our country for two hundred years. But think about it—should we blame the British or should we also dwell upon the blindness of the Indian? The one who walked with the lamp of liberty for two hundred years and still stumbled into the abyss with his eyes wide open.

The British did exactly what was expected of them, one would be foolish to expect anything else from a foreign ruler. The fault lies in our own mentality; even after two centuries of experience with British machinations, we were unable to evade the trap they laid for us.

For three quarters of a century, hundreds of thousands of patriots rallied under the banner of the Congress to wage a non-violent campaign that eventually defeated a power as mighty and cunning as the British empire. But did we really think that they would accept the verdict honourably, pack their bags and sail back to England? If he were to behave honourably, he wouldn't be called the Angrez, now would he? No sir! He had one final move up his sleeve and when he played that move on the chessboard of Indian politics, we saw our winning hand turn into crushing defeat.

And what was this diabolical move? To pull back all his pieces and push forward a pawn called Jinnah. This was like offering to kill the snake poised on your enemy's chest. If the blow kills the snake, you profit. And if it kills the enemy, you profit still.

On one hand, Independence was finally knocking on India's door. And on the other, you had Mr Jinnah beating his little drum and shouting 'Pakistan! Pakistan!' at the top of his voice, even as he practised the dictum 'We won't play, and neither will we let you play.' One side was chanting slogans of Akhand Bharat while the other was conspiring to carve up the country into pieces. And while the British embarked on the charade of inviting the parties to set up an interim government as a first step in the transition to full independence, the Muslim League stepped up its own campaign. Its shrill cries for Pakistan were now accompanied by dire threats of violence.

The British had been working for a while to prepare a fairly detailed plan to accord dominion status to India, but each attempt to move forward was thwarted by Jinnah's insistence on Pakistan. Some of the country's finest political minds grappled with this conundrum but failed to come up with a viable solution.

The Congress leaders tried to placate Mr Jinnah with a series of concessions in the hope of keeping the country together, only to face disappointment after each meeting. Jinnah's demands kept growing and his jaws appeared to open ever wider to swallow each offer of compromise. The structure of an interim government was ready, but couldn't get moving until the representation of the Muslim League in the government was settled. From Lord Wavell and Lord Mountbatten to Pandit Nehru—everyone tried their best. Even a great leader like Mahatma Gandhi took the initiative to personally go across and meet Jinnah. But like a novice drummer's monosyllabic rhythm, Jinnah was stuck on his 'I will not accept; I will never accept' refrain.

With no resolution in sight, the British government resolved to get around the intransigence of the Muslim League with an announcement on 15 August 1946 inviting the Congress to form the interim government. Jinnah's storm troopers responded with unrestrained fury. Muslim League leaders across the length and breadth of India started to deliver incendiary speeches that often ended with chants calling for 'Direct Action'. You may have thought that this was just a moment of insanity, but when a Direct Action Day was announced, you could see it take a menacing shape before our very eyes. Sure enough, the first round of this infernal cannon was fired in Calcutta by none other than Huseyn Suhrawady, prime minister of the Bengal Council. A week of relentless violence left the streets of the metropolis littered with corpses. Some twenty thousand persons were killed and around fifty thousand left wounded. The damage to property alone was estimated at around ninety crore rupees.

But the embers of the communal fire ignited in Calcutta didn't remain confined to the city. Fanned by the inflammatory speeches of Suhrawady and Jinnah acolytes, the flames rapidly spread to Assam, Delhi, Dhaka, Bombay, Nagpur and Noakhali. They engulfed Bihar and scorched the United Provinces before entering our land, Punjab.

The Muslim League had intended to use their Direct Action campaign and its accompanying spectre of communal violence as a political tactic to scare the country's non-Muslim population, and to gain additional leverage over the Congress. But it turned out to be a double-edged sword and the ravenous flames of religious passion didn't feed on the non-Muslims alone; they also turned towards the Muslim community and consumed many of them. The attacks on Hindus in Bengal were avenged against Muslims in Bihar; the Frontier Province settled scores for Bihar, and Punjab retaliated against the violence in the Frontier Province. Death and destruction were spreading through the country and every attack and counter-attack stripped away a layer of compassion from the soul of India. Young men were being killed for no fault of theirs and mothers around the country were grieving their loss, but Mr Jinnah was unmoved; each conflagration seemed to make him harder, more implacable.

The Congress leadership, meanwhile, had accepted the invitation from the British, and on 1 September 1946, an interim government, headed by the Congress, assumed formal charge. The Muslim League also formally announced its decision to boycott the government, adding fuel to the communal riots raging across several states. The result was entirely predictable. The interim government failed to get off the ground, and the expanding circle of violence led the British to renew their efforts to broker a compromise between the Congress and the Muslim League. But Jinnah remained adamant, and the stalemate continued.

Jinnah's obduracy eventually forced the Congress to bend. Senior leaders of the Congress who had resolutely proclaimed that 'there would be no negotiations with Mr Jinnah until he gave up his demand for Pakistan' now started to sing a different tune. To be perfectly honest, they surrendered to Jinnah's will by accepting his claim for 'Pakistan' and burying forever their own dream of an Undivided India.

But let's move on and turn our attention to the state of affairs in our own province of Punjab, where another battle was taking place—this one between the Muslim League and the coalition government. The League was desperate to head the government in the Punjab, but had failed to achieve its ambition. The formation of a coalition government in Lahore meant that Jinnah's desire to see the Islamic banner unfurl across the state remained a mirage. Neither the Sikh leaders nor the Hindus were so naive as to take Jinnah's promises at face value and extend their support to the League. Gruesome stories of the havoc wrought by Muslim League zealots on the Hindu and the Sikh communities in towns and cities across Alanabad, Pothohar and the Frontier Province were still too raw to contemplate such a thought. The League had mobilized hordes of poor and uneducated peasants in the name of Islam and incited them to go on a rampage against the non-Muslim minorities in these regions. Their homes looted and destroyed, thousands of Hindu and Sikh families had been forced to leave their ancestral lands to join caravans of refugees snaking across the countryside towards the relative security of eastern Punjab.

The concessions and assurances being offered by Jinnah to the Hindu and Sikh leaders in lieu of their support for a Muslim League government in Lahore were categorically rejected. The actions of the Muslim League towards the minorities spoke louder than its words. There was no way that the Hindus and the Sikhs would accept a subservient status under a party that had already revealed its true colours.

The swearing in of Malik Khizar Hayat as chief minister of a coalition government supported by the Congress and Akali Dal sent a wave of anger through the Muslim League. They decided to move heaven and earth in opposing the coalition, launching a campaign of civil disobedience and even threatening Direct Action.

For the satanic cabal of the League, Punjab was now the stage where they could perform their diabolical campaign to sow chaos and unrest. Laws were broken with impunity, and it wasn't until their gangs started to board trains without tickets and rob unsuspecting passengers that the government machinery started to rouse itself from its slumber. The Muslim National Guard was declared an unlawful organization and several senior League leaders from the Punjab, including Sir Firoz Khan Noon, Nawab Mamdot, Begum Shahnawaz, Shaukat Hayat and others, were placed under arrest. But if the government expected the Leaguers to back off, it was sadly mistaken. Their agitation started to acquire a menacing character even as they stepped up their Direct Action campaign against the Khizar government.

It was perhaps too much to expect the feckless Khizar Hayat to stand firm amidst these swirling currents. As demonstrations against his government spread from Punjab to the neighbouring Frontier Province, Hayat beat a hasty retreat by removing all restrictions on the activities of the Muslim National Guard and ordering the release of the League leaders. And if we needed any further evidence of his pusillanimity, he provided it by going across to the governor on 1 March 1947 to unceremoniously tender his letter of resignation.

The reactions were quite predictable—jubilant celebrations among the Leaguers and a wave of anger and disappointment among the Hindu and the Sikh communities. Master Tara Singh joined several Hindu and Sikh leaders at the Assembly Hall in Lahore on 4 March to shout 'Death to Pakistan!' and other similar slogans. Later on the same day, a huge crowd of Hindus and Sikhs gathered at the Guru ka Bagh grounds in Amritsar and swore that they would lay down their lives to prevent a Muslim League government from being foisted upon them. That gathering also came up with a chilling new slogan:

> *If it's Pakistan that you want*
> *It's the graveyard that we grant!*

Khizar's letter of resignation had clearly opened a Pandora's box in Punjab. The furtive manner in which it was delivered gave rise to all manner of speculation and the air was rife with conspiracy theories.

As the sun rose on 5 March, its rays glistened on the crimson hues of blood that had been shed on the pious earth of Amritsar. For the first time since anyone could remember, the people of Punjab turned upon their own brothers. What an irony that it happened to be Holi! The festival of colours was being celebrated in the most macabre fashion with the blood of friends and neighbours!

It would be no exaggeration to say that this accursed day of Holi, on 5 March 1947, marked the beginning of sectarian violence in Punjab. The riots quickly spiralled into an unending cycle of attack and counter-attack, prompting the governor to invoke Section 93 and assume direct control of the government.

The reins of the government, of course, were always in the hands of the British. But did they do anything to stem the tide of violence? To halt the rivers of blood that had started to flow alongside the five rivers of the Punjab? No, sir. They had always wanted to create chasms between the people of India, and were secretly pleased to see their plans come to fruition. This was evident in the way Jinnah was propped up as a leader who would campaign for the division of India. Didn't the astute British rulers know the consequences that would follow when they drew up plans for the partition of Punjab and Bengal? Of course they did! How could we have expected them to stop the sectarian riots spreading like wildfire across the Punjab? The blood of innocent victims was coagulating into clumps of mud as it flowed down the grimy streets and bazaars. A wave of shootings, stabbings, bombs and arson was turning thriving neighbourhoods into rubble. But who cared? Certainly not the one who was busy packing his own bags to leave the country.

The tempest of sectarian violence continued to sweep across the Punjab for weeks and the death toll kept mounting. But Governor Mr Jenkins, that self-righteous captain of the ship of our state, seemed utterly oblivious to the carnage around him. Yes, the very same governor, who would crack the whip if the ceremonial dagger of the Sikh exceeded the prescribed length, was now presiding over a state where bombs, rifles and pistols had become as commonplace as bricks and stones. Wah! What a governor we have! You saw all this happening around you and turned a blind eye to everything.

And it wasn't just Jenkins who was asleep at the wheel. So were Mr Bennet, the Inspector General of Police, and General Rees, the Supreme Commander of the Punjab Boundary Force. They were all cast from the same mould. From the junior-most man to the highest official—the British all seemed to have the same approach, 'Observe but take no action; mind your own business.'

These are the same high and mighty rulers who were making tall declarations before the sectarian violence started. 'We will not tolerate a single drop of blood being shed on the land of the Punjab ... We will impose martial law and crush the heads of the hooligans ... We will sacrifice our own lives to maintain law-and-order in the state...' At that stage, the declarations weren't mere words; they were also accompanied by a show of force, with the armed forces displaying their formidable squadrons of fighter aircraft and tanks to send a clear message to the public. But when the time came, those brash declarations turned out to be a damp squib. For months on end, sectarian flames raged unabated. They consumed one neighbourhood after another, one town after another. Every bazaar, every street had its own stack of corpses providing eloquent testimony to the collapse of law and order. But where were the fighter planes and the tanks meant to instil fear into the hearts of the rampaging mobs? Maybe the planes and the tanks had rusted while waiting for orders; or maybe their pilots and drivers had vanished into thin air. God alone knows the truth.

Why did this happen? Why did the senior officials present at the scene remain so quiescent? Was it because those dying were mere Indians? Had senior British officials shown such deceit, such apathy and such blatant disregard towards human life in any other country, I am sure they would have faced the hangman's noose. It wouldn't have mattered whether their names were Jenkins, Bennet or Rees.

So that was the backdrop for a particularly gruesome drama for which the Punjab provided the stage.

This novel was written in those desperate times when our country seemed to be playing a game of blood and fire, when the Muslim League had become a pawn on the English chessboard, when the League's actions had forced the non-Muslim communities of the Frontier Province and the adjacent district of Rawalpindi to flee their ancestral lands, and when this pestilence of ethnic cleansing was also spreading into eastern Punjab.

In its initial part, the novel is set in a small village on the banks of the Soan river in the Pothohar area near Rawalpindi. The different communities of this village have always lived in harmony as members of one large family, ready to sacrifice their own lives to protect their neighbours. The story that I narrate isn't merely the product of a writer's imagination, nor is it based on hearsay alone. It reflects characters and events that I know personally or about which I learned from the direct experiences of some of my close friends.

As I make this humble attempt to recount the tragedy of Punjab to my readers, I readily concede that I cannot claim to be a historian. I am also aware that eminent historians will look closely at the events that unfolded to piece together an authoritative account of this period. But I am impelled to write this book because of a fear that the prevailing climate of sectarian hatred might sway the narrative in a particular direction. A Hindu or a Sikh writer may not be able to do full justice in presenting both sides of the picture. Or a Muslim author may present a picture that exaggerates the violence perpetrated by Hindus and Sikhs, even as it glosses over the carnage wrought by the Muslims. About my own attempt in this novel, I can only say that I have done my best to stay impartial. I have not hesitated from bringing out the misdeeds of any sect or community that has transgressed.

A novel cannot claim to be a strictly historical narrative, nor is a novelist expected to weave all relevant historical incidents into his story. A novelist has the license to maintain the flow of the story by abbreviating some incidents, even as he expands on others, all the while trying to stay true to the essential facts.

I would accordingly request that my readers neither place this book in the fiction category nor see it as a historical text. They could, perhaps, see it as a novel based on historical events, a story that flows naturally between the two banks of imagination and reality.

Amritsar
20 February 1948

HYMNS IN BLOOD

A tree of love starts to blossom

A LIVELY HALF-MOON was playing a gentle game of hide-and-seek with a mass of grey clouds, its lovely silhouette ducking behind the dark curtain before appearing suddenly to reveal the outline of a small village. But only for a minute or two before sneaking behind the curtain and leaving the village hidden beneath the shadows of the night. It was midway into the second quarter of the night and the deserted lanes of the village were in deep slumber, the silence broken only by sounds emerging from the open grounds—the exuberant voices of girls singing in unison, their songs blending with the rhythm of their dancing feet and floating gently into the sleeping village. The only other sound was the soft murmur of the Soan river as it flowed besides the village, its girth swollen to twice its usual size by the bountiful rains.

It was late July. The sky was overcast and the cool breeze was fanning the joyful energy of the maidens. The evening had seen a bit of a drizzle and that unique monsoonal fragrance from the moist earth permeated the air. The younger girls had broken up into pairs, each one crossing arms in front of her like a pair of scissors, clasping her partner's hands and getting ready for a game of kikkli. She would start with the folk song, '*Kikkli Kaleer di, te pag mere veer di...*' and soon, the duo would start spinning like a top. Round and round they would go, gathering speed with each twirl, laughing and singing and spinning until one would get so dizzy she would stumble or fall. Did that hurt? Who cares, when you are under the intoxicating charm of the game!

The older girls were in an equally boisterous mood. Away from the prying eyes of men and inebriated by the magic of the moment, they shed their inhibitions and sang with full-throated abandon. The fields soon resonated with melodies about the joy of meeting one's beloved and about the sorrow of separation, songs that tugged at the heartstrings of the young women. The most powerful, though, were the songs about the newly wed brides who had gone off to the distant homes of their husbands and were pining for the familiarity of their own village, remembering not just its lanes and alleys but even its little puppies and kittens.

The revelry continued for a while longer but was beginning to taper off as the night's second quarter came to an end and the third one was ushered in. The young women started to become conscious of the late hour, and of their own vulnerable age and situation. Tunics were buttoned up and dupattas were retrieved to cover the bosoms. Their youthful faces were flushed with exhaustion and beads of sweat were glistening on their foreheads.

The peals of laughter subsided, and the melodies started to fade into the silence. They were being replaced by voices that seemed both worried and annoyed. 'My mother-in-law will start barking at me the moment she sees me ... I didn't even tell my aunt I would be away ... My mother had told me to place the dung cakes under the big pot, but I completely forgot … I hope the cat hasn't polished off the milk by now…'

'Let's go! It is past midnight and we'll be in trouble,' said one. The lively group dispersed within a matter of minutes as the girls started to head back towards their homes.

The half-moon had again parted the clouds and was shining bright on the maidan. An ancient peepul tree stood in the middle of the open field as moonlight weaved its way through its dense foliage to create thousands of intricate patterns of light and shade on the ground.

One of these illuminated spots revealed a slender form leaning against the trunk of the peepul tree. From a distance, her body seemed to be wrapped in the same intricate patterns, giving it a particularly attractive aura.

The girl wouldn't have been much older than thirteen or fourteen. Her slim frame nestling against the huge girth of the peepul gave the appearance that it had been painted by an artist who had only used the moonlight and the shadows of the night as his palette.

How long had she been standing here? How did she manage to dodge her friends and stay back, alone and fearless, when they were returning to the safety of their homes? Were any of her friends aware that she had quietly snuck away?

Her fair skin and innocent face were lit up by large, luminous eyes that were anxiously scanning the horizon, impatiently waiting for someone. Her expression reflected a constant ebb and flow of emotions, changing within moments from a sense of anticipation to one of anxiety. Tired of standing, she would sit for a while on the old stump of an acacia tree, before getting up quickly to hide again in the shadows of the peepul lest someone should see her alone at such a late hour.

The lines of anxiety etched deeper and deeper on the girl's face and her impatience grew with every false alarm. Finally, a hint of a smile appeared, suggesting that her vigil might be coming to an end. A light blush spread over her delicate features as she saw a shadow hurry towards her.

'I thought you must have left with the girls,' a boy of fifteen or sixteen blurted, as he came up to her and grasped her hand. 'I don't want to talk to you,' the girl replied, snatching her hand back. Turning her face away from his, she remonstrated, 'Half the night has gone by waiting for you; my legs have turned to stone standing here for such a long time.'

There was something about the boy's garb that belied his rustic roots and carried a whiff of the city-dweller. Instead of the usual slippers, he wore an inexpensive pair of shoes. The customary flowing tahmat around the waist was replaced by a creased pair of pyjamas, while a plaid Ludhiana jacket conveyed a hint of prosperity. He had a lean but muscular physique and a face that still reflected his adolescence, a wispy darkness above his lip only adding to his attractive visage. Although his countenance and his restless blue eyes alluded to a certain turbulence of character, there was something decidedly magnetic about his appearance that invariably drew attention to him.

He seemed completely unperturbed by the girl's annoyance and took it in his stride with the air of one who has endured such criticism all his life. Instead of trying to assuage her, he busied himself with a small package that he was carrying. It was a large kerchief, and he slowly opened its knot to reveal a hefty Langra mango of the Banarasi variety. Presenting it to the girl, he smiled, 'Here, Seema. I went especially to the bazaar to get this for you. Don't you remember what I said to you when I was leaving for Rawalpindi with my uncle? That I would get you something special from the big city.'

'Such a large mango!' the girl exclaimed as she clasped the fruit in her own hands and gazed at it in wonderment. The sheer novelty of the fruit seemed to make her forget her exasperation. In all fairness, it was quite an extraordinary mango—must have weighed at least half a kilo, its exterior a dazzling blend of gold and blush, and its powerful aroma slowly enveloping her.

The girl's gaze had moved away from the boy and was now focused entirely on the mango. She was looking at it as though it were a mirror and not a mere fruit. In the mirror, she could see her own reflection, interspersed with images from that time a year and a half ago when the boy had left the village with his uncle and moved to the city, that time when he had come to see her just before his departure.

'Ranjheya,' she whispered, eyes still transfixed on the mango. 'Honestly, I've never seen a mango of this size. Are the city mangoes really this big?'

They were now sitting on the stump of the old acacia, the boy clearly pleased with the praise being showered on his present. 'This is nothing, Seema. They have mangoes that can weigh a kilo or more. Besides, these are not the kind that you squish and slurp. You take a knife and cut these up into slices and eat them the way you would a melon.'

'Really?' she murmured, clearly impressed with this new insight into mangoes. 'And I bet they are really sweet too.'

'Not just sweet! They are pure honey! Your lips sort of stick together after you've eaten one of them. And they are pretty expensive too.'

'So how much was this one for?'

'This one? I paid seven annas for it. Truth be told, I visited the bazaar just for this. Went from one shop to another till I found the right kind. I didn't really have the money, but I knew that I just had to share the taste of a Banarsi mango with you. So, I waited for my uncle to go to sleep and took eight annas from his jacket.'

The girl had been quite enchanted by the size of the mango, by its beauty and aroma, and by the boy's comments about its exceptional taste. But her face fell when she heard his flippant remark, that he 'took eight annas from his jacket'.

Her eyes, which had been suffused with her feelings towards him, were now blazing with anger. Their fury struck the boy like a bolt of lightning as she cried, 'So you still haven't given up your habit of stealing? Here! Keep your mango. I don't want it.' The boy felt the ground slip beneath his feet as she handed the mango back to him. Mortified, he lowered his eyes and when he finally raised them to look again at the girl, they seemed contrite and apologetic, seeking forgiveness. He was also cursing himself for having revealed the bit about stealing the money. He should have remembered that he had been at the receiving end of her ire whenever he had behaved similarly in the past.

But seeing the impact of the humiliation that she had wrought on her young lover was a bit too much for our tender-hearted lass. Her hand shot out to retrieve the mango from him as she murmured, 'Are you upset?'

The boy's eyes had clouded with remorse, but these three words were like a sponge that quickly soaked up his misery. 'Old habits die hard! And you still have yours, it seems,' she said, as she let her right hand rest on his shoulder. The warmth of her touch sent a tremor through his frame, and he found himself being swept off his feet by her kindness.

'You are just so wonderful, Seema,' he gushed, and lifting her hand from his shoulder, held it tight within his own palms. 'Please forgive me this time, Seema. I will never steal again.'

'Yeah, sure,' the girl replied in a tone that mixed the tender voice of the mother with the stern notes of the teacher. 'I know your false promises pretty well!'

The boy knew that he had been given a reprieve, not by the girl's words but by that look which carried a message of forgiveness along with an unspoken warning: 'There will be no place for you in my heart if you ever behave that way again.'

Perhaps neither of them wanted to dwell any longer on the unpleasant topic. Their eyes fell on that mango whose controversial acquisition had led to this fuss in the first place.

Lifting his eyes from the mango, the boy fixed his gaze on the girl's delicate countenance and asked, 'Seema! Weren't you afraid, standing all alone in this place?'

'I am only afraid of you. I don't fear anyone else.'

'Me? Why?'

'Because of the way you've been since we were kids. When you would start beating me up over the slightest thing. I told myself that you would beat me up again if I didn't wait for you and so I…'

'Don't be silly!' he interjected. 'You still remember those trivial things? I am no longer that foolish kid, nor are you the same little girl that I could start beating you up.'

Hearing from him that she was no longer a little girl, she stole a quick head-to-toe glance at herself before replying bashfully, 'I haven't grown that much! You are the one who has bloomed, tall and strong like a soldier.'

'Maybe you haven't seen yourself, silly!' the boy laughed at her innocent comment. 'You would know if you saw yourself through my eyes. Honest, Seema! You have really blossomed of late. It's barely a year and a half since I left the village and you were a mere chit of a girl then, hair all askew and barely conscious of your dupatta. But look at you now … now…'

He stopped mid-sentence, suddenly unsure if the girl would see his words as a compliment or an affront. Their eyes met and their peals of laughter broke the silence of the night. The girl's laugh suggested that she had taken his unfinished comment as a compliment. But it also bore a new-found coyness emanating perhaps from a sense that she had now crossed the threshold of childhood and was becoming a young woman.

Stepping in before he might have made a fool of himself by blurting something about her good looks or about her age, she quickly changed the subject and asked, 'Okay, let's leave this stuff. You were going to tell me something, weren't you?'

'Not really. Nothing.'

'But you sent a message that you wanted to see me alone.'

'Yeah, but there's nothing really important to say.'

'In that case, couldn't you have dropped in at our home? Mother was getting upset, saying she'd heard you arrived yesterday but haven't bothered to come over. Like you need to swim a river or something to meet her.'

'It isn't about swimming across a river or any such thing, Seema. I wanted to meet Maasi as soon as I set foot in the village but … but I just felt a bit shy.'

'Shy?' the girl asked in astonishment. 'Since when does one feel shy before his mother or maasi, you moron?'

'I was just a bit shy about the prospect of seeing you, not your mother.'

The girl laughed out loud when she heard his comment, before teasing him, 'You are an absolute Ranjha, aren't you? Why should anyone feel shy before his sisters or cousins, you fool?

The boy responded in a timid sort of voice, 'I really can't fathom what's wrong with me, Seema. It's like I am afraid of coming face to face with you. Allah knows that I am dying to see you and that's why I asked you to meet me in a secluded place like this. I knew that in a day or two, I'd have to return to the city and this was an opportunity to sit with you and chat to our hearts' content. Honestly, Seema, I miss you a hell of a lot ever since I've moved to the city. There are times when I am trying to sleep, and I drift back into our childhood when we played on the banks of the Soan. Do you remember that well, the one where I used to give you a ride on the seat of the water-wheel? In my dreams, I often...'

'Come on now! Let's drop this silly talk. Let's get up and move; Amma is going to be really cross with me,' the girl interrupted him, even though she had been listening to him speak with unblinking attention.

The mango was still nestling in her palms and she was unconsciously rubbing it as they got up from the stump. When they had walked ten or twelve steps away from the trunk of the peepul, the girl looked towards the boy. His gaze was fixed on the mango, as though his unanswered questions would now be directed towards the fruit.

'What are you staring at, Ranjheya?' she enquired.

'Nothing,' his lips replied without any conviction. The yearning in his eyes told a different story, and the girl could sense there was definitely something going on.

'You are lying,' she said with the authority that springs naturally from an old friendship.

'No,' he gave a flustered response. 'I was just saying ... saying ... saying...' He found himself unable to complete the sentence.

'What? What are you trying to say?' the girl asked impatiently. 'You have really become a bit weird since you've gone to the city. What did you want to say?'

The boy coughed, as though trying to remove some unseen blockage from his vocal cords and expel a few words. 'I was saying that we should sit here for a while and enjoy this mango.'

'Really? Is that all?' she smiled gently. 'So why feel shy? Get your pocket-knife and let's slice this mango.' She handed the mango to him and started to walk back towards the acacia stump.

They sat back on the stump and he passed the mango back to her. 'You should taste it first, Seema.'

'Taste it just like that? Like squeeze the mango and slurp on the pulp? I thought you wanted to slice it like a melon. Don't you have your pocket-knife?'

'I do. But ... but I thought it would be nicer if we could take turns sipping on the nectar from the mango?'

'You and your silly ways haven't changed one bit, Ranjheya.' She took hold of the mango and started kneading it with her fingertips until she could feel its soft pulp. She removed the remnants of the stalk with her fingernails to create a small hole and placed her lips on it, sucking out the juice and pulp with great relish.

'You should stop calling me Ranjha. I really mean it,' the boy said as he watched her gorge on the fruit.

His remark went unnoticed and the girl took another two or three gulps before passing the mango to him and proclaiming, 'Wah! This is incredibly sweet. Like pure honey, nothing less.'

The boy sucked on the mango a couple of times before handing it back to the girl. 'Here, now you polish off the rest, Seema.' But the girl refused to take advantage of his offer and the two continued to take turns in devouring the mango and didn't pause till its pit had been licked clean.

'Look, Ranjheya,' she said as she held out the pit for his examination before tossing it aside. 'Ya Allah! Such a slender pit from such a huge mango! Our mangoes here are half the size but the pits are larger than this one. I say, if we take the seed out of the pit and sow it here, we might just get these lovely mangoes in our own village!'

'And why not! Our region has also started to grow some great mangoes now. Not far from where we live in 'Pindi, quite close to my uncle's workshop, lives a Sikh landowner who has a large orchard. Seema, he has planted different varieties of mangoes in the orchard. I've been there a couple of times with my uncle because the gardener there is a friend of his. He was telling me...'

But the girl's mind was racing ahead. Unable to restrain her enthusiasm, she interjected, 'So I must plant it in our courtyard,' and reached out to retrieve the pit. Removing the bit of soil and grass from its surface, she held it out for his examination and asked, 'Ranjheya! I haven't seen any decent mango trees in our neighbourhood. Do you think this one will bear fruit?'

'Of course it will! Why won't it? We would have had proper mangoes here if our people had bothered. You know Thaneela village? It isn't that far, and I've seen lovely mango trees up there. The key point, Seema, is that the mango sapling needs a lot of care during its early days. It can't tolerate extreme cold, nor does it do well if it gets too hot. So, you have to protect it from the cold in December-January and from the heat in May-June. If you can help it through its first year, it will never die.'

'But how do you protect it, Ranjheya?'

'Some people plant a few banana trees around the mango sapling. The large fronds of the banana provide pretty good protection from the extremes of our weather. Others create a kind of a tripod from reeds of elephant grass and drape it like a curtain around the sapling.'

'And do you plant it the same way as we would with our ordinary mangoes?'

'Exactly the same way. Though the gardener in 'Pindi says that pouring some goat's blood in the roots of the sapling can do wonders for its growth.'

'That shouldn't be a problem at all,' the girl exclaimed. 'Nabi the butcher lives next door and I am sure I can get some goat's blood from him.'

The boy pulled out his kerchief to wipe his hands before offering it to the girl to do the same. 'Ranjheya! Let's start moving. It is really late,' she said, getting up from the stump.

The boy started to get up but then sat back, as though the girl's use of the term 'Ranjheya' had somehow glued him to the acacia. 'Seema! Please sit down and hear me out.'

'What?' the girl asked as she sat beside him.

'Didn't I just say you should stop calling me Ranjha?'

'Why? Have you suddenly become some lordship? The whole village calls you Ranjha.'

'What the people of the village say is another matter, you idiot. You won't understand this.'

'Okay. So, help me understand.'

'See, some of my friends from our village gave me this nickname. Later, others picked it up and everyone started calling me Ranjha. But that's not my real name.'

'If everyone else can call you Ranjha, why can't I?'

'You shouldn't call me that, Seema.'

'Why?'

'Do you know why my friends gave me this nickname?

'How would I know?'

'They started calling me Ranjha because of you.'

'Because of me?'

'Absolutely! You were just a kid then, but I remember it so well. We were inseparable. Always together, playing or chatting. Even in a group, we would sit together. That's why the boys started calling me Ranjha. They also had a name for you, but they never dared call you Heer out of fear of your mother's temper. But among themselves, they would always say that Seema is Ranjha's Heer.'

It would be hard to find a Punjabi who is unfamiliar with the legendary love story of Heer and Ranjha. Seema had also heard of it without being aware of all the details. All she knew was that Heer and Ranjha were lovers and references to Heer–Ranjha often came up in the lyrics of various folk songs. But hearing that she was being described as some Ranjha's Heer sent a wave of embarrassment through her being. He is absolutely right in asking me not to call him Ranjha, she thought. Both lapsed into an uncomfortable silence, broken only when the boy chirped up, 'But Seema, if you like to call me Ranjha, why don't you actually become my Heer?'

'Actually become your Heer?' she was startled and also a bit nervous. 'What kind?'

'Just like Ranjha's Heer.'

'What? What did you just say?' Her face was turning crimson with a mix of shame and anger.

Taken aback by the girl's reaction, the boy froze into silence. He was already remonstrating himself for having gone too far. 'Heer was an unmarried girl who took Ranjha as her lover. You … you want me to be the same? Aren't you ashamed of yourself?' she fumed as she got up from the stump and walked away, standing at the kind of distance that one would maintain from a leper. The sound of her laboured breathing could be heard at a distance.

The boy tried to compose himself before speaking, 'What is there to be ashamed of? Can't we be in love like Ranjha and…'

'Shame on you! Is that the kind of stuff you have learned in the city? Don't you dare talk to me again!' she huffed, as she moved further away from him.

Seeing that her anger was only increasing, the boy felt a pang of guilt and scrambled to make amends. 'I am really, really sorry, Seema. Please forgive me. I am ready to fall at your feet,' he pleaded as he clutched her hand to pull her closer.

The boy beseeched her and swore that he would behave, but his entreaties fell on deaf ears. He wanted to make peace, but his appeals only appeared to harden her resolve. Suddenly, he snapped. With a deliberate push, he jerked his hand away from hers and snarled, 'Go to hell, then. The more I plead with you, the worse your attitude gets. Now let me tell you something. I won't speak with you till you've said sorry to me. Or I am not my father's son.'

'Even my slippers won't say sorry to a lecher like you,' she roared as she moved away from him. The boy pounced on her and delivered a ringing slap on her cheek. 'Come here, you daughter of a pig! Let me show you the taste of a slipper. What do you take me for?'

A smothered cry broke the silence of the night and disappeared into the darkness. Without uttering a word, she turned her back on him and bolted along the path towards the village. The boy stood still, nonplussed.

Some three or four houses before reaching her own home, the girl sensed something unusual in her hand. It was the slender pit of the mango. She paused to look left and right. On her left lay the abandoned ruins of an old house, its front yard cluttered with all manner of litter. She raised her arm above her head and flung the pit into the yard with all her strength.

It was almost dawn when a ploughman was heard exhorting his mules as he passed the abandoned house. 'Who's there? Is that you, Seema? My girl, what are you trying to find in this garbage at this time of the morning? And be careful you don't get bitten by something. This is the season for all manner of insects and vermin.'

'Nothing, Chacha,' the girl replied even as she held a lamp in one hand and rummaged through the litter with the other. 'I've lost my kajal stick. I thought I might have accidentally dumped it here after I swept our courtyard last night.'

1

'ISN'T IT TERRIBLE, Chaudhryji? We must reflect upon this. We all have our sisters and daughters to worry about. Incidents like these can create absolute havoc. We've lived here all our lives and never had to deal with such irresponsible behaviour. He acted like he is the only one to claim the license of youthful indiscretion!'

A small village, surrounded by the hills of the Pothohar highlands—a place known for its natural beauty. A village whose charm was enhanced by its location in a wide plain surrounding a phalanx of huge, irregularly shaped cliffs. A community nestled around the small Soan river whose shallow, crystalline waters magnified every pebble on the riverbed, whose constant flow created its own music, whose banks were drenched with the ballads of true love. Like a poet once said about another river, 'Must be something magical in the love-soaked waters of the Chenab/Playing on its banks turns kids into lovers.'

In a somewhat similar fashion, the Soan too was considered the younger sibling of the mighty Chenab when it came to the history of colourful romances. Its verdant banks had heard the young maidens of the village tell many a tale—of letters written by lovers who had gone off to distant lands, or of heartless men and their uncaring attitudes.

Like the music of Ranjha's flute, the restless waters of the Soan seem to have this magnetic energy that can swell the turmoil of an expectant lover into the turbulence of a volcanic eruption.

These days, it is winter and the waters of this blessed river have receded a fair bit. And yet, there is something maddeningly attractive about its mildly intoxicated, swaying flow—something that impels a passer-by to approach its banks for a closer look. Standing on the silky sands of its banks, the visitor can see miles of lush green fields cradling a nascent crop of wheat. The hills that frame the luxuriant farms add their own charm to the village and its surroundings in a way that is bound to tug at one's heartstrings.

Although the terrain is hilly, there is an abundance of wells and their waters allow the farmers to grow a wide variety of crops. The local population, as a result, is fairly prosperous.

This village called Chakri is located on the unpaved road that links Rawalpindi with Talagang. It is about thirty miles from Rawalpindi and abuts two railway stations—Dadhiyal and Fatehjung.

As the warm rays of the afternoon sun in early December provide some much-needed succour and as the planting of the wheat crops in the farmlands gathers momentum, a small group of elders and notables starts to gather for a meeting in a largish, prosperous-looking house that stands in the middle of the village.

The village has a large majority of Muslims, many of them affluent landlords who control sizeable estates. There is a relatively smaller number of Hindu and Sikh families, who are broadly called 'Khatris', because of their preponderance in trade and finance. They are also fairly well-to-do and several of them have expanded beyond their traditional occupations to become landowners.

Bhane Shah is a wealthy businessman whose family has enjoyed prosperity over several generations. Affectionately known as Baba

Bhana for his age and wisdom, he is not only regarded as the head of the Khatri community but also held in high esteem by the Muslims of the village. It was in Baba Bhana's sprawling haveli that the Muslim and Khatri elders had assembled.

Around seven or eight Muslims sit at a short distance from their Khatri brethren, possibly to avoid bothering them with the smoke of their hookah. The hookah's pipe is passed around and a wreath of smoke carrying a distinct whiff of tobacco and jaggery wafts towards the open door behind them. They appear to be waiting for someone, but amid energetic puffs on the hookah, an animated conversation is already underway.

Baba Bhana is around seventy, but his respect amongst the denizens of the village transcends his age, experience and wealth. He heads the village panchayat, acts as a last-resort lender, functions as the local hakim, helps out with writing deeds and legal documents, produces some perfumes, and contributes to much else. But his special status in the village stems from yet another attribute. His knowledge of Urdu and Persian languages makes him indispensable for anyone who needs to submit an application or engage in any kind of official correspondence. Let's admit that his proficiency in Persian may not stand the test when compared to someone with a formal education in the language, but that did not diminish his standing in the village. His people looked up to him as a man of letters.

Baba Bhana didn't have the privilege of studying in any government or private school. In the era when he was growing up, even the towns and cities in these parts rarely had a proper school. Education in villages was usually provided through the local mosques and both Muslims and non-Muslims sat together for their classes.

The Baba had studied under the tutelage of the Moulvi at the village mosque. But he hadn't stopped there. He had also borrowed some books on traditional medicine from the Moulvi, in particular, the Persian classics *Tibb Akbari*, that focused on the treatment of infectious diseases, and *Ilaj ul Ghuraba*, that dwelt on the therapeutics of rare conditions. Urdu and Persian were considered the most useful languages in these parts and acquiring a working knowledge wasn't too difficult. People used to say that if you had read just two books— Sheikh Saadi's *Gulistan* and *Bostan*—you were deemed proficient in Persian. Or to put it another way, one's study of Persian started with *Gulistan* and culminated with *Bostan*. Studying these two books was mandatory for all students at the mosque and it applied equally to Hindus, Sikhs and Muslims. The Muslim students, however, also received additional classes on the holy Quran.

It was a far cry from the formal education provided in today's schools. Classes were limited, and so was the curriculum. Mats, usually long and narrow, would be spread out in the courtyard or the verandah of the mosque and the Moulvi would have the students line up in two separate groups—a Persian class for general students, and an Arabic one for those pursuing the holy Quran. And that's where the students sat from morning to evening, imbibing the Moulvi's tutorials, their torsos rocking gently as they tried to absorb his words. The classes would wind up in the early part of the evening with one final ritual—each group would stand up and recite from memory whatever they had been taught during the day. A couple of the brightest students would usually be placed in the front row to lead the rest of the class in a melodious recitation of verses from *Gulistan*…

> *O save me, my Lord, have mercy on me*
> *I am trapped in a web of desires*
> *To appeal for help, I have none but You*
> *For You alone can forgive me for my sins.*

This would be followed by sonorous notes echoing across the courtyard of the mosque from the Arabic class as the students recited the siparah from the Quran that they had learned during the day:

> *Praise be to Allah, Lord of the Universe*
> *The most Merciful and Compassionate*
> *Sovereign of the Day of Recompense.*

At the ripe old age of seventy, the Baba smiles fondly when he thinks of the Moulvi, his first mentor. And even now, when he wants to give an example to illustrate some particular aspect, he often starts off by saying, 'And as our Moulvi sahib used to say…'

You couldn't call the Baba a religious fanatic in the way some zealots are. And yet, he was an ardent believer in his own special way. He could be heard chanting something before he went to bed, when he woke up in the morning, when he took his bath, before he had his meals, when he left his home, and so on. He had learned a few shlokas in Sanskrit from the Gita, some verses from the Sikh scriptures and a mishmash of sayings attributed to poets of the Bhakti movement. Together, they constituted the essence of his prayers and meditation, with the mantra, 'Sri Namo Bhagawate Vasudevaya.'

His family had lived in this village for several generations. He hadn't travelled much, but thanks in part to his reading habits and in larger measure to the experiences acquired over seven decades, he managed to sound knowledgeable on most matters. He was also known for his acumen and integrity when it came to running his own business.

When we look at our towns and cities today, we have this notion of the municipal commissioner being called the father of the city. But to compare this modern city father to our old man would be to compare a trinket with something made of pure twenty-four-carat gold. Baba Bhana could be called the father of the village in the truest sense of that expression. This was reflected in the respect that he received from the residents of the village, Hindu and Muslim, the elderly and the young.

He may not have the formal training of a hakim but pretty much everyone in the village agreed that he could not merely diagnose your ailment but also dispense the right medicine to cure it.

For any function in the village—a birth, a wedding or a funeral—the Baba was the first to be invited by the family. This wasn't just out of respect for his stature but also because he was the one who could guide the family on the appropriate rituals and ceremonies for both Hindus and Muslims. What gifts should be given when the husband comes to take the bride from her parents' place in the village? How should a family conduct a nikah ceremony? Without the Baba's counsel, the families would be in sixes and sevens.

If it were time for a bride to be given a formal send-off in her palanquin, the Baba could be seen coming down the path with his walking stick. He would dip into his waistcoat and place a rupee in the bride's palm, stroke her head and say, 'May your husband live long; may you enjoy the cool breeze; don't you forget us when you go to your in-laws.' His face would crinkle up in a serious expression when he said that last sentence. When the palanquin was lifted for the farewell, one of its four poles would rest on the Baba's shoulder. Despite the remonstrations about his age by friends and family, he would rely on his walking stick for support and insist on escorting the palanquin to the edge of the village. Once the kuhars took charge of the palanquin for the remainder of the journey, the Baba would go across to the bridegroom sporting the scarlet turban and accost him with the solemn message, 'Listen carefully, young man! Make sure you treat our daughter like the petals of a rose. Look after her because she is the goddess Lakshmi of our village. Lakshmi, do you hear!'

When a new bride was received in the village, it was customary to first stop at the Baba's haveli. The bride would kneel her head at his feet to seek his blessings, prompting the Baba to hurriedly pull his feet back, lift the girl's head and place a rupee along with a piece of coconut in her wedding dupatta with the words, 'May you enjoy the luxury of bathing in pure milk; may you have many sons; may you live a long and happy life with your husband.'

The village's Khatri community was fairly small in comparison to the Muslims. But their lives were closely interconnected in so many different ways that neither community could imagine a life without the other.

Baba Bhana lives in a fairly spacious home, easily one of the finest in the village. His son and daughter-in-law are the only other residents of the house, giving it an empty sort of a feeling. There are times the Baba misses the vibrant presence of grandchildren, but he pauses to admonish himself. What am I complaining about? Aren't all the sons and daughters-in-law of the village like my own offspring? And all their children are like my own grandchildren! The thought brings a reassuring smile on his face, particularly as he reflects on the small family of three that lives in an outhouse behind his home. The affection that he feels towards them, the special bond that he shares with them makes them an extension of his family. Indeed, their presence next door substantially makes up for the small size of his own family.

The good lord made the Baba wait for many a year after his marriage before he was blessed with offspring. A son and a daughter, that's all he had to be content with. But the good lord turned out to be even more miserly than that. Fate snatched his daughter from him at an early age, leaving Boote Shah as his only surviving child. If that weren't enough, Boote Shah too is still without child though he must be over thirty years old and has been married for quite a while.

People like to say that their sons are more precious than their daughters. But for the Baba, the death of his daughter Krishna was a tragedy larger than the loss of seven sons. He was so utterly devastated after her passing that he may not have survived long if another girl hadn't miraculously appeared to take Krishna's place. That's what his friends and neighbours avow.

The Baba's home—made largely of expensive hardwood and fine stone—was built around five or six years back. Boote Shah, in fact, spent a fair bit of money on the façade and also on the aesthetics within the house to give it a pleasing appearance.

Baba Bhana's old house was located behind this new building. It's low ceilings and elaborately carved wooden doors are testimony to the stature of its previous dwellers. It is now occupied by a middle-aged widow and her young daughter.

The elders of the village had by now been sitting for close to an hour, making small talk and puffing on their hookahs even as they awaited the clack of the Baba's walking stick heralding his arrival. A few of them were also beginning to show their impatience over the prolonged delay.

Passing the pipe of his hookah to Deena the gardener, Chaudhry Fazal Karim stroked his henna-tinged beard as he spoke, 'I must say that Babaji is running pretty late today. I have to go to the tehsil office, and I also had to pass by the fields where the seed-planting team is waiting for me.'

Juma the carpenter piped up, 'Relax, Chaudhryji. The tehsil office isn't going to run away. It's important to settle this festering issue today. Fortunately, all of us are here today. And if it comes to our errands, I've probably got the most pressing one. The wedding of the Haqqanis' daughter is just around the corner, and I still have to finish their bed and couch. I've been working on the lathe since the Fajr prayers and was just about finishing the legs of the couch when I got your message.'

The Chaudhry turned towards Bhagta the brahmin and asked, 'Ojhaji, why don't you go inside and check where exactly Babaji has gone? Is it a long way off? I can't see Boote Shah at home either.'

Bhagta was still tugging at the elbows of his old wool jacket and beginning to get up when they heard the clack of the walking stick in the adjacent room, accompanied by the murmur, 'Sri Namo Bhagawate Vasudevya.' He returned to his seat as the attention of the visitors gravitated towards the door.

One hand on his waist and the other holding a stick that seemed somewhat taller than him, Baba Bhana hastened towards the group and exclaimed, 'Welcome! Welcome! I hadn't gone very far but you know how it is. You visit someone and it ends up taking a little longer than you'd thought.'

Baba Bhana was of average height but seemed a bit shorter because of a small hump in his back. His ruddy countenance, framed within a neatly trimmed, silvery beard seemed to place him at some intersection between the young and the elderly. Imagine him with a black beard and you'd have to say that he was actually in pretty good shape.

A simple tunic of hand-spun cotton, a waistcoat with faint, thin stripes that looked a bit like a Nehru jacket, and a brownish coat with a Kashmiri trim added to Baba's impressive appearance. He wore a white dhoti, again made from crisp homespun cotton and a closer look at his walking stick revealed an interesting contrast: the bottom part was frayed from prolonged contact with the ground, while the area where he gripped the stick was smooth and burnished, revealing the small depressions that his fingers had created over the years. From the tidy locks that spilled on to his neck, an elegant silver mane was discernible under the folds of his turban.

'Babaji!' Gulab Singh Kohli remonstrated with a hint of a smile. 'I thought we would grow old waiting for you. What kind of errand kept you so long?'

The Baba, meanwhile, had set his stick aside to take his customary seat in the room. His fingers were subconsciously engaged in twirling his luxuriant moustache and keeping the gravity-defying tips of the whiskers pointing upwards. 'It wasn't any errand, my brother. The mother of Safi the potter has been feeling under the weather for a while. The old lady is pretty frail now; has been bed-ridden for over a month and a half. I thought I must go and see if we could do something.'

Changing the subject, he turned towards the Chaudhry and said, 'What brings you to our humble abode, Chaudhryji? Hope everything is okay?'

'What's okay, Babaji?' the Chaudhry exclaimed. 'To be honest, I wonder if one should continue staying in this village much longer.'

A worried frown crept across the Baba's face. His head seemed to sink a bit lower under this new burden and he was on the verge of posing a question to the Chaudhry when Bhagta the brahmin piped up. With his index finger determinedly scratching his clean-shaven chin, he spoke, 'It's absolutely dreadful, Babaji! I've never heard anything like this since the day I was born. Haven't we all seen our own youth? But we never saw such appalling behaviour. The fellow has neither any concern for a daughter nor any respect for a sister's honour.'

'But who are you talking about, Ojhaji?' the Baba asked a trifle testily.

'We are talking about that ruffian,' Mir Baksh Bhatti responded. He seemed to have applied some fresh butter to his unruly hair and his hand worked tirelessly to suppress a few wayward tufts. 'That Yusuf, son of Langa the blacksmith. A classic case of good parents, bad kids. The father has never done a wrong in his life and look at the conduct of the son. Biting the hand that feeds him!'

'He was a rotten apple to begin with,' Heera Singh Kochchar commented as he tried to adjust his precariously perched turban. 'Now these added airs of a policeman's uniform have turned him from bad to worse. He is simply insufferable. If I can be candid, Babaji, your leniency is partly responsible. After all, he claims to be the blood brother of Boote Shah. Had it been anybody else...' Realizing that he may have gone too far in the presence of the Baba, he froze mid-sentence.

It was Chaudhry Fazal Karim who stepped in to provide the Baba with a detailed account of the incident. The Baba's anger mounted as he heard the facts, his flushed face acquiring the hues of heated copper. As a matter of principle, he had always treated every girl in the village like his own daughter when it came to protecting their honour. But when the name of the girl involved in the unfortunate incident was mentioned, it pierced his heart like a bullet. A wave of rage surged through his body. His eyes appeared bloodshot and the veins in his forehead started to throb on their own volition. He took a deep breath to bring his runaway emotions under control. When he finally spoke, his voice gave no indication of the tumult within him. 'Is there anyone who actually saw this or are we depending merely on hearsay?'

'Hearsay?' Niaz Gakhkhar spoke as one hand emerged from the pocket of his khadi kurta to tug at the hookah's pipe. 'The eyewitness is sitting before you. Ask him to take a solemn oath before he tells you what he saw.' He looked to where Allahditta was seated.

'Allahditta!' the Baba addressed him with a quiver in his voice. 'You are a Muslim, right?'

'Praise be to Allah! I am indeed,' Allahditta replied with a touch of fervour.

'Take your oath then!' the Baba ordered.

Allahditta brought his hands together, palms facing his chest and recited:

La illahalilallah
Muhammadurasoolallah

Eyes closed in devotion, he moved his fingertips from his forehead towards his lips.

'So, tell us truthfully what you saw. Remember that you are answerable to the Prophet and to the Almighty,' the Baba said sternly.

'Babaji,' Allahditta lifted his eyes with reverence. 'May I burn in the fires of hell if I utter a single word that is untrue.

'It was last Thursday that I had gone to my mother's place in Kauliyan. My nephew had been unwell, and I'd gone to see him. I left Kauliyan before dawn today and it was still pretty early in the morning when I was approaching our village. I was passing the grove near your place when I heard some voices. It seemed like some altercation. My first reaction was that it must be Ida your gardener having an argument with his nephew. The two of them are always at each other's throats. I decided to pass through the grove and see what was going on, just in case someone was injured and needed some assistance.

'The voices were coming from the direction of the cowshed within the grove. I looked inside and—Allah is witness that the scene I beheld left me boiling with fury—Yusuf had locked Naseem in an embrace and the poor girl was shouting curses, scratching and biting him and tearing his clothes as she tried to free herself from his clutches. Before my eyes, Naseem slapped him a couple of times and bit him so hard I could see his arm bleeding.'

'And then?' the Baba quizzed breathlessly.

Allahditta paused for a moment before responding.

'Yusuf let go of the girl the moment he saw me. Naseem took advantage and ran out of the grove towards the village. That left this upstart free to confront me. I swear by the thirty siparahs of the Quran that all I did was to tell him, "What's going on, Yusufa? Aren't you ashamed that you are forcing yourself on a young girl?" And he turns on me and shouts, "Get lost or I'll rip you apart." You would agree, Babaji, that all of us are nourished by the same kernel of grain and I also have the same blood running through my body. How could I remain unmoved by the sight of a girl being molested? And now, the villain was trying to browbeat me! So, I rolled up my sleeves and said, "Fine. Let me teach you a lesson or two." I gave him a couple of solid blows and you could see that his guilty conscience had sapped his strength. Within moments, he was pleading at my feet, saying, "Allahditta, for God's sake help me bury whatever happened. You are like my brother, aren't you?"

'I was enraged, I must confess. So I caught him by the throat and shoved him to the ground. "Let me show you what your brother is like," I told him. By now, the lout was beside himself with fear and he was again imploring, "Allahditta, please do what you can to save my honour." I responded, "You bloody rogue! You think your honour is more important than the honour of a daughter of this village. You thought this girl doesn't have the protection of a father so you can do whatever catches your fancy? I swear I'll gouge the eyes of anyone who casts a dirty look at our daughters and sisters." That put him in his place, and I swear by Yusuf's mother there wasn't a peep out of him after that.'

'Who says,' the Baba crackled, 'that the girl doesn't have a father's protection while this old man is still alive? How dare anyone call her an orphan?'

'It is true, Babaji,' Fazal Karim hastily intervened. 'You have done more for her than any father could have done. Everyone in this village acknowledges this fact. Who knows what terrible fate awaited mother and daughter if you hadn't been around to protect them! To be very frank, you've managed to pull the family out of the abyss. You are no less than a father to all of us too, Babaji. That's why we are so restrained in bringing up a subject like this in your presence. I still can't believe that a tramp like Yusuf would have the guts to accost her like this. He must have been instigated by someone.'

'Instigated by someone?' the Baba's eyes were burning with the intensity of fresh embers. 'And who might have instigated him?'

'Let's keep this matter under wraps, Babaji.'

The Chaudhry's reticence only added fuel to the fire raging within the Baba. But he maintained a calm demeanour as he replied, 'This panchayat is a representation of the Lord Himself. We can speak freely here and don't have to keep anything under wraps. Please don't hesitate to name this individual.'

'Babaji,' the Chaudhry spoke. 'I don't know how to allow my lips to utter something like this. To be honest, my own heart insists that this cannot be true. But the facts speak otherwise.'

'No, no!' the Baba spoke in a commanding tone. 'This is no time for soft pedalling or beating about the bush. It would be a sad reflection on all of us if incidents like this start to occur in our own village. I won't pardon the offender, no matter who it might be. I won't care if it is my own son. Now go ahead and name the fellow who instigated Yusuf to act like this.'

'So, Babaji,' the Chaudhry whispered softly, 'what if this actually turns out to be about your son?'

'In that case...' the Baba's lips quivered, and his pitch increased as he spoke, 'in that case, I would immediately disassociate myself from him and I ... I...' By now, the Baba's voice had risen so high that he started to sputter.

'So, forgive me, Babaji,' the Chaudhry spoke diffidently. 'It was Boote Shah who took Naseem to the grove around the time of the Fajr prayers. This much I saw with my own eyes.'

'What?'

'Indeed.'

'Boote Shah accompanied her?'

'Yes.'

For once, the Baba was lost for words. He seemed to have lost the power to speak, or even to raise his eyes and look at those sitting around him. He shut his eyes, denying them the opportunity to peer into his emotions. They could only see his frame trembling with rage.

A suffocating silence pervaded the room, hanging heavy over the heads of the participants. No one had the courage to break it and who knows how long it might have continued if it hadn't been for the intervention of the one whose name had caused it. Hearing the sound, the Baba lifted his head and opened his eyes. He leapt towards the door from which he had entered the room to retrieve his walking stick and roared, 'Bootey! Oye Booteya.'

A voice came from the other side.

'Yes, Babaji. Coming!'

2

I SUGGEST WE leave the panchayat meeting in Baba Bhana's place for a while and switch our attention to a few related matters. It is important that my readers are acquainted with these and I hope they won't mind this digression. In fact, it may even add to their appreciation of the story.

Rahim Baksh was a prominent landlord who owned around a hundred acres of land. Now, anyone who is sitting on such a large tract of fertile land in these parts can be described as prosperous. And if we go back some fifteen or twenty years, it would be fair to say that a man like that would be considered amongst the wealthiest persons of the village.

So Rahim Baksh had seen his share of good times and the bonds between his family and that of Bhane Shah went back quite a few decades. Rahim Baksh's forefathers had engaged in the lucrative practice of employing indentured labour and, over time, the profits from their operations had enabled them to acquire these large land holdings.

But Fate played a funny trick on Rahim Baksh and he managed to squander the accumulated wealth of his family with one roll of the dice. You see, he had joined hands with one of his friends to venture

33

into the contract farming business. Together, they leased a largish tract of land in Multan district. The rains that year were bountiful and timely, and a part of the land also had access to water from a nearby canal. The crop was abundant and after paying the contracted amount for the lease, the duo made a profit that far exceeded their expectations.

The transition from landowner to contract farmer hadn't been easy. Oh, the scorn he faced when he had brought up the idea of handing over his own land to share-croppers and taking up the new land in Multan! His friends and neighbours had been scathing in their criticism. 'Look at this fool,' they would say, recalling the proverb: 'He sells his buffalo to buy a horse. He loses the milk and has to deal with the dung.' But Rahim Baksh was made of sterner stuff. Paying no heed to the barbs, he packed his bags and moved with his family to the leased farmland in Multan.

The handsome profits from his very first venture in contract farming had him hooked. In his mind, his success had shown that he was on the right track. The fact that he had enjoyed exceptional good fortune in the Multan venture and that it was a fluke that may not repeat itself was completely lost on him. Avarice triumphed over judgement, as he also dumped his partner and decided to go solo on his next venture. He entered into an agreement with a retired army subedar in Sheikhupura and took a massive five hundred-acre tract on contract for a period of five years. The quality of the land wasn't all that great, but he reasoned that getting such a vast expanse for an annual rent of only three thousand rupees was a terrific deal. If he got a decent crop of cotton on even a hundred acres, he would be rolling in cash.

One part of the land was ready for cultivation, while another was relatively barren and needed a fair bit of work before it would be ready for planting. If he had thought like a farmer, he would have started off with the parts that were ready to go. But greed can make a mess of logical thinking, and he decided to start with the part that was barren, without realizing that the ground below was hard and rocky. Tilling this land was a tough and arduous grind and by the time it was ready for planting, it had consumed most of his cash and family jewellery. He now needed a lot more cash to buy the seeds and hire labour to sow the land. A wiser man might have taken a step back, but our Rahim Baksh was stubborn as they come. Throwing caution to the winds and paying no heed to advice from his family, he returned to his village and sold off his ancestral land.

He now had the seeds, the workers and the animals needed to plant the cotton crop, and he embarked on the task with great vigour. But his luck had run out. Just as the crop started to flower, a vast swarm of locusts emerged out of nowhere to devour everything that came in its path. Several districts of Punjab were devastated by the attack. The swarms not only destroyed fertile farmlands but even left the trees bare of any leaves. Many a wizened elder of the region swore that he had never seen a swarm of this size in living memory.

For poor Rahim Baksh, this was the last straw. He slumped in despair, bemoaning the hand Fate had dealt him. But crying wasn't going to solve his problems. Besides, there was an even larger catastrophe lurking around the corner. You see, he had only paid half the contracted amount for the land, with the promise that he would pay the rest upon harvesting the first crop. He summoned the courage to visit his landlord, hoping against hope that the man would understand his plight and give him some grace period to make the payment. The subedar, though, was completely unmoved. Bringing all his military bearing to the fore, he responded, 'That's not my problem. The terms and conditions of the contract are explicit and don't you know what they say? "Whether you get a crop or not, you are obliged to pay the requisite amount on time.'"

The unfortunate man found himself in an absolute quandary. His one remaining asset was a piece of land that he had bought some time back. But that too had been mortgaged to a local landlord to finance his venture. He had nothing left.

As the deadline for paying the subedar approached, Rahim Baksh found himself sinking deeper into the morass. Where on earth could he find such a large sum of money? Who in this world would spare one thousand and five hundred rupees to bail him out?

News of Rahim Baksh's predicament soon made its way to his village and reached the ears of Bhane Shah. Without wasting any time, he made the necessary preparations, packed his old money-belt under his waistcoat, and set off for Multan. He was shocked beyond words when he saw the abject condition of his friend and his family.

Bhane Shah quietly approached the subedar, settled the dues and escorted Rahim Baksh and his family back to their home. They were greeted by the village in utter disbelief. By daybreak, the topic was on everyone's lips. In hushed tones, they murmured, 'Now that's a real man for you … That's what you call a true friend … Can you imagine the fate of Rahim Baksh and his family if the Baba hadn't…'

But Bhane Shah wasn't done yet. Holding Rahim Baksh in a warm embrace, he chided him, 'Don't you dare despair, Rahim Baksh. Even the kings and queens can become victims of misfortune. And don't bother about the cash. Money is evanescent by nature. It's here today, gone tomorrow. Look after your health, and the money will come in due course. So, stop worrying, go home and look after your wife and children. The travails of distant lands have reduced the poor fellows to half their size. By the grace of God, there is enough land to be tilled. Choose any of my fields that catches your fancy, take a plough, and get to work. You should make enough to look after your family and if there is something beyond that, we can share it. And don't fret if you don't. Since it is your brother's land, you have the same right to it.'

They say that a drowning man will clutch at any straw to save himself. But in this case, the drowning man not only found a boat but also a boatman, extending his hand to pull him aboard. With tears running down his face, Rahim Baksh prostrated himself at Bhana Shah's feet and sobbed, 'Shahji, from this moment you are not just my older brother but also my mother and father. I know I won't be able to repay your generosity till the end of time. But I want to assure you that Rahim Baksh comes from a lineage of repute. If water is needed, he will offer the sweat of his toil and if that isn't enough, he will offer his blood. May Allah look after you till eternity.'

The years rolled by, but the vicissitudes of life had taken their toll on Rahim Baksh and he never recovered his health. Knowing one day that his end was approaching, he called for Bhane Shah and asked him to sit by his side. Placing his young daughter Naseem's hand in the Baba's, he wheezed, 'My brother! You've already done so much for us. Now, the honour and dignity of these children are in your hands, too. You'll have to make sure that they never have to extend their hand to receive alms from anyone. That's my last request to you…'

Bhane Shah stopped him in his tracks. Stroking his friend's emaciated chest, he gently admonished him, 'God will give you good health, Rahim Baksh. There's no reason to utter such depressing thoughts. And as far as the family is concerned, Sugara is like my sister and Seema and Aziz are my own children. Your girl always appears like a replica of our Krishna and reminds me of the daughter that I desperately miss. Seema is about the same age as Krishna, and were

Krishna around today, I would have been thinking of her wedding. Alas! Fate didn't give me that opportunity. Now I want to make up for it by arranging Seema's marriage with the same fanfare. But why are we even discussing these things! You are going to be absolutely fine. Take the Lord's name and rest assured!'

Rahim Baksh passed away that night and Bhane Shah made it a solemn mission to look after the family and ensure that all their needs were met.

Rahim Baksh's house was situated in an isolated part of the village and was in a fairly dilapidated condition. The roof, in particular, was in terrible shape—during the winter rains or monsoon in summer, Sugara found herself busy trying to plug the holes with a thick paste of mud and dung. The fact that she also suffered from asthma didn't help matters. Bhane Shah wanted to find a solution to this constant nuisance. He was also concerned that Seema, who was becoming an adolescent, lived in an isolated neighbourhood. He resolved both problems by asking the family to move into his own old house, which was located right behind his current abode. He also bought them a milch cow for two hundred and thirty-five rupees, thereby ensuring that the family would always have plenty of milk and butter. Then there was the matter of arranging regular fodder for the cow. To avoid burdening Sugara or Naseem with this chore, he entrusted the responsibility to Sundru, an old and trusted worker on his land.

Naseem's brother Aziz was about two-and-a-half years older than her and had moved to Rawalpindi a couple of years ago, to take up a waiter's job in some restaurant. He knew that he didn't have to worry about his mother or sister while Bhane Shah was around, but nevertheless made it a point to take leave every three or four months to visit the family. Bhane Shah had also used his extensive network to arrange for Aziz to be engaged to a girl from a neighbouring village.

This happened around six months ago, and they might have been married by now if it hadn't been for an unexpected hitch. The girl's father was in Burma and some unforeseen work commitments had led him to postpone his return. Bhane Shah was beginning to get impatient with the delay and wanted to make sure that one way or the other the marriage took place before the Vaisakhi festival next April.

Once the marriage of Aziz was out of the way, Bhane Shah planned to concentrate on Naseem. She was now seventeen and he was mindful that the clock was ticking. But he also didn't want to rush things; the honest truth was that he hadn't yet found the right match for a girl as beautiful and well-educated as his foster daughter. He had personally tutored the siblings in Urdu and Persian. It would be fair to say that he wasn't just their foster father but also their teacher.

Boote Shah gazed adoringly at Naseem as she rolled up the sleeves of her grey tunic and leaned into the trough to mix the hay, straw, oil cakes and water. Her delicate hands, supple wrists and ivory-hued forearms moved in unison, occasionally lit up by the rays of the setting sun as they fell on the golden straw. A speckled cow, it's udders heavy with milk, strained at the rope as she impatiently eyed her meal. Gently pushing her away as she tried to force her way towards the trough, Naseem said, 'Stop rushing me, will you? I still have to mix the oil cakes for you.'

The small calf tied nearby seemed even more anxious as it stretched its slim frame to reach for its mother's udders.

Naseem carried a spirit that reflected the very essence of her name—a cool and gentle breeze. Her slim face was defined by her large, expressive eyes—eyes that were steady and serious; eyes that displayed an intense curiosity; eyes that seemed ready to question. Her tall frame tended to lean forward when she walked, giving the appearance that she was being affected by the weight of her adolescence. The film of moisture around her rosy lips only added to her attractive countenance.

She was working without the customary dupatta and a thick braid was snaking its way below her waist, occasionally picking up the golden hues of the evening sun. Her vigorous moves to mix the meal in the trough made the braid lurch from one side to the other, often falling in front of her and threatening to dip into the messy mix. This prompted a swift shake of the head that yanked the braid back to its original position.

After mixing the meal, she untied the cow and calf and went to the kitchen to pick up the milk can when she sensed someone entering the courtyard.

'Seema,' Boote Shah smiled affectionately as he came inside.

Boote Shah must have been a little over thirty. He was of average height but had a sturdy physique. The calm demeanour of his eyes and the gentle smile on his lips reflected the quiet confidence of his lineage. Or let us just say that in terms of his attributes, his nature and his deeds, Boote Shah was an exact replica of his illustrious father. His simple attire was no different from any other member of the local Khatri community and gave no indication of his wealth or stature.

It wasn't just Bhane Shah who had found his daughter Krishna in Naseem. Boote Shah also doted on her with the same intensity that he had once reserved for his younger sister. To the point that he would sometimes address Naseem as Krishna before hastily apologizing for his error. It wasn't right to use the name of a departed soul for one who was very much around, he would chide himself.

Naseem felt a little awkward that she was bare-headed in his presence, but not enough to make a hurried dash for her dupatta.

'Bhaaji!' she brushed off some bits of hay and straw from her clothes and rolled down the sleeves of her tunic as she approached him.

'Were you going to milk the cow?' he asked somewhat shyly as he approached his youthful sister.

'Not yet. There's no rush. I've just mixed their meal. But why are you standing there? Do come inside please.' She placed the milk can back in its place and deftly moved ahead of him to pick up a lilac dupatta with a light green border from the bed and cover herself.

'Chaachi isn't home?' Boote Shah asked as he entered the room and sat on the side of the bed.

'She left a little while back,' Naseem said, sitting near the foot of the bed. 'Chacha Ram Singh Kohli's son has brought his bride from her parents' home for the first time since their wedding. The barber's wife came with this news.'

'And you, silly girl?' Boote Shah glared at her in mock anger. 'Why couldn't you have gone? It's freezing outside and she is hardly in the best of health. What if she catches a cold…?'

'I did ask her not to go, Bhaaji,' Naseem replied with a hint of annoyance. 'I told her that I would go but she does as she pleases.'

Naseem was going to ask him if there was anything pressing that had brought him over, but he pre-empted her by starting, 'Seema! Just as well that Chaachi isn't home. I wanted to have a private chat with you.'

She was surprised when she heard this. But the surprise was not tinged with any sign of doubt or mistrust.

'With me?' she asked.

'Yes,' Boote Shah responded, adjusting his position to make himself more comfortable.

'But first, you must agree with something that I ask,' she spoke tenderly. 'Let me quickly go and milk the cow. Have a glass of fresh milk, nice and warm.'

'I can never drink fresh milk, Seema. I feel bloated when I do.'

'Bloated? Really? How can fresh milk cause that? Just give me a minute and I will get some for you.'

'Sit down, you silly girl. Sit down, I say! There's much that I have to tell you and I must do it before Chaachi returns.'

His comment deflated Naseem's enthusiasm. She thought of pressing her point once again but decided against it after she observed the resolute expression on his face.

'Okay! Go ahead.'

'Why don't you sit comfortably on the bed?'

Naseem clambered on the bed and made herself comfortable.

'Seema?'

'Yes.'

'How is Aziz related to you?'

'Why do you ask this, Bhaaji?'

'I have my reasons. Just answer me.'

'The same way that you are related to me.'

'Do you really see me as an older brother the same way that you see Aziz?'

'Even more than Aziz, Bhaaji. Because you are older than him.'

'In that case, Seema, I presume that as your older brother, I can ask you anything I like?'

'Sure, Bhaaji.'

'And you will give me honest answers to my questions?'

'Of course. Why wouldn't I do that?'

'Seema! Do you know your age?'

'About eighteen years,' Naseem replied in a guarded tone.

'So, we should be thinking seriously about your marriage, right?'

Naseem felt a protective wall of modesty rise around her upon hearing these words. She blushed, lowered her eyes and shrank into herself without giving any response.

'Didn't you agree, Seema? That you would reply candidly to me? There is no reason to be so bashful on this matter.'

His soothing tone started to lower the wall that she had drawn up. She gradually lifted her eyes but remained speechless.

'Fine! I am not going to force you, Seema,' Boote Singh started to rise from the bed. 'If you don't want to speak...'

Naseem leapt across the bed to grasp his arm and pull him back. 'Are you leaving because you are upset with me? Please don't go, for God's sake. I'll answer whatever you ask.'

'So, tell me.'

'What?'

'Answer my question.'

'I really have nothing to do with these matters, Bhaaji. It is your responsibility, so you know best.'

'I am not insane that I should come here and ask you these questions if you had nothing to do with the matter.'

'So, please go ahead and ask me whatever you have in your mind.'

'Seema, I came today to seek something from you. Will you give it to me?'

'What do I have that I can offer you, Bhaaji? The little that we have belongs to you and to the good Lord.'

'So, I can ask you for anything?'

'You don't have to ask. You can take whatever you like.'

'What is that, Seema?' he pointed to the young mango tree in the courtyard. Its leaves had turned a pale yellow in the winter cold and it was swaying gently with the breeze.

'What?' Naseem asked.

'That one. Whose leaves are drying up and falling.'

'A mango tree.'

'And who planted it, Seema?'

'I did.'

'Why?'

Naseem froze. That small monosyllabic question burrowed its way deep inside her to nip at her heart. A secret that she had hidden under layer after layer in a nook of her heart had been prised open. She felt her face blush once more. A string of memories started to unfold before her eyes as she sat in stunned silence. A tiny crack opened up in the tightly shut doors to her heart and a faint silhouette could be seen emerging. A few moments later, it seemed to be standing right in front of her, in flesh and blood.

'Why don't you speak up, Seema?'

She remained silent.

'If I am not mistaken, that tree is a symbol of someone's love, isn't it?'

Naseem started to bow her head.

'Seema, I am not sure if you are aware of this fact but Yusuf is like my blood brother.'

Naseem felt a tremor run through her lips.

'Seema, right now you are the only one who can save my friend's life.'

Like droplets of morning dew on grass, a couple of large teardrops were glistening on Naseem's eyelashes. Her lips were clenched tight between her teeth.

'Seema! I know that you hold him responsible. I know that he has insulted your love. But can you please forgive him, for my sake? I know that he is a flawed person, that he has many bad habits. But my dear sister, I also know that he will be devastated if … If…' Boote Shah paused when he saw that Naseem was holding her head in her hands and sobbing.

'Seema!' Boote Shah found his own voice cracking in pain as he saw the grief on Naseem's face. 'I've probably said a lot more than any brother should say to his sister. I think it is best that you hear the rest from him with your own ears. He will be waiting for you near our well in the morning. You could say that you are going out early to get some fresh mustard leaves or something. Or I could escort you there if you like. And if you are reluctant, let me not force you to do something that you don't want to.'

Naseem said nothing in response. Boote Shah could hear the tempo of her sobs reach a higher pitch. Getting up from the bed, he caressed Naseem's head and said, 'What's the point of crying, silly girl! Come on now. Get up and milk that cow of yours.' He slipped on his shoes and left.

3

THERE ARE TIMES when emotion starts running counter to reason. When this happens, we find that our life's journey has meandered away from its original course and placed us on some unknown path. There is a fork in the path, and we are unable to decide which way will be comfortable, and which one will be fraught with hardship. Our emotions often try to lead us astray, while the strength of our reason tries to bring us back to the right path.

Naseem spent much of the night undulating between the two currents. Boote Shah's words had left her in a state of turmoil. Her attempts to analyse the situation logically were beginning to falter and she found herself being drawn ever deeper into the quagmire of her emotions.

Yusuf was her childhood friend, a headstrong fellow about whom she possessed a bucketful of memories, good and bad. Although she couldn't erase those memories, she had somehow succeeded in setting them aside so that she could continue with her life. And yet, here he was again, seemingly present in every pore of her consciousness.

Before moving to Baba Bhana's house, Naseem had lived in her old home that was next door to Yusuf's place. The only child in his family, Yusuf had been spoilt silly by his parents and grandparents and developed a reputation for being aggressive and a bit of a bully even when he was a little boy. But he was also the clear leader amongst his contemporaries when it came to popular sports like kabbadi and gulli-danda. Growing up in the village, he had a robust physique, fair complexion and blue eyes that always sparkled with a hint of mischief.

Naseem and Yusuf had been friends since childhood, but at some point that friendship turned into affection and the affection bloomed into love. She wasn't too sure about the timeline of this progression. But she was aware that her relationship with Yusuf was a bit like that tale of the man who bought a baby monkey because he found it cute. He showered his love and affection on the baby monkey, but as it grew up, its destructive antics became quite intolerable. The man still loved the monkey, but he also knew that they had to part. He eventually ended up paying some money to divest himself of the burden.

It is said that love blossoms when there is a meeting of minds. Naseem and Yusuf were as far apart in their character as the sky is from the earth and yet, there was some invisible thread that seemed to bind them. A girl as gentle as Naseem in love with a fellow as mercurial as Yusuf? The ways of the Lord are truly beyond the ken of mere mortals!

That night seemed endless. A multitude of thoughts assaulted Naseem's consciousness, each wave cascading into a thousand streams. Images from years gone by rolled before her eyes, a new film playing every hour, usually featuring Yusuf in some form. The sequence of random thoughts and images continued until she heard the night watchman sound his customary 'Beware!' The three taps from his stick told her that three quarters of the night had passed, and dawn was approaching. Her eyes felt raw and gritty, as though sleep had taken the form of tiny grains of sand.

There is a certain sweetness about sleep but there is also a bitter taste when it eludes you. Naseem's eyes were brimming with the two contrasts, as was her heart. Did she love him or did she loathe him? Or was it both? Like a pool of pure nectar that has been sullied by adding the venom of a snake. Her mind sifted through page after page of the book that captured every detail of her relationship with Yusuf. Each incident linked with Yusuf was examined minutely in an attempt to prepare a balance sheet of love and loathing. Did it show that love was the dominant sentiment? Naseem couldn't be sure.

In evaluating Yusuf's behaviour, Naseem acknowledged that he would do things for her that he wouldn't deign doing for anyone else, things that no one could possibly associate with him. Who could imagine this impish lad, insouciant to the core, searching for new ways to win Naseem's affections! And what about his other side? The slightest argument between them would provoke him into violence. Always the same story. He hits her. She cries. He can't bear to see the tears in her eyes. He kneels before her and pleads that she forgive him.

And then? Then her heart melts. The anger and tears in her eyes are replaced by warmth and affection. Oh! How many times did they fight and make up in this manner? Only the Lord knows.

Lying in her bed, Naseem's thoughts went to an incident during the harvest season when they were kids. Both families' kept their harvest of freshly winnowed corn next to each other's and someone had to keep an eye on the large heaps to prevent the odd thief from decamping with a sackful. This was a nice excuse for the elders to get together with their hookahs and gossip late into the night.

Yusuf and Naseem would take advantage to scamper off to a large lasura tree nearby and chat for hours, narrating stories or talking about other boys and girls. The conversation would often turn towards exotic fruits or other delicacies. Something like, 'Our melons last year were just amazing! This April should see our jujube tree, the one near the well, flower quite nicely...' etc.

That evening, Yusuf suddenly exclaimed, 'Hey Seema! Have you ever seen those Shimla peas? The ones that Ida's family have planted? I must say that I was absolutely amazed when I saw them.' Joining his fingertips together to extend his palms, he nudged her, 'Look, Seema! Their pods are this big! And the peas taste so good ... as sweet as our jaggery. God knows where they got the seeds?'

'Ida's chacha lives in the city. He must have bought the seeds there and sent them across. I've seen the plants, but I must say I haven't tasted the peas,' Naseem replied.

They met again at the lasura tree the following evening and Yusuf reached behind the tree trunk to pull out a small bundle. Carefully opening the package, he spread out a dozen or so pods of the Shimla peas before her.

'Where did you get these from, Ranjheya?' Naseem asked in surprise.

'Near Ida's well.'

'How come?'

'For you, of course.'

'Did you steal them, Ranjheya?'

Yusuf was silent.

'Please take them away,' Naseem said in a tone that an affectionate mother might use with an errant son.

'But I've brought them for you. Please try them, Seema,' he implored.

'Eat these? Eat these stolen peas? Are you crazy? Don't you remember what Baba Bhanaji told us during our lesson the other day? He said that stolen property is akin to pork for Muslims and beef for Hindus. Go on, my dear fellow. Put these back in your bundle and leave them where they belong. Please do it or I'll never speak with you again.'

Naseem's request was completely unpalatable for Yusuf. Her entreaties fell on deaf ears. Yusuf was adamant that he would not return the pods. The argument continued for a while, ending only when a resounding slap landed on her cheek.

And the pods? They were angrily flung to the ground and Yusuf didn't rest till he had crushed every single one of them under his shoes.

In Naseem's eyes, Yusuf had not only erred but made matters worse by covering up for his sin with unwarranted aggression. Her tears seemed the only deterrent that worked and she soon found Yusuf kneeling at her feet and seeking forgiveness. The entire episode— from argument to aggression, and from contrition to compassion— must have lasted no more than fifteen minutes.

There was also that other incident around the time of the Eid festivities when all kinds of firecrackers were being sold in the village. Sometime earlier, she had casually mentioned to Yusuf, 'You know what, Ranjheya?' Extending her hands about a foot and a half apart from each other, she continued, 'I long for the day when we have so, so … many firecrackers. So many that you and I can sit right through the night of Eid ul-Fitr and play with them to our heart's content.'

Naseem had made the remark in passing but Yusuf had made a mental note of it. Sure enough, soon it was the night of Eid ul-Fitr and he went up to her home and whispered, 'Come along! I have a surprise for you.' He led her to the backyard of his house and pushed aside a bale of hay to reveal an old carton. She was stunned to see that it was full of fireworks of different kinds—crackers, sparklers, ground spinners, fountains and what not. But her wonderment quickly turned to anger as she got him to admit that he had stolen the money from his mother's piggybank to buy the fireworks. Kicking the carton aside, she raged, 'You shameless wretch! Stealing during the holy month of Ramzan! You will burn in the fires of Hell!'

Yusuf stepped back in trepidation. His mother would no doubt be angry when she discovered the theft but right now, he was more anxious about Naseem's reaction.

'But I've already bought them,' he explained plaintively. 'What do I do with them now?'

Naseem thought for a while before responding with barely concealed fury, 'Just hand it to me, you dimwit.' She took the carton and marched off to her house.

Later that night when Yusuf was busy playing kabaddi with the boys, she took the carton back to his place and approached his mother. 'Chachi, I am going to ask you for something. Will you agree?'

The entreaty of an innocent, beautiful young girl, expressed with such transparent sincerity! Even the most heartless man would find it hard to say no. There was no way that a woman, a mother would refuse her.

Once Yusuf's mother had nodded in agreement, Naseem continued in the same earnest manner, 'Chachi, Yusuf has committed a crime. And I've come to ask you to please, please forgive him.'

'A crime? Yusuf?'

'He has, Chachi. For God's sake don't get cross with him. Didn't the Prophet say in the holy Quran that if you forgive an errant person's sins during the month of Ramzan, you will get twice the blessings?'

Yusuf's mother pulled Naseem to her bosom and held her in a warm embrace. Kissing her forehead, she said, 'What can I say, my dear? The Lord knows everything. What's new if he's done something foolish today? He's been like that since the day he was born.'

Memories of incidents like these, incidents big and small, flashed across Naseem's mind as she lay still in her bed. Her thoughts drifted to another time, the day when she started to see Yusuf through the prism of romance and not merely as her childhood compatriot. She must have been around fourteen, making that transition from childhood to adolescence. Yusuf had also grown quite a bit taller and the hint of a moustache could be seen on his face. Those carefree days of playing together till late in the evening, of sitting in a quiet corner and chatting for hours ... those days seemed to be receding like a distant dream. Yusuf had left the village and moved to Rawalpindi to work with his uncle.

Naseem heard one day that Yusuf had arrived in the village for the first time in a year and a half, and he was staying only for three or four days. The news hit her with the force of a tidal wave, overpowering her heart with a surge of emotions that she had never experienced before.

She spent the rest of the day and much of the night waiting for her sweetheart. She had been so sure that after a year and a half's separation, he would turn up at her doorstep as soon as he arrived. Her spirits drooped with every passing hour, and it wasn't till the following morning that the young daughter of one of their neighbours showed up with a message. 'Yusuf asked you to come to the peepul tree in the grove once the other girls have finished playing.'

And what happened next? I don't think there is any need for me to repeat all the details. Let me just say that in the four years that had elapsed, the dainty little seed of that Banarsi Langra mango has grown into a young tree which is swaying gently in Naseem's courtyard, waiting perhaps to flower after the next monsoon rains.

Naseem hadn't forgotten those moments before they parted, the crazed desperation with which he had sought her, the anger with which he had attacked her, the burning imprint of four fingers across her cheek as she had bolted from the grove.

But that imprint, that mark of revulsion didn't stay very long on her cheek. It was washed away by a steady stream of tears and as the night progressed, the pain of the slap was also buried under the thoughts of the mango and its slender pit.

Somewhere in Naseem's heart, an intense feeling of love for Yusuf started to grow. And along with that, the little mango pit also started to develop its own roots in the welcoming bosom of Mother Earth. Soon enough, a little plant began to emerge from the embrace of the mother, and a similar sapling of love also started to blossom within Naseem's breast.

But the sapling of love was still a juvenile when it received a shock that sent tremors down to its very roots. Naseem had just heard that Yusuf had joined the police. The police! For as long as she could remember, the very mention of the words 'police' or 'policeman' had been enough to trigger her ire. News that Yusuf had joined the police force was akin to sprinkling a large measure of poison over the bubbling spring of her love.

But there's this funny thing about humans, old or young, educated or unlettered, all of them possess two strong emotions—love and hate. The degree or intensity can vary but the presence of the two emotions can't be denied. Isn't it curious that Naseem hates ninety per cent of Yusuf's habits but her love for him continues to endure? His joining the police had tilted the scales even further towards the other side, but not so much that the other feelings etched into the slate of her heart could be erased.

There are countries where the police is respected and perhaps even liked by the people. But not in our country. Here, every single police official is an object of loathing. Strange, isn't it? That a department established with the avowed purpose of protecting our life and property evokes this kind of sentiment in us? That the very sight of the red turban of a policeman can either make us fearful or get us to turn our faces away in revulsion. But why should it be so? Are we at fault or is it the nature of the police department itself? Maybe neither of us should be blamed because the responsibility really lies with the British government. They should reflect carefully on the kind of persons they choose. It is true that every now and then, some decent folks do somehow land up at senior positions in the department. But if you get down to the level of constables, you will be hard-pressed to find a single one who conveys a sense of decency, honesty or even a respect for the law. This shouldn't come as a surprise because constables are mainly recruited on the basis of their robust physique and other superficial attributes. You could, of course, complain to the government—that it ought to recruit better educated persons with sound moral character. The government has a ready response for you. Its doors are open for such persons; the problem is that well-educated and decent individuals don't want to join the police department. So how can you blame the government?

But is that argument good enough to exonerate the government of its culpability? After all, the government can afford to pay as much as a hundred rupees per month to an ordinary mechanic in a workshop. It can even pay two or two and a half rupees a day to an unskilled female who serves them. And for the ones chosen to protect us? The government says that it can't afford to pay them more than thirty or forty rupees a month. What does that tell us about the mentality of the government itself?

The public's biggest grievance against the police relates to bribery and corruption. Indeed, bribery appears to be synonymous with the police department and it is easy to lay the blame on the miserly salaries of the policemen. But what about the public? Shouldn't they also bear a part of the responsibility? Why can't people understand that giving a bribe and receiving a bribe are two sides of the same coin? When you raise this issue with the bribe-givers, they have a simplistic response—that bribes enable them to surmount unnecessary hurdles so that they can go about their business. Take the case of a typical government contractor. He can play fast and loose with the law and make as much as two hundred thousand rupees of illegal profit from a single contract. And if his transgressions come to light, he happily gives a small part of his ill-gotten gains as bribe to sort things out. In the rare instance that the bribe doesn't work and the matter goes up to a court, the judge may impose a penalty of some two thousand rupees or so. That's as good as getting a license to engage in corruption. Keep making your illicit profits and if you get caught, pay your tithe to the government and go back to business as usual! When the system is rotten to the core, who do you blame for what?

Enough said! It is what it is. Young Naseem may not have been aware of all these intricacies but she was pretty clear in her mind that policemen are bad characters, that they have a reputation of being brutal and violent, and that people have good reasons to either hate or fear them. Her impressions weren't just based on hearsay either. She had seen the police abuse and beat people with her own eyes. Like the day the police had thrashed a poor labourer so badly he remained unconscious for quite a while. And that other time when a posse of policemen had rained blows on some perfectly respectable persons, apparently because they were investigating a theft and were frustrated they couldn't find the thief.

So Yusuf had joined the police! Her body trembled with the shock. He could also have joined the army, gone off to war and gotten wounded by an enemy bullet. Would that have been a bigger shock for Naseem? Maybe not.

As the weeks went by, Naseem forced herself to reconcile with the new reality. She thought that the effect of the poison sprinkled into the bubbling spring of her love was wearing off and she could again nurture a positive feeling about Yusuf. That was when a second bombshell dropped.

Yusuf, it was rumoured, had settled in Rawalpindi after marrying a woman of ill-repute. The news left the young girl's dreams in tatters. Her hopes of a life of bliss with Yusuf had rapidly evaporated. 'Could anyone imagine that he would act in this fashion?' she asked herself. But life doesn't unfold according to one's expectations—there are times when it runs counter to them. And there are times when the improbable, even the impossible, happens before our very eyes.

There is a part of our personality that we guard jealously from prying eyes. We try to make sure that it is safely hidden away behind a thick curtain. But that doesn't prevent a strong gust from lifting the curtain in a way that a section of the portrait becomes visible to the public, warts and all. Reports of Yusuf's latest indiscretion had arrived like that gust, revealing other facets of an individual whom Naseem thought she knew so well from childhood. As tongues started to wag in the village, more stories about him began tumbling in by the day. Tales about his thieving, his gambling, and his whoring that poor Naseem had to listen to from women young and old. And she cursed herself for being such a fool, lamenting her own blindness in the face of so much evidence. But did she manage to expel Yusuf from the innermost recesses of her heart? The embers were still there—she thought the pain-drenched breath from her sobs would be enough to extinguish them for good. Instead, it seemed to stoke the fires.

That tree ... that mango tree in the courtyard! That tree is the root of all my woes, she thought to herself. No matter how reprehensible

Yusuf's character, she wouldn't be able to get him out of her system unless she tackled the source of the problem.

She spent the afternoon pondering over the dilemma. The sun had started to wind up its business for the day and was moving towards a secluded corner, when Naseem leapt from her bed with new resolve. She went to the rear of the house and soon emerged with a woodcutter's axe. Heading straight for the young tree, she lifted the axe and delivered a blow on its slender trunk.

She didn't miss her target, but neither did the blow have the force to fell the tree in one stroke. Perhaps the delicate arms didn't have the required strength for the task. Perhaps the trunk wasn't as thin as she had imagined it to be. Or perhaps, during the split second between lifting the axe and delivering the blow, Naseem had lost the will to finish the job. Her arms had the power when she lifted the axe, but her hands were lifeless by the time the axe struck the trunk. An ugly gash emerged at the point where metal had met wood. She banished any thoughts of raising the axe a second time and hurriedly put it aside. Eyes transfixed on the trunk, she gazed fearfully at the wound she had inflicted on it. The mango tree no longer appeared as inanimate; it had become an embodiment of a sentient being.

A few minutes later, Naseem was kneading some mud and cow dung together into a thick paste which she applied in layers on the laceration. Her prayers were answered and the tree continued to flourish in her courtyard.

The lacerations in her own heart were also beginning to heal, albeit gradually. She felt that the pain constantly gnawing inside her was beginning to subside. Naseem was convinced that since Yusuf had already exited from her world, it was only a question of time before he would clear out of her thoughts too. But the unexpected was again lurking around the corner, this time in the form of some fresh reports about Yusuf. 'That wretched woman, the one with whom Yusuf had a marriage contract … Well, she's left him. And not just that. She's also cleaned up everything she could lay her hands on.'

The stories brought a fresh turbulence to Naseem's fragile state. Yusuf's name was once again on the lips of the village folk. Tales of his previous misadventures were retold with great relish, each one providing the fodder for a renewed round of entertainment. A few days passed, the novelty wore off and the gossip slowly died.

Barely a month had passed before the village was once again aflutter with news that some of its residents had recently seen Yusuf. He looked a different man, they said. He was Mister Mohammed Yusuf, Police Constable, now. Tall, handsome and well built, attired in a policeman's uniform.

Naseem felt a burning rage when she heard that Yusuf was in the neighbourhood. A volcano was building up inside her, it's fiery lava barely contained within the rim. She would have been ready to slap anyone who even dared mention Yusuf's name within earshot. But did she dare to slap the one who had sat by Yusuf's side for hours, taking his name ever so sweetly?

And so, her mind flitted from one thought to another as the hours of the night ticked away and the watchman could be heard calling out 'Beware' to announce the third quarter. Naseem's eyes felt raw from lack of sleep but she told herself that she had taken a firm decision. There was no way that she was going to meet Yusuf; she would not see his face, nor would she let herself think about him. And yet, no sooner had the rooster crowed than she sprang from her bed and was out of the door with the alacrity of one who is chasing a thief.

4

A LITTLE WHILE later, the stirring notes of 'Allahu Akbar …
Allahu Akbar' could be heard from the village mosque, as the
muezzin called the faithful to their morning prayers. Naseem was
hurrying along the street when she heard the call. By the time the
azan ended with the words 'La ilaha illallah,' she could be seen walking
along a grassy trail that ran between the cultivated farmlands. She
was so lost in the soothing, spiritually uplifting notes of the azan that
she had left the village and was approaching her destination without
having noticed that someone was following her.

She heard the footsteps behind her as the azan ended. Startled,
she looked over her shoulder before exclaiming in a reassured tone,
'Bhaaji?'

Boote Shah walked up to her before responding, 'I thought I
would come along, lest you are scared or something.'

Feeling a bit awkward, Naseem continued to walk towards the
well in silence. Boote Shah also didn't make any effort to strike a
conversation and the two walked up the trail, one behind the other.
They had only walked a short distance when they caught a glimpse
of someone in white clothes in the adjacent tract of farmland, which
extended all the way to Chaudhry Fazal Karim's well, near the banks

of Soan river. Suspecting that it must be the Chaudhry himself, out for a walk in his estate, Boote Shah quickly took a detour, with Naseem following behind him.

The well was located inside a small grove and as they approached its periphery, Boote Shah could see Yusuf pacing up and down, impatiently. 'I am going across to our fields to take a look,' he told Naseem and left.

Yusuf had lost his father at a very young age. Abdullah, or 'Dulla' as he was known in the village, was a blacksmith by caste. He used to have a job in the workshop at Golra railway station, but he lost his leg in a railway accident while he was still a young man. He was sent to hospital and paid a modest sum by way of a provident fund. But the hospital discharged him prematurely and upon his return to Chakri, he continued to suffer the after-effects of amputation. The poor man spent six or seven months in agony before the injury prematurely claimed his life. Fortunately, Yusuf's maternal uncle Sikander was doing fairly well in Rawalpindi those days. He had a small business repairing horse carriages, and gladly offered to support his widowed sister and young nephew. He would send some money each month to help them meet their expenses. The family also had a small piece of land that they gave to a sharecropper. The produce from the land and the financial support from the uncle enabled them to make both ends meet until Yusuf reached the age of thirteen. He had entered his fourteenth year and had already developed a reputation for being something of a rascal. Sikander thought he would solve the problem by taking him along to Rawalpindi. The blithe environs of the village were replaced by the grind of long days at his uncle's workshop, with a hammer and chisel as his constant companions. He hated it but didn't really have too many options at that stage.

He would get a chance to visit the village every six or eight months but only for a few days. His mother wanted him to stay longer but the uncle would insist on his early return, apprehensive that lack of supervision and the company of unruly friends in Chakri would lead him back to his old ways. Sikander had managed to get Yusuf on the straight and narrow by directing his energies into work and he wanted to keep it that way.

Not long thereafter, Yusuf's mother fell ill and received the inevitable invitation from the Angel of Death. Her passing also took away the principal reason that had pulled Yusuf towards Chakri. He had no particular attachment to their small mud house. It was the streets that he remembered more often. The alleys where he had spent much of his youth would appear in his dreams every now and then.

But this visit to the village was different. It was taking place at a time when his life had taken several difficult turns. His decision to join the police had led to an unpleasant altercation with his uncle and aunt, and forced him to leave their home. His infatuation with the dissolute wife of a cobbler had been an unmitigated disaster. Rudderless, he felt the tug of his roots, the urge to find an anchor on familiar turf.

It isn't easy to be granted leave so soon after joining the police force. It had spent barely six months in the job, but Yusuf managed to persuade his bosses to let him take a week off. On reaching the village, he first went across to meet his closest friend Boote Shah and poured out his heart. Boote Shah had heard of Yusuf's escapades and some of the stories had left him quite distressed. But his tale of woes was enough to neutralize Boota's angst and he found himself recalling the old saying, 'It is the friend's friendship that matters, not the friend's traits.' And so it was that he embraced Yusuf at a time when the young man was down and out. Not only did he embrace Yusuf, but he went a step further and made a promise that even today sends a shiver down his spine—the promise to help Yusuf fulfil his desire to marry his foster-sister. He reasoned that this was best accomplished by creating an opportunity for Naseem and Yusuf to meet face to face and resolve their differences directly. He knew that he would not force Naseem into the marriage against her will, but he had also heard enough from Yusuf to recognize that Naseem too was fond of him. He reasoned that once they had met and sorted things out, he would be able to take the proposal for their marriage to the elders and seek their blessings.

Boote Shah left after escorting Naseem to the grove. She lifted her eyes and wondered, 'Is this really the same Yusuf?' Her thoughts went to the poet Gul Marsool's rendition of the legend of Yusuf and Zuleikha that she had read some time ago, and she could discern the similarities between this Yusuf and the Yusuf of lore. He did look exceptionally handsome, and she felt compelled to lower her gaze for a moment or two. That was enough time for that familiar cloud of hatred to emerge from the morning skies and cast a dark shadow over her emotions. With a deep sigh, she mused, 'How I wish this Yusuf was like Zuleikha's Yusuf—pure and noble like that son of Yakub!' Her eyes shifted their gaze from the ground only when she heard a plaintive voice, 'You … you've come, Naseem?'

Naseem didn't respond. She felt her mouth dry and her heart pounding in her ears.

'Come inside,' he said from the entrance of the thatched hut inside the grove. Naseem found her unsteady legs drag her to the entrance.

A cot made from rough twine was positioned at the side of the hut. Responding to his signal, she gingerly sat on the edge of its wooden frame.

An uncomfortable silence prevailed, broken eventually when Yusuf said, 'Naseem!'

Her lips didn't utter a sound but her eyes lifted. They had the look of a deer caught in the sights of a hunter. A thin film of moisture appeared on them.

'I really thought you wouldn't come,' Yusuf continued as he read the message of pain writ large on her face.

'How could I not come?' Naseem had to clear her throat before she could voice the few words. Her damask lips had blanched to resemble the petals of the nilofar water lily. Head bowed, her slender fingers were nervously tugging at the inky fringe of her dupatta.

'Naseem!' Yusuf slid a couple of inches closer to her. 'Are you still angry with me?' Naseem raised her head and lowered it again, as though trying to convey, 'Is there any doubt on that score?'

'Come on, Naseem! You are acting like you have marbles in your mouth. Who should I speak with?'

'Go on, please,' she managed to say. She realized that the 'please' was an afterthought, a word that would never have occurred in earlier conversations with Yusuf. But he was no longer the errant lad with whom she could speak so informally. The suffix appeared appropriate, particularly since he too was addressing her as Naseem and hadn't called her Seema the way he used to.

'What can I say, Naseem?' Yusuf found himself getting tangled in a web of shame and guilt. 'You must have heard a lot of stuff about me and…'

Naseem's eyes lifted again, this time digging her gaze firmly on the young man's face. She wanted to hear his side of the story.

'It is true, whatever you've heard. I am a sinner in Allah's court, and in yours too. Forgive me, Naseem.'

Naseem could see that Yusuf's eyes were brimming with remorse. His earnest confession and the transparent sincerity shining in his eyes had started to dissipate the miasma of loathing that Naseem had accumulated. But a reckoning of her own self-esteem and religious beliefs arose like a dense mist to cloud even those parts of the mirror had started to clear up. The crimson flames of lava were once again rising within her and she saw them take the form of words as she spoke, 'Who am I to forgive or not forgive you?' The rage within her was melting her eyes and she could feel the searing heat of her tears streaming down her cheeks.

'Believe it or not, Naseem,' he whimpered, 'the devil had taken over my mind and I...'

'Please tell me,' Naseem interrupted with an edge in her tone. 'Why did you ask to see me? Please hurry up because I have a lot of chores waiting for me.'

'I asked to see you so that I could remind you of our deep love for each other.'

His words only aggravated her agitated state. What a scoundrel, she told herself. After trampling on his own love and discarding it without a second thought, he has the nerve to come here and remind me of my love for him? She felt the veins in her forehead dilate with anger and her instinct told her to get up immediately and make a dash towards home. But she also needed to unburden herself before she could get up. The embers of her rage crackled as she spoke, 'Love? What love?'

'Have you forgotten, Naseem?'

'Aren't you ashamed to be saying this? How mulish can a man be?'

Yusuf winced at the insult but swallowed his pride. He bit his tongue and held himself from retorting, 'How dare you speak like that, you who has been raised on the crumbs of others!' Keeping his habitual aggression in check, he said in a gentler tone, 'Let bygones be bygones, Naseem. My actions have already shamed me enough.'

'But I am not the one responsible for your actions,' Naseem replied in the same fiery hue.

'Naseem,' he pleaded. 'Please don't wreck my life.'

'Why would I do that? Allah punishes those who go about destroying the lives of others.'

Yusuf's sense of self-esteem was yelling at him, 'Do you have no self-respect, you contemptible man? Why are you allowing this chit of a girl to heap such insults on you?' But he hadn't given up hope yet. His restraint was once again able to push aside his surging ego as he implored, 'Naseem, I swear by my mother that I will always remain faithful to you. If you can just once…'

'I've heard such oaths many a time,' Naseem retorted and turned her face away from him. 'Those who take a false oath invite the fury of God Himself,' she continued sternly.

'Naseem!' Yusuf crackled as he found himself losing his battle for self-control. Naseem anxiously turned her face towards him. She could see a ferocious anger building up in his eyes. Annoyed by what she had observed and also a little bit concerned by his reaction, she got up from the bed and signalled that she was ready to leave. Her eyes glared at him in defiance.

She had barely taken a couple of steps when Yusuf leapt forward and caught her arm, pulling her back towards the cot, saying, 'Look Naseem! Such disdain isn't good for anyone. Sit down for a while so that we can chat about a few more things.'

The powerful grip of his hand on her arm sent a tremor through her body. Her senses warned her of impending danger. But without any further protest, she sat down again on the cot.

'Naseem!' Yusuf spoke with a conscious effort to add a touch of honey to the bitterness of his voice. 'I had asked you to come with the hope that you would apply some balm to my wounds. Had I known you were going to sprinkle salt and aggravate them instead I wouldn't have come.'

'I don't know about your need. My brother asked me to come, and I couldn't say no to him.'

Yusuf recoiled at the harshness of her response. A rising tide of anger swept aside the reason he had summoned to pull her back so they could complete their conversation. His lips quivered as he growled, 'Brother? Which brother of yours are you talking about?'

'The same one that brought me your message.'

'And how is he your brother, Naseem?'

'The same way that Aziz is my brother.'

Her blunt response knocked another hole into the reservoir that was holding back Yusuf's anger. He felt his pent-up frustration tumble into his words as he spoke menacingly, 'And why not! That Hindu becomes your brother and I become a complete stranger.'

'Stop it! Don't you dare say a word against Bhaaji. You insult him again and you'll see what I do to you,' she hissed.

'You! And when did you become such a beloved of your brother?' Yusuf roared. His face had turned ochre with rage as he snarled, 'Did your mother secretly give birth to him?'

'Don't you dare cross the boundaries of civility. If Bhaaji hadn't asked me, I wouldn't be here to even spit on you.'

'Watch it! You are the one crossing boundaries. Looking at your arrogance, you must think you are some kind of angel from the heavens.'

'You won't find your houris in these villages. But I am sure you can find them in the windows of the brothels in your city. Why don't you look for them over there?'

'Shut up, you bitch!'

'Who are you calling a bitch? Your mo—' The word 'mother' was still on Naseem's lips when his palm came crashing on the side of her face. The impact of his heavy hand reverberated through her ears. She felt her head spinning and a darkness enveloping her. It took her a few seconds to regain her bearings and when she did, she found his powerful arms crushing her against his body. She kicked and slapped and pinched to free herself from his grip, but her efforts were like those of the tiny sparrow flapping its wings and screaming in vain as the viper tightens its hold.

'You bitch! You low life! You illegitimate progeny of a swine!' Yusuf hurled the curses in a single breath even as he splattered her face with kisses. The animal in him was unleashed and he might have continued if he hadn't noticed someone appear at the entrance of the hut. His arms involuntarily loosened their grip, allowing Naseem to escape his clutches. She bolted straight through the door and through the grove without pausing to see the face of her saviour.

'What do you think you are doing, you nasty piece of work?' young Allahditta rumbled as he leapt towards Yusuf with the agility of a leopard.

Yusuf was rather proud of his physique and also stood a couple of inches taller than Allahditta. But the intruder was exceptionally muscular, and his stocky frame was hard as iron after years of tough manual labour. He placed one hand on Yusuf's throat and pushed him out of the hut. 'Let me show you what happens when you mess around with girls from our village,' he warned.

'Get lost,' Yusuf twirled his moustache as he growled. 'Or you'll find yourself leaving this place with a broken jaw.'

'Really?' Allahditta said as he rolled up his sleeves. 'Let's settle the matter then. We've had enough of your nuisance. It's time someone taught you a lesson.'

As the two went at each other, Yusuf found it hard to believe that his shorter opponent could possess such strength. Within minutes, he had pummelled Yusuf to the ground, ripped his clothes and boxed his face black and blue. After being released from Allahditta's brawny arms, Yusuf looked sheepishly at his feet.

Allahditta brushed the dust off his clothes and warned, 'Blacken your face and get lost, you son of a swine. If I ever see you in our village again, I promise you I'll shove that police uniform of yours up your arse! Son of a bitch! Even the most depraved know where to draw a line. And you … you had no qualms about assaulting a daughter of your own village? If you ever return to this place, I will make sure that your face is blackened and you are paraded on a donkey. I swear that if I don't do that, I am the offspring of a bitch and not of my mother.'

'Allahditta,' Yusuf pleaded as he used a section of his turban to stem the flow of blood oozing from his teeth. 'Please forgive me, brother. I've made a mistake,' he panted.

'Made a mistake?' Allahditta scowled. 'This isn't the first time you've behaved like this! We know your habits well, you scoundrel.'

'Alright, brother. But I implore you to protect my honour this one time. Please don't breathe a word about today to anyone in the village. And if I ever do something wrong again, you can treat me like a bandit and give me the same punishment.'

'Not tell anyone in the village?' Allahditta asked incredulously. 'And what about the poor girl that you have assaulted? What will she say? That her village folk have all vanished? No way! I suggest you take the track outside the village and make your way to Rawalpindi without uttering another word. That's your safest bet. Or else…'

5

AFTER DROPPING NASEEM at the grove, Boote Shah decided to walk across the farmlands to his own cotton plantation. He was in a particularly pensive frame, questioning the rationale of his recent actions and apprehensive that matters could well take an unexpected course. The night had also been equally restless as he fretted over the import of delivering Yusuf's message to Naseem. 'What have I done?' he pondered. 'How can any brother so brazenly discuss such a delicate matter with his sister? If Krishna had been around, she would have been Naseem's age today. Would I have dared to have a similar conversation with Krishna? And what about the person whose message I am carrying with such earnestness? Does he deserve my recommendation to become the life-partner of a girl like Naseem? Just a few days back, the entire village was buzzing with tales of his misdeeds. And here I am advocating that we place our trust in a character with such an unreliable reputation? That doesn't say much for my own wisdom, does it? Okay, agreed that I may have done the right thing as a friend. But is my sister's life less precious than my fidelity to my friend?' Over the course of the night, Boote Shah's mind often drifted to elements of his conversations with Yusuf. 'I have done no wrong,' he would reassure himself. 'If Naseem also loves Yusuf the same way, why shouldn't we help them come together? After all, we have the responsibility to make sure that Naseem gets married. If we find some other suitable match for her, don't we run the risk that the death of her first love could cloud the rest of her life?'

He spent much of the night mulling over these issues. Naseem's first reaction on hearing about Yusuf last evening had given him the confidence that he could be proud of his initiative. But he had a change of heart as he thought more deeply about the matter. Yusuf's mercurial nature was well-known and his nikah with that woman in Rawalpindi was evidence that his professions of love for Naseem could also prove transient. If Yusuf could turn his back on his childhood love and get infatuated with some debauched woman, where's the guarantee that he wouldn't do the same again? That made up his mind. He would go across to Naseem's place and persuade her not to see him. Leaving home early for his morning constitutional, he was heading for her place when he saw that Naseem was already on her way to the grove. His mind flipped once again. If Naseem is going on her own volition to see Yusuf, she must have been pining for him. Instead of trying to discourage her from going, he decided to accompany her to the well. As he walked with her, he reasoned that he wasn't setting aside his reservations about Yusuf. He was what he was. But no one could have any doubt about Naseem's character. Let the two meet and she could decide on the next step.

And yet, there was a sense of disquiet as he went about his work. It had taken him around two and a half hours to finish the round of his farm and he was sure that Naseem would have returned home by now. But he found his legs unwittingly pull him back towards the grove.

The hut was empty and Boota's heart sank as he looked inside. He bent low to pick up fragments of golden yellow glass bangles scattered across the floor. He found it hard to breathe as he looked at the pieces he was clutching in his palm. Something terrible has happened, he thought. His heart was thumping in his ears and he could feel his legs buckle. His eyes brimmed with the pain of death itself.

Taking a deep breath, he pulled himself together and started to run towards the village. The news had already spread like wildfire. 'Yusuf has molested Naseem.' It was on everybody's lips.

He ran into Allahditta as he was entering the village. The young man narrated the entire sordid episode in detail, adding that Yusuf hadn't dared to enter the village. He also mentioned that a bunch of hefty young men from the village had gone out with their sticks looking for him.

Allahditta's account gave Boote Shah some comfort. An altercation had taken place but fortunately, Naseem was safe. He thanked Allahditta profusely for saving the honour of his foster sister, showered blessings on him and set off for his home.

Boote's grief over the unfortunate turn of events was overshadowed by an even larger fear of his father's reaction. How would he handle the shock when he heard about the assault on Naseem? He thought it best to head straight home even though he wanted to drop in at Naseem's and check on her. Upon entering the haveli, he heard the voices of some of the village elders who were sitting waiting for Baba Bhana. A few others had joined them.

He got the drift and decided that it was best to tiptoe around them and wait quietly in his room. A little while later he heard the Baba, who had been tied up with a patient all morning, enter the haveli. A few more minutes elapsed before he heard a crackling voice, 'Oye Boote! Come here right away.'

It was his father's voice alright, but there was a harshness to it that he had never previously heard from his mellowed personality.

'Coming, Bapuji,' he said and froze in his tracks when he entered the room and saw the expression on his father's face. His eyes were burning with rage and there was a tremor on his lips that was causing his beard to shudder.

The Baba's right hand was clasped around his walking stick and as soon as Boote Shah appeared before him, the stick came crashing on his back. He staggered under the force of the blow and the Baba was getting ready to lift the staff again when some of the guests got up to grab his arms.

Finding himself restrained by several pairs of hands, the Baba roared like a lion, 'May you rot in hell, you wretch! Look at the muck you've rubbed on my grey hair. What did I do to deserve this kind of ignominy at my age? Now, come clean and tell us where you took the girl at the crack of dawn.'

A few of the visitors got up to tend to Boote Shah, massaging his injured back and urging him to sit with them. He felt his head spinning, partly due to the injury and in larger measure due to a sense of acute shame. The walls of the room appeared to be spinning before his eyes.

'Go stand there amid the shoes,' the Baba bellowed again. Like a puppet following its master's commands, Boote Shah went to the corner where the visitors had left their shoes and slippers before entering the room.

'Did you take Seema to the well?' the Baba barked as he gnawed at his lips in anger.

'Come on, Babaji,' Chaudhry Fazal Karim placed his hand on the Baba's shoulder, rubbing it gently as he spoke. 'Don't be so harsh on the boy.'

'Harsh?' the Baba rolled his head from one side to the other as he crackled. 'Chaudhry, you are telling me not to be harsh after the way he's muddied my reputation? All these years, he's never given anyone the slightest opportunity to complain. I used to count my blessings. I would even tell people that they should wish for a son as decent as mine. A soul so gentle that you wouldn't notice his presence. And now? He thinks he's one of the local thugs! How I wish this boy had never been born! If I had any inkling that you would turn out like this, I would have given you poison while you were still an infant. Get out of this house right now, you wretch. Or bring me a handful of cyanide and I'll do the rest.'

Boote Shah felt as if a paralysis had gripped his vocal cords. He wanted to speak but the words refused to emerge from his lips. He finally croaked, his voice sounding like one of those flutes that has a crack running through it, 'I made a mistake, Bapuji. But there was nothing wrong with my intentions.'

'Nothing wrong with your intentions?' the Baba sneered. 'Oh sure! What could be wrong with your intentions? After all, you only took the girl on a pilgrimage to see a well-known holy man! Can't I see what you are up to? First you commit a sin and then you try to cover it up.' His temper had flared up again and a hint of froth could be seen trickling down the corner of his lip.

'Speak up! Why did you take the girl to that fellow?' he raised his voice in irritation when Boote Shah didn't respond. Boote Shah remained mum. The Baba moved to grab his stick from the Chaudhry's hand and roared, 'Who's stolen your voice? Answer me now!'

'Bapuji!' Boote Shah tried to moisten his lips with his tongue as he stood in the corner amidst the many pairs of shoes. 'I will tell you everything. And if you still find me guilty after listening to the entire story, I will blacken my face before these elders, get on a donkey and leave this village in disgrace.'

'No, young man! Please don't say such things,' the Chaudhry admonished him before walking across and pulling Boote Shah's arm, urging him to take a seat beside him. 'No, Chaachaji. I won't move from here unless Bapuji asks me to.'

'Sit down,' the old man's lips quivered as he thundered. Boote Shah left the corner and sat on the floor near the Chaudhry's knee.

He had barely sat down that the Baba's hand again moved towards his stick. The Chaudhry moved quickly to grasp his arm. 'Enough, Babaji. Leave that cane alone. I have stayed quiet out of respect but…' he spoke firmly.

'Don't worry. I won't do anything to him.' The Baba's trembling hands clasped the cane and left his seat. Without saying a word to his guests, he headed for the rear door that led into the house. They waited in silence, none daring to question where he was heading.

A few minutes later, the sound of the walking stick could be heard again. The Baba was carrying a round brass pitcher which had a somewhat dirty and fraying cord wrapped around its neck. The mouth of the pitcher was sealed with wax and a tin foil.

Holding the cord in his hand, he went across to Boote Shah and placed the pitcher on his head. 'Booteya! What have I placed on your head? Do you understand its importance?' he demanded.

'It's holy water from the Ganga, Bapuji.'

'Then swear by the holy waters of the Ganga that you will speak the absolute truth.'

'I swear by the holy water and I also swear by your feet that I will tell everything truthfully,' Boote Shah bent to touch his father's feet as he spoke.

The Baba removed the pitcher from his head and slung it from a hook on the wall behind him before returning to his seat.

Boote Shah started to outline the case in his defence. 'Everyone in this village knows that Yusuf is my closest friend. Although he is a few years younger than me, we have been friends from the very beginning and the bonds of this friendship have only become stronger over the years.

'You also know that I look at Naseem as my own sister and have a special affection for her, especially since Krishna's death. I have often thought that the Lord snatched Krishna from us and sent us Naseem in exchange.

'You would remember the house in which Sugara Chaachi and Naseem used to live before they moved here. I mean their old house. Yusuf was their neighbour at the time, and while he is a good three years older than Naseem, the two grew up playing together. We always knew that they were fond of each other, but it was only recently that I learned that they are in love.

'I won't hide anything from this august gathering. I still care very deeply about Yusuf but I can't say the same about his habits. While he was in the village, he was always involved in some nuisance or the other. When his maama took him to Rawalpindi, I heaved a sigh of relief even though I often missed his company.

'After he had left for the city, his mother hinted to me on at least a couple of occasions that it would be wonderful if we could arrange his marriage with Naseem. I liked her suggestion but I also worried that marrying her to this ruffian would lead to a life of misery for poor Naseem.

'Yusuf's mother passed away and Yusuf was tied up with his maama in the city. That was the end of the matter, I thought. But Yusuf started sending me long letters from Rawalpindi in which half the narrative was about Naseem. He went to the extent of writing to me that he would take his own life if Naseem refused to marry him. I didn't pay much heed to his entreaties initially. But after reading quite a few of his letters, I started to feel his pain. I also reasoned that he now had a job of sorts and if I were to take the proposal to Bapuji and

Sugara Chaachi, I might get their consent. I decided to informally broach the subject with them. Sugara Chaachi was very clear in her mind that it was up to Bapuji to take a view on this matter. I then took it up with Bapuji. He was distinctly lukewarm about the idea and said, "The boy is a bit of a vagabond. I don't want to do anything that might wreck the girl's life." And that was it. I never had the nerve to raise this subject again with Bapuji. But I also wasn't unmindful of the turmoil through which my friend was passing. This was manifest in every letter of his, often declaring that he was counting on me to sort this out and warning that I might see him dead if I didn't.

'I would reply to his letters with the advice: "Yusuf, first make yourself worthy of Naseem. If you do, I will do my best to help you. God willing, you will get what you cherish." I also advised him that instead of working at his maama's workshop, where he'd spend the day beating iron with his hammer, he ought to look for some kind of government job. If he managed to get in at a young age, he could reach a position of some consequence. He followed my advice and managed to get a job with the police. But God alone knows what came into his mind that he fell into that woman's trap...'

Boote Shah paused for a second as he mulled over his choice of words. He was in the presence of elders and didn't want to use any uncivil vocabulary. Of course, the audience already knew about this particular matter, but he continued his narrative in a more circumspect fashion. 'Yusuf's action came as a real shock to me and I soon found myself developing a strong aversion towards him. And yet, when he came to the village this time, he just poured his heart out. He kept crying about his miserable life. He was so emotional that I was also moved to tears. I should also confess that I might have played a role in his misadventure in the city. You see, I made the mistake of writing to him that Bapuji will never agree to his marriage with Naseem and it would be best for him to give up this dream of his. That might have been the reason he fell into the web of that woman. He told me the whole story when I saw him the day before yesterday.

'I'd thought that he would go on and on about Naseem but that wasn't the case. He did mention her, but in such a way that it really touched my heart. He said, "Brother Boote, I am convinced that I can keep trying my best till Judgement Day, but I won't be able to make myself worthy of Naseem. I have given up my dream of having Naseem as my life-partner. But I also know that I won't live very long after losing Naseem. So, I've come today to bid farewell to you and to take your help in delivering one last message to Naseem. I have tormented her on so many occasions and I really want to seek her forgiveness…"'

Boote Shah's voice choked with grief and he found it hard to continue. Pausing for a while, he cleared his throat and swept his hand over a fold of his turban before resuming, 'To be honest, I didn't see any trace of duplicity in Yusuf's words. I was convinced that this fool might actually take some extreme step, and that I had to do what I could to save him.

'Now let me come to the matter of taking Naseem to the grove. I don't deny that I accompanied her to the grove, but I believed I was doing this to help both of them. I wanted to give them the chance to come face to face and decide what they wanted to do. If Naseem were to give her consent, I thought I would once again take up the proposal with Bapuji and try to persuade him. How could I have known that he would turn out to be such a lowlife? So here I stand before you. If you feel that I have sinned, please feel free to unleash your shoes on my head…'

Boote Shah lowered his head before the audience and continued, 'I agree that it was inappropriate for me to have acted in this manner.

The very fact that I am discussing such personal details about my unmarried sister is wrong. But I have sworn by the holy waters of the Ganga, and also by Bapuji's feet that I would tell the whole truth. Otherwise, I would rather have torn my tongue out than spoken about such matters.'

A murmur of approving sounds went around the room as several voices heartily endorsed Boote Shah's remarks about Naseem's innocence.

Boote Shah continued, 'I was absolutely convinced that no matter how depraved Yusuf might be, he could never bring dishonour to his friend's sister. But that devil acted absolutely contrary to my expectations. I was wrong about him, but I was right about something else. When I was escorting Naseem to the grove, my heart told me that irrespective of any misbehaviour by Yusuf, I had the fullest confidence in the virtuousness of my sister. I was sure that even Satan himself couldn't weaken Naseem's resolve. I am happy that on this count, at least, I was absolutely correct.'

As he completed his defence statement, several members got up to pat him on his back. The Baba seemed embarrassed that he had acted in such inordinate haste, but the embarrassment was compensated by a sense of vindication that his son had done no wrong.

'We always knew that Boote Shah could do no such thing,' the Chaudhry exclaimed. 'He's grown up before our eyes. We know him much too well for such a trait to be hidden.'

Trying to atone for his own outburst, the Baba said, 'You are absolutely right, Chaudhry. That's the very thought that made me blind with anger. Otherwise, how could I think such a thing about my own son!'

The panchayat ended its meeting.

Boote Shah heaved a sigh of relief.

6

BOOTE SHAH HAD managed to establish his innocence before
his father, and he was happy that the elders of the village now
understood his position. But he had also lowered himself in Naseem's
eyes and his own shame from the sorry episode was stuck like a thorn
in his side. He knew that his actions had thrust Naseem into ignominy.
Had he not urged her to meet Yusuf, she would have escaped the
physical and emotional trauma inflicted on her by that fiend.

Without waiting to have his dinner that evening, Baba Bhana went
across to Naseem's house to comfort her and offer his unreserved
support. Naseem's mother told him that her daughter had gone to
pick some fresh mustard leaves when Yusuf waylaid her and dragged
her into the grove. Naseem had to fight with all her strength to save
her honour from that ruffian. The old man's face had a volcanic look
about it even though he had already heard the full facts of the incident
from his son. His only regret was that he hadn't been able to lay his
hands on Yusuf.

Meanwhile, Boote Shah's statement to the elders of the panchayat
had made it clear that blame for the unfortunate happening must fall
squarely on Yusuf. This put a stop to the unsavoury tales that some
of the womenfolk were spinning about Naseem's role in the episode.

Their wagging tongues were silenced, and their gossip was replaced by a new-found respect for the girl. A new story could be heard on the lips of all and sundry in the village. About the courage of a young girl who had fought like a tigress to protect her honour from that brute of a man. In the eyes of the village, she had emerged as an idealized heroine. But was Naseem happy with all this adulation?

Boote Shah also wanted to visit Naseem the same evening, but was held back partly by his lingering sense of shame and partly because he knew that his father would also be going to see her. He wanted to catch her alone so that he could express his heartfelt apology and ask her to forgive him. This left him no option but to wait till the evening of the following day.

The sun was setting, its last slivers of light leaving after extending an invitation to the darkness of the night to take their place. One of the last rays was falling on Sugara's emaciated face, making it look even more pale and deathly. Her frail arm could be seen moving a broom as she sat on her haunches and swept the courtyard. The mouth-watering aroma of saag being cooked from fresh mustard leaves was wafting through the entrance to the kitchen. In a smaller mud oven, a slow fire from a handful of cow dung cakes was keeping a pot of milk simmering. A large wooden churner stood in a corner; the remains of butter fat stuck in its grooves attracting a stream of little brown ants. Some leaves and stems were lying in a winnowing basket, intended perhaps to feed the cow. The speckled cow that had recently been separated from its herd was tied next to the feeding trough. It was trying to stretch its rope towards its calf, the young fellow tied a few feet away from her, and straining to get some milk. The juvenile mango tree stood in the middle, swaying in the evening breeze like a tipsy young man. A few dozen golden-hued leaves were scattered beneath the tree and a new one would glide down every minute or two to add to their number.

'Chaachi!' Boote Shah called as he entered the courtyard. 'Why are you busy with the broom today? Hasn't Bapuji cautioned you against doing anything strenuous? This is just the kind of thing that aggravates your asthma.'

'Come inside, my dear son,' she said as she abandoned the broom and stood up to greet him. 'Nothing to worry. I had just picked up the broom to clear out the mess left by some kids who were playing here. I thought I would be very gentle as I—'

'And where's Seema?' Boote Shah interrupted her, 'I don't see her around.'

'She's lying down in her room,' Sugara brushed the dust off her hands and gestured towards the door.

'Is she alright?' Boote Shah asked with a troubled expression.

'She's okay, I guess. She said she had a headache and I advised her to rest for a while.'

'Anyway, you carry on with your chores,' Boote Shah muttered as he went inside. Sugara picked up the broom and continued where she had left off.

'Seema,' he called as he stepped inside the house. 'What's wrong? Why are you in bed at this hour?'

Naseem snapped out of her bed and called, 'Please come in, Bhaaji. Just had a bit of a headache. Do sit down. Why are you still standing?'

Boote Shah immediately realized that his assessment was way off the mark. He had imagined that Seema's face would reflect her angst, if not an outright dislike for him. He had thought long and hard about the words and phrases he'd need to use to regain her confidence. But all of that became redundant when he looked at his foster sister's face. Like always, her eyes had lit up with that familiar expression of filial affection when she saw him. As though nothing untoward had ever happened.

He sat beside her on the bed for a couple of minutes, taking the time to collect his thoughts before murmuring, 'Seema! Won't you forgive me?'

Naseem looked up and observed the deep sense of guilt and remorse in his eyes. 'Forgive you for what, Bhaaji? Why are you looking so depressed?'

'Seema,' Boote Shah's voice appeared to echo his pain. 'It's all my fault. Otherwise, why would I have taken you to…' The burden of his own guilt and a recollection of Yusuf's hideous act combined to choke the words in his throat. Seeing the tears well up in his eyes, Naseem moved across and put her arm around him. Gently caressing his shoulder, she said, 'What are you saying, Bhaaji? How are you at fault in this? Would you ever do anything to hurt me?'

'No, Seema,' Boote Shah's gaze was transfixed on the door as he spoke. 'Of course, it's all my fault. I would never have thought that rogue … that…' His sense of propriety stopped him mid-sentence.

'Please don't look so despondent, Bhaaji,' Naseem gently caressed his back as she spoke. 'I'll stop speaking with you if you go on like this.'

Boote Shah's expression remained unchanged as he silently cursed his own role in the unfortunate affair.

'So, you won't listen to me, Bhaaji?' she asked with a hint of despair, as she peered at his glum countenance. 'Why do you want to break my heart?'

Boote Shah's eyes finally left the door and moved to Naseem's face. Speaking directly to her eyes, they appeared to say, 'How could I ever try to break your heart, Naseem? Me, who is wrestling with the challenge of fixing your broken heart.'

Observing that Naseem's eyes were also drenched with emotion, he said, 'You truly have a very big heart, Seema. Any other sister would have found it hard to forgive a brother who has transgressed the way I have.' His hand moved to her head to gently comfort her.

Sugara finished sweeping the courtyard and perched herself next to Naseem on the bed. 'What's this intense conversation between sister and brother today?' Looking at the moist eyes of both, she could deduce the topic at hand.

'Nothing, Chaachi,' said Boote Shah, turning turned his face away from Naseem towards her mother. 'We were talking about yesterday's incident. I was telling Seema that she shouldn't allow it to pull her down. The one who has sinned will pay for it.'

Sugara's sunken eyes were set within dark circles on her gaunt face. They fluttered with the nervousness of a hen trying to protect her chicks from the predatory eyes of an eagle. The bluish veins on her frail neck appeared to become even more prominent as she sighed, 'What can I say, my son ... I swear I didn't sleep a wink last night. Just lay in my bed wondering why Allah wanted us to see a day like this. We've spent our entire life in this village and we've never seen anyone so much as disturb a bird's nest. God knows what happened to that rogue! How could he forget that they have grown up playing with each other like siblings? He didn't even think that...'

'Forget about it, Chaachi,' Boote Shah intervened, 'my only regret is that we couldn't catch hold of him. He would have met a fate worse than a stray dog. But fortune favoured him and he managed to escape.'

'May you enjoy your youth forever,' Sugara smiled in gratitude. 'It is thanks to the blessings of Allah and the grace of your family that we have managed to survive. Otherwise, who would have bothered about this poor widow. May you live long. As long as Babaji and you are around, we know that we are safe. These are difficult times and even the closest relatives turn their face away. It is the mercy of Allah that he provided your comforting shade to me and my two kids, otherwise…'

'Leave it now, Chaachi,' Boote Shah remonstrated. 'There is absolutely no need to say such things. If Krishna had not died so young, I may not have felt the same kind of affection towards Seema. But the Lord has given me Seema in Krishna's place. Bapuji also likes to say that Seema has the same disposition as our Krishna. The same innocence. You knew her equally well, so I am sure you see this too.'

Comforted by his words, Sugara spoke gently, 'My son, may Allah protect you. Of course, I was equally attached to Krishna. Who can forget such a vivacious girl? It was in a matter of days that she flowered into this beautiful angel. You couldn't take your eyes off her. If Allah hadn't broken the thread of her life, she would have been absolutely matchless. But my son, we have to keep living even after her loss. And Seema is yours before she is mine. Anyway, let bygones be bygones. Before you go, please advise your sister to refrain from going alone in the fields. There are plenty of girls around who can offer company. She should take someone along when she goes that way. Times have changed, my son. Our village might still be better than hundreds of others but as the wise say, "Eat what you like but live as the world expects." Why should we become the topic of conversation for others?'

'You are absolutely right, Chaachi,' he said and turned towards Naseem. 'There is no need to go alone, Seema. If you don't find anyone to accompany you, just ask your bhabi. She is right next door. All you have to do is shout for Rukman and she'll be there.'

Naseem looked at him with renewed respect but didn't speak. Her eyes were conveying her feelings.

As Boote Shah returned to his place, he felt that a huge burden had lifted from his shoulders. He felt lighter, more alive.

7

IF A GARMENT keeps absorbing dirt over a period of time, it is bound to lose its original beauty. Indeed, it gets so discoloured that it would seem impossible to dye it any other colour. But does that mean that the garment has permanently lost its capacity to adorn a different colour? No, it hasn't lost that capacity. It's simply been buried under layer after layer of dirt. Give it a proper wash with some detergent and it will regain its sheen, along with the capacity to absorb different colours on its fabric.

The human mind can be a bit like that garment, discoloured by a multitude of sins, to a point where it starts looking like a dirty rag. But honest remorse can act like the detergent to cleanse it of its sins and restore it to its pristine state.

Nothing within us ever goes waste. As Guru Nanak says in the Japji Sahib, 'Everything in this universe was created at the same time.' The Lord has made sure that we humans are endowed with all noble attributes. Malevolence and evil traits are not an integral part of our make-up. They are external elements and, no matter how powerful, do not have the capacity to kill our innate goodness. At most, they can suppress our divine and virtuous nature for some time.

Granted that there are times when the dirt has leached itself deep into the weave of the fabric. Or let us say that a multitude of sins have sullied the conscience to a point where it seems beyond redemption. But can we really say that there is no remedy for it? When the garment gets utterly filthy and detergent alone doesn't work, you must resort to heat as an additional element. Let the garment soak in some water with the detergent, heat the water till it starts boiling and then see it emerge fresh and clean.

And when our conscience has been tarnished beyond repair by a series of crimes and transgressions, detergents like advice and punishment won't work. But a major accident or a tragedy can start generating a kind of heat within us, the heat that comes from genuine remorse, the heat from sincere penitence. The power of this heat can burn every particle of dirt from the fabric of our conscience, cleanse it of our sins and make it sparkle once again.

Yusuf's conscience had reached that extreme state where it seemed utterly beyond redemption. Neither friendly counsel nor threats of punishment could cleanse his soul. But the sheer gravity of the incident in the grove had triggered a chain reaction within him and the heat emanating from it was enough to have his conscience boiling in a cauldron, the particles of muck being incinerated.

Some seven or eight days after the incident, Boote Shah received another letter from Yusuf that left him stumped.

The envelop contained two letters, one addressed to Naseem and the other to Boote Shah. What was his mental state after reading the two letters? From the moment he learned about the assault on Naseem, every pore in his body had throbbed with an uncontrollable rage towards Yusuf. This was completely at odds with his innately gentle disposition, but the very thought of Yusuf seemed to trigger an urge towards violence. Had he run into Yusuf, he would have been impelled to charge at him even though he knew that Yusuf was probably strong enough to dispose of a couple of Boote Shahs. But as he read Yusuf's letter, each line seemed to narrate its own saga of remorse and repentance. Boote Shah's emotions flipped once again; his searing sense of anger being gradually replaced by a deeper feeling of sympathy. As he went on to read the letter addressed to Naseem, he found it hard to keep his eyes dry. 'Ah! You unfortunate man!' he sighed.

He delivered Naseem's letter to her that evening but not before he had shown it to his father. He had not forgotten the old man's ire and didn't want to risk it a second time. The Baba thought long and hard before allowing his son to take the letter over to Naseem. He knew after reading the letter that the girl was also attached to Yusuf and understood the kind of hurt that his actions must have caused. He also recognized that the letter might provide a healing touch to her injured soul. 'Go give it to her,' he advised gruffly as he handed the letter back to his son.

A woman's heart is generally a lot more tender than a man's. And the heart of a woman in love? You could say that it is delicate as a flower with soft petals.

Naseem's hand was trembling as she held the three pages of the letter. A steady stream of tears was snaking its way down to her chin. Her blurred eyes were trying to concentrate on this para:

Naseem! You told me the other day that you don't ever want to see my face again. Inshallah, your wish will come true. You will never see me again. But I do want to let you know that if you don't forgive me, my soul will remain tormented even after I am buried in my grave. I know that my crime is not one that can be forgiven easily. But for one who has already forgiven me for many smaller transgressions, it might be possible to forgive a bigger sin as well...

Naseem read the rest of the letter, wiping the tears streaming down her face as she moved from one paragraph to the next. She had finished the letter, but the tears would not stop.

She stepped out into the courtyard after reading the letter with the feeling that a huge burden had lifted from her, only to be replaced by an even larger one. The letter had succeeded in dissipating the deep animosity that she had nursed towards Yusuf since the unfortunate incident. There was a new sense of empathy seeping into her consciousness. Not just empathy but also the gentle flicker of a flame that might thaw her frozen emotions towards Yusuf. At the same time, there was a growing burden on her heart, one that was directly linked to her anxiety about Yusuf's well-being. Her thoughts kept returning to those words in his letter that were drilling tiny holes into her skin: 'You will never see me again ... my soul will remain tormented even after I am buried in my grave.'

'Is Yusuf preparing to take some extreme step? God forbid he takes his own life! He can be pretty hot-headed but ... but...' Her mind refused to move any further, but she could see a sliver of a thought entering her head. 'What if I were to send him a short letter?' No way, she shook her head as she tried to shake off this strange feeling. Her eyes fell on the mango tree for the first time in a week. Her feet started to draw her under its branches as she looked up. The young tree appeared to have aged within the space of a week. The leaves had crinkled and turned yellow—a phenomenon caused by the onset of the autumn winds. But she blamed herself and her indifference towards the tree over the last few days.

She tried to make amends by fetching the water pitcher and pouring some water into its base, but it did nothing to diminish the ache in her heart. Restless and on edge, her thoughts continued to drag her in a direction that she wanted to avoid. It wasn't until she had fetched some paper along with her pen and inkpot and started to write that a sense of calm descended.

They had an early dinner and Sugara went off to sleep. That left Naseem free to complete her letter. Once she had finished writing, a fresh worry crept up on her. How would she send it? She had no idea of Yusuf's address. Maybe he had intentionally left it out of his letter because he wanted her response to come through Boote Shah. But could she really hand this letter over to Boote Shah? A wave of embarrassment swept over her as she pondered over the prospect. Did she have any other option?

After some deliberation, she neatly folded Yusuf's letter and her own response, and tucked the letters in the trunk where she kept her clothes. She spent the better part of the night tossing and turning as she grappled with the dilemma. Should she send the letter or should she hold it back? And if she chose to send it, what was the best way? And if she didn't, what if Yusuf were to really take a drastic step?

The morning broke and Naseem was still wrestling with her doubts and anxieties. She wanted to save Yusuf from destroying himself and that remained the main argument for sending the letter. True. But there was also a second reason for her restless mood. In the ten odd pages that she had written to Yusuf, she had tried to persuade him about her true and eternal love for him. She assured him that she would consider it a real accomplishment if she could spend the rest of her life by his side. But that would only happen if he acquired the goodness and virtue of his namesake Yusuf, the son of Yakub. If he could do it, Naseem would happily be his till her last breath.

In writing these pages, Naseem had expressed her profound love, outlined her aspirations, and even set out all her hopes and desires for the future. Had she done all this so that those pages could sit at the bottom of her trunk? No, she needed Yusuf's address. She could ask Boote Shah, of course. But wouldn't her foster brother see it as an insult? That she didn't trust him to post her letter? Or that she had something to hide and wanted to send the letter secretly?

The morning gave way to the afternoon and Naseem was still lost in her thoughts. She was carrying a heavy burden and she felt that it would only be lifted once the letter was in the post.

She finished lunch and went to the room at the rear to steal a quiet moment. Sugara had gone to the haveli, having decided to visit Rukman after quite some time. Naseem sat on her bed and pulled out the two letters from the trunk, starting first by reading Yusuf's letter, slowly and line by line. She moved on to her own letter, examining each line critically to make sure that there was nothing that could hurt Yusuf's feelings at a time when he was already being swept away by the whirlpools of depression.

She had barely gone through half the letter when she heard a voice call out, 'Seema!' She quickly hid the pages under the bedspread and replied, 'Coming, Bhaaji.'

Boote Shah was standing at the door. Naseem asked him to come inside and sit for a while but he declined. 'There's no time to sit today. I have to go to Lattiphala for some urgent errand. I've dropped in only to deliver an important message from Bapuji.'

'Please tell me, Bhaaji.'

'He said that you should not respond to Yusuf's letter.'

Naseem gasped. 'Why?' she wanted to ask but couldn't. Boote Shah was quick to see that Naseem was perturbed and wanted to know the reason behind the restriction. Without waiting to be prompted, he started, 'As you know, Seema, I had shown Bapuji the letter Yusuf has sent you. In fact, I delivered it to you only after obtaining his consent.

I don't know what went on in his mind last night but first thing in the morning, he called me and instructed, "Go across to Seema's place and advise her not to reply to his letter."

'I was stunned when I heard this,' Boote Shah continued. 'I asked him, "Bapuji, if he doesn't get a reply to his letter, God forbid he should do something terrible." Bapuji replied, "You don't have to worry about that at all. These pathetic persons are capable of doing many things but sacrificing their life isn't one of them. You know what kind of person can sacrifice his life? One for whom his word is his honour, one who would gladly give up his life than violate a promise. But this man's character is so fickle that there is no reason to be afraid for him." Bapuji also gave me strict instructions that I should not correspond with Yusuf for the next month or so. I guess Bapuji wants to send him a tough message. Be that as it may, we have to accept one fact, Seema. Bapuji has a lot more experience than me. He must have thought over this deeply before giving such categorical advice. I think it's best that both of us follow it.'

Naseem had lowered her head and was staring at the ground as Boote Shah continued, 'But Seema, I don't want to break your heart. If you really do want to send him a reply, I'll scribble down his address for you. You can post your letter to him. I won't say a word to Bapuji about it.'

'No, Bhaaji, no,' Naseem's hands covered her ears as she spoke. 'Bapuji must have thought this matter through before giving this advice. We may think we are pretty smart but compared to him, we are just kids. I have seen on numerous occasions that when Bapuji says something like this, it is the last word on the subject. I am sure he had my welfare at heart when he sent this message. I won't post the letter, you can assure him.'

Boote Shah was astonished by the faith that the girl had in the judgement of her adoptive father, particularly since he himself was pretty unhappy about his father's intervention. But Naseem's words convinced him that his father's prediction was accurate, that Yusuf wasn't going to take his own life.

He went off to complete his errands, leaving Naseem to retrieve the papers from under the bedspread. She wanted to rip the letters into tiny fragments but couldn't muster the strength. She felt sad and disappointed, but she viewed it as the pain that must be endured when the surgeon removes a festering sore.

8

AND SO, THE December–January month of Poh rolled by in our blessed little village, sprinkling the land with splashes of winter rain. The following month of Magh was eagerly awaited by young and old alike, because it ushered in the much-anticipated festival of Lohri and its long night of music, dance and festivities.

Lohri, like most other festivals in these parts, was celebrated together by the Muslim, Hindu and Sikh communities. There was something particularly intoxicating about the magic of Lohri night. Folks could spend half the year reminiscing about the enchantment of the last Lohri and the other half in feverish anticipation of the next one.

A couple of timely rains had done wonders for the season's crops. The lush green carpet of wheat fields extended to the furthest edge of the village and the joy on the face of the villagers was a sight to behold. 'God willing, the harvest this year will be the best in the last twenty years. Haven't seen such a rich growth in quite a while,' the old-timers proclaimed as they pointed to the stalks leaning forward under the weight of the grains.

'How many days till Lohri?' the youngsters would ask. The countdown had begun, and each passing day heightened the air of excitement. Groups of young boys traversed the village with cries of 'Sunder Mundriye' as they went from door to door to solicit wood, dung cakes and other fuel for their Lohri bonfire. Bands of young girls went around on a similar mission, singing, 'Give us some wood, o lady ... may your daughters live long, o lady.' Every little addition of a log or a handful of dung cakes to their kitty fuelled their single-minded determination, 'This Lohri, we must have a bigger bonfire than the boys.' Every home was fair game, and the boys and the girls would stand on the doorstep singing at the top of their voices until the residents gave them what they wanted.

Naseem's house was a special target for these groups because her brother had recently gotten engaged to a girl from a neighbouring village. One evening, a band of some twenty or twenty-five young boys and a similar sized group of girls landed up at her place around the same time. The courtyard was soon resonating with their songs, the rising crescendo making sure that each group drowned out the voices of the other. One song led to a second and to a third and for a while, the two groups merged into one. Naseem's mother stepped towards them with a plate of raw sugar and a one-rupee coin for each group.

'What? Just one rupee to celebrate Aziz's engagement? No way, Chaachi ... You might as well take it back ... we aren't going to accept this pittance...' The game of bargain, reproach and accusations of stinginess might have continued for a while, but a silence descended as soon as they saw Boote Shah enter the courtyard. He quietly placed a five rupee note in each tray.

Six rupees was a princely sum, certainly a lot more than they had expected. They whooped in joy as they left the place.

Last year, the boys had managed to build a much bigger bonfire than the girls, and had exercised their bragging rights over the last few weeks. There were rumours, of course, that the boys hadn't exactly won fair and square. Their collections of wood had been quite meagre until some enterprising fellows managed to steal some extra wood from here and there. But the fact that they had the better bonfire still rankled with the girls.

With two days to go, the girls redoubled their efforts. Anyone passing their way, young or old, Hindu or Muslim, would be accosted by their band. The younger girls would tug at the passer-by's clothes while the older ones would start with their songs, 'Don't want your change, don't want your pennies … a rupee, a rupee will do just fine.' Rare was the person who could escape their entreaties without paying his tax.

The Khatri community in the village wasn't very large but they made sure that every Muslim home in the village received a tray laden with the seasonal bhugga sweetmeat, a bowl of vermicelli pudding, lumps of the season's fresh jaggery and more. It was the other way round on Eid when the Khatris would receive more sweets from their Muslim neighbours than they could consume during the entire month.

The long wait finally ended. It was Lohri and everyone seemed busy preparing for the festivities. There was no time to tend to the fields, except to fetch some ripe sugarcane sticks for the evening.

Nooran, the one who roasted the corn kernels in her clay oven, had been working nonstop through the day without time to even scratch her head. She had set up an additional oven and had brought in her husband Haadu to lend a helping hand. There was an unending stream of girls coming with pouches of kernels that they had hoarded over the days in order to savour Nooran's fresh popcorn. A few waited patiently, while others dashed off to Mohra's oven. They knew that Nooran was slow at the best of times, while poor Haadu suffered from Parkinson's and his nodding head could take forever to roast a handful.

The small shops in the village were busy selling soap, vegetable dyes and a powder made from crushed glass.

An abandoned old mansion known as the Haveli of the Anands stood near the centre of the village and was usually the preferred venue for the Lohri festivities. Behind the slim red Nanakshahi bricks of its crumbling boundary wall lay a large open courtyard which came in handy for gatherings large and small. From the occasional evening with a visiting minstrel to performances by a travelling magician, puppeteer or acrobat, the haveli was the place where everyone came together. It hosted engagement ceremonies and weddings and many a marriage procession had assembled at its premises before setting off to its destination. Full moon nights often attracted groups of boys who would play games or yak away till late in the night. And every now and then, the older ladies of the village would get together to exchange some gossip and enjoy the winter sun.

The haveli was buzzing with activity that afternoon. There was a time not too long ago when the entire village celebrated around one large communal bonfire. That split into two when the youngsters separated themselves from the elders. And a couple of years back, a third bonfire emerged when the young girls decided to have their own party. They had resented the fact that the boys contributed little by way of firewood but tried to dominate the evening with their noise. But truth be told, there was another reason too. The girls were constrained by the presence of boys and felt that they couldn't sing or dance as freely as they would have liked.

And so, the practice of three separate bonfires spread across the expansive courtyard became part of the village's Lohri celebrations. Small teams of boys and girls worked feverishly through the afternoon to stack up their firewood for the evening, each lot keeping a jealous eye on the other to make sure that they stayed ahead of the game.

A walk through the village that afternoon would reveal that almost every home had washed the clothes for the evening. Colourful turbans and dupattas, freshly dipped in a mix of corn starch and crushed glass powder were being tugged at on both ends to stretch and dry out. They seemed to be embedded with a thousand tiny diamonds as the glass powder shimmered in the rays of the late afternoon sun.

The three bonfires were lit soon after sunset and for a while, the haveli's spacious courtyard appeared to shrink as it struggled to accommodate the growing mass of visitors. The elders, neatly attired, were the first to come and form their own group. Then came the young boys, resplendent in their bright turbans, each with a little plume on top and a yard of the fabric nonchalantly cascading down the shoulder. The girls, of course, came in their own group, dressed in rustling silk tunics and salwars, the shimmering starched dupattas struggling to stay on their heads. They were also beaming with satisfaction that their bonfire was visibly better than the one put together by the boys. The boys, of course, weren't going to take this lying down and a couple of them complained, 'Stolen goods. Half their firewood is stolen.' The comment was heard by one of the girls who swung around and retorted, 'Stolen? What do you mean by that? You lot, who go around uprooting the neighbours' fences in the middle of the night and then say that you've collected firewood? Sure! Only a thief thinks everyone else is also a thief.'

'Why don't you swear on the Quran?' challenged one of the boys. 'Take an oath and tell us when you've seen any of us uprooting a fence.'

The argument escalated into a shouting match between the two sides and might have continued if they hadn't been interrupted by a booming voice from the elders' bonfire. 'Boys and girls! Behave yourselves, will you? Or I will have to come over and box a few ears.'

The warning had its effect, and both sides fell silent for a while.

The Khatri women were the last to arrive, carrying bundles of corn kernels, chidwa savouries and the coin-sized rewris made from jaggery and sesame seeds. Richly attired and with dupattas pulled low, covering their faces, they created an instant stir as they went around the three groups dispensing their goodies.

Each bonfire was now crackling with a healthy blaze, its warmth spreading to the groups squatting around it, adding its own magic to the evening. Their faces looked radiant, lit up in the golden hue of the fire. An enchanted cloud appeared to descend from the heavens into the haveli's courtyard.

'Listen folks,' someone spoke from the elders' party. 'We haven't seen Babaji today.'

'His eyesight is failing, and he didn't want to stumble over the rough ground. That's why he stayed at home,' Boote Shah responded.

'And what's the point of having you boys, then,' Chaudhry Fazal Karim turned around towards the boys' bonfire and said tauntingly. His son Fatta was among them and was the first to get up even before his father had finished saying, 'Go across and carry the Baba here on your shoulders.'

Within minutes, Fatta was at the head of half a dozen strapping young men as they left the bonfire and headed out of the haveli.

A peal of laughter went through the three groups when they saw the Baba's mode of travel as he entered the haveli. 'Babaji has arrived … look guys, Fatta is carrying him on his back … look girls, Babaji has come riding a two-legged horse … Wow! I wouldn't mind having a ride like that…'

'Don't set him down yet, oye Fattya!' the Chaudhry called. 'Give him a nice little spin around the three bonfires first.'

A young man called out, 'This round is in the name of my parents, this one's for…'

That was the cue they needed. Baba Bhana found himself being passed around like a parcel from one sturdy back to the second and then to the third, each one spinning around in the name of his parents. The haveli's courtyard resonated with the enthusiastic clapping of the girls and the laughter of the boys.

'Oye! Stop it! Set me down now. You boys are out of your minds, I…' the Baba was shouting but no one was paying any attention.

The merriment finally ended with the Baba being brought back on terra firma. He appeared a bit wobbly and out of breath, beads of sweat lighting up his face in the light of the bonfire as he gingerly made his way to the elders' bonfire and took a seat among them.

'Babaji! We've gone grey waiting here for you and you are happily sitting at home?'

'What can I say, Khudabaksh!' the Baba replied as he paused to catch his breath. 'My eyes have deserted me. Up until a few weeks back, I could still manage. But they've become absolutely useless now. Otherwise, can you imagine me sitting at home on Lohri?'

'Why don't you get your glasses made, Babaji?' asked the Chaudhry who was sitting next to him. 'Last year that fellow, what's his name … that Illahi's father … he couldn't see a thing … Used to sit like a statue all day. Look at him now, running around everywhere.'

'I saw the doctor recently,' the Baba replied, 'he told me the cataract is still pretty fresh. Wait for a couple of months, he said. But I've decided I can't wait much longer. I'll get the glasses made by March or April. This life becomes pretty meaningless if you can't see a thing.'

'Absolutely. As the saying goes, there is no taste without the teeth and no world without the eyes.'

Embers from the bonfire were rising towards the sky and the crackling of the firewood was mixing with the joyous sounds of firecrackers being burst by some of the youngsters. The boys were craning towards the girls' party, trying to discern the owner of a lyrical voice softly singing a popular melody.

The elders' party had also warmed up, with animated conversations covering everything from personal adventures to the state of the world. One topic led to another and to a third, often jumping to a new subject while discussion on the previous one was still underway.

The warmth from the bonfire was adding it's own heat to the conversation which currently revolved around a recent spate of thefts and robberies in the region.

Moola Kocchhar, whose addiction to opium made him look a lot older than his forty odd years, picked up a fat jaggery-filled rewri and rolled it around in his toothless mouth as he spoke, 'You must know Mahtab Singh Bhasin from Gheelan village. Some burglars came and stole his milch buffalo the other night. He'd paid three hundred and fifty rupees for it not long ago. And what a buffalo it was! Like a portrait that you could keep gazing at for hours. The crooks thought they would outsmart the search party by walking the poor buffalo for a mile and a half down the Soan river. But hats off to the trackers who went after the crooks, especially one old cobbler from Dhakwan village. He was relentless and didn't pause till he had tracked down the gang. To cut a long story short, the search party returned by dawn with the buffalo, which is now back with the owner.'

'Must have been the man's honest, hard-earned money that he got his buffalo back,' Bhagta the brahmin commented as he gathered some popcorn from the base of the bonfire. 'Otherwise, who's ever heard of thieves returning stolen property.'

'They are quite amazing, these trackers. I heard a story from around Lyallpur the other day. The cattle thieves covered the hooves of the animals with tart as they left but all credit to the trackers—they still managed to follow the trail and nab the thieves!'

'These aren't real thieves, my friends,' interjected old Deena the carpenter. Sitting on his haunches with a small blanket draped around his knees, he continued, 'Sadly, you haven't seen the real burglars. These ones passing off as burglars are no better than the urchins who steal your slippers.' His voice rose as he emphasized the last bit, triggering a bout of coughing. He cleared his throat and carried on, 'You aren't a real burglar if you get caught so easily. We've seen experts in our times who could steal the kohl from your eyes, and you wouldn't know it.'

'Oh, come on now! There should be a limit to these tall tales. Are you talking about a thief or a magician?' piped up one outspoken fellow.

Baba Deena flared in anger. Turning his steely blue eyes on the upstart, 'Why don't you sit quietly, young man! What do you know about the world? Still wet behind the ears and he wants to share his experience!' He turned towards the middle-aged Arju Sabherwal and said, 'You won't believe it, Arjana! Let me tell you something that I've seen with my own eyes. We'd gone to this big Vaisakhi fair and as luck would have it, I ran into an old friend of mine who was acknowledged as a genuine master thief. That's right, a master thief.' The old man turned his face to let out a loud burp before continuing, 'He was known in those days for pulling off thefts one can barely imagine. Anyway, we decided to spend the night under the open skies near a rose garden. Like me, he had also spread his rough cotton wrap on the grass and was lying down. We kept chatting till about midnight as he regaled me with stories of his escapades. I observed that a couple of Khatris had spread out near us and my eyes were drawn to the sheet on which they were sleeping. To be honest, it looked less like a wrap and more like a stole that a princess would adorn. It had bright red corners woven from a silk thread that were wider than both my palms, with these gorgeous yellow stripes running along the sides. Indeed, its rich fabric and fine embroidery would have made it a fine present for a king! The more I looked at it, the greater my temptation grew. I finally turned to my friend and said, "Look Umardin, you've been telling me some great stories. But I'll believe that you are a real thief only if you manage to steal that wrap from under the Khatris and bring it to me."

'Folks, telling a fib in an august gathering like this is worse than going to a whore, so let me continue. My friend didn't demur for a second. He got up and said, "Come on, that's hardly a challenge. It's the kind of job that I would assign to my apprentice." And he quietly walked across to the sleeping Khatris and somehow managed to slide between the two of them. He lay still for a while, with neither of them aware of the interloper's presence. I saw him spend the next few minutes gently pushing one guy a few inches, before turning his attention to the other one. Each time the fellow moved a bit further, he would pluck out a bit of the wrap from under him.

'Before I knew it, he had managed to pull out the entire wrap and was standing next to me with a wide grin. The two Khatris were now sleeping on the grass, snoring away without the slightest idea of what had transpired. Now that's what I mean when I say that a real thief can steal the kohl from your eyes.'

'Wow … Now, that's really something … What an artist…' The old man's eyes lit up as he heard the murmurs of appreciation from the audience. Scratching his ash-grey beard with the index finger of his right hand, he continued with a renewed burst of energy, 'This was actually child's play for him. Let me tell you what happened the following day.'

'The next day, we were part of a huge crowd that was making its way to the big local fair to see the wrestling competition. We were all being shoved and jostled as we walked along a narrow track between the farmlands. That's when I noticed the person walking ahead of me. He seemed one of those wealthy Pathans, a Khan perhaps. But what caught my attention was his footwear. He was wearing a traditional jutti, richly embroidered with gold thread. It looked brand new. Must have been worth twenty or twenty-five rupees, at the very least. I turned to my friend and joked, "Just take a look at that jutti, Umardin! Imagine the intoxicating pleasure of floating around the fair in a pair like that." He looked at me and said, "So should we get you to experience that pleasure? Here, give me your jutti for a bit." I was perplexed as I reluctantly handed over my simple jutti to him and began walking barefoot. What was he planning now, I wondered!

'He pushed his way a few yards ahead and headed straight for a thorny bush that was growing on the side of our dirt track, bending low to quickly pluck a few bristles before returning to my side. We were again following the Khan sahib. His jutti appeared a bit loose and I saw Umar bend once again and slip a couple of bristles into the Khan's right jutti. The Khan walked a few steps before he felt the bristles pricking his heel. He stood on one leg as he raised his right foot to remove the jutti and shake out the bristles. No sooner had he placed the jutti on the ground to slide his foot into it than Umardin replaced it with mine. I swear by Allah that it happened in the blink of an eye! The Khan had no idea what was going on. Mindful of the crowd behind him, he quickly donned my jutti and continued walking. A couple of minutes later, Umar again used the same ploy to switch the other jutti. He then tugged my arm, led me away from the crowds towards a quiet spot and smiled, "Here's your gold embroidered jutti, my friend. I hope that satisfies your hunger." Now that's what I call a real thief! Not these amateurs who sneak into a farm and walk away with a buffalo. Nor the ones who will ambush you with a knife and force you to hand over your possessions. Those bastards … they aren't thieves by any definition. They are bandits, pure and simple.'

Tara Singh Chadha, who had slid back a couple of paces to avoid the direct heat of the bonfire, removed his expansive woollen shawl and commented, 'It is one thing to steal a buffalo or to ambush a poor sod. But what about the sectarian bandits that are cropping up these days, the kind who will waylay a traveller and stick a knife into his back?'

'Evil, pure and simple. That's what it is,' Baba Deena responded. 'And such are the acts of bravery in these times.'

Reacting to Baba Deena's observation, Bhagta the brahmin remarked, 'The fact, Baba Deenya, is that these knife-wielding bandits aren't the real culprits. That responsibility unfortunately rests on the shoulders of our leaders, the ones whose rousing speeches drive communities against each other so that they sit back and enjoy the spectacle. Look at the bloodshed in Bengal and ask yourselves who was behind it? And then it was Bihar's turn. If the Hindus were the victims in one state, it was the Muslims in the other. Did the leaders lose their offspring in these riots? No, sir! It was the innocent sons of mothers from the two states. Have you seen any of the leaders die in these riots? No, sir. They will quietly incite the people to go at each other's throats while they watch the carnage from a safe distance.'

'You are absolutely right,' Sant Chandioke commented as he used his hand to shade his face from the bonfire's heat. 'I don't know when our people will grasp this reality. Or do these so-called leaders want us to battle with each other and finish off this country!'

Baba Bhana had stayed quiet till now, perhaps trying to recover his breath after being spun around by the boys. Having regained his composure, he replied to Chandioke. 'The real issue, Santya, is that all leaders are also not the same. There are leaders who feel the pain of both the Hindu and the Muslim communities, but who listens to them? Gandhi went on a fast unto death to restore peace between Hindus and Muslims in Bihar. Nehru threatened to call in the army and destroy the rioting Hindu mobs if they didn't cease attacks on their Muslim brethren in Bihar. And the two leaders didn't leave Bihar until they had managed to restore a semblance of peace. But it takes both hands to clap, doesn't it? If the leaders on the opposite side had made a similarly earnest effort, these riots would have died out in no time.'

'Don't involve yourself in sectarian matters, Babaji,' an angry voice crackled from the other side of the bonfire. 'You have no right to blame our Muslim leaders.'

The group's attention turned towards the new entrant in the conversation.

The orange flames of the bonfire were rising higher, forcing the members of the group to move some distance away. The circumference of the group was growing larger with the warmth of the flames.

The man who had replied so insolently to the Baba was Munshi Abdul Rahman, a teacher at the middle school. A man of medium height and brisk manner, he had been late in joining the bonfire that evening.

Abdul Rahman lived in the neighbouring Koliyan Hamid village which was no more than a mile and a half away. He would walk down to the school every morning carrying a small packed lunch with him and return to his own village in the evening. Of late, though, he had occasionally started spending a night or two in Chakri and there was a reason for this.

Since Baba Bhana and Boote Shah were among the only literate souls in the village, they had taken the initiative to subscribe to a newspaper that arrived by the regular post. For those interested in developments in the world, the arrival of the post was the signal to assemble at the Baba's haveli and hear him read out the latest news. But over the last few weeks, the attendance at the Baba's assembly appeared to be thinning out, because Munshi Abdul Rahman had started to receive a Muslim daily.

The Munshi had begun in a fairly circumspect fashion, confining himself to reading out a few chosen stories for his audience. He built up an audience of regulars to his assembly and once he had achieved this objective, his tone and language began to undergo a metamorphosis. Over the last week or two, he had taken it upon himself to issue a grim warning to his audience—'Muslims who paid attention to the newspaper of the Hindus could not claim to be real Muslims. They were kaafirs.'

The tempest of sectarian riots that started in Bengal was now moving rapidly towards Punjab and there were signs that its arrival in these parts was imminent. Worrying reports of sectarian violence were already emerging from the neighbouring Hazara region.

Baba Bhana and the other senior members of the Khatri community were mindful of the disturbing trends but saw no reason to panic. They felt confident that the generational ties between the communities of the area were strong enough to withstand any passing gust of sectarian violence. But as the Munshi's activities gathered momentum, a sense of disquiet could be felt.

The unexpected rudeness of the Munshi's reply to the Baba had turned everyone's eyes on him.

'Young man,' the Baba spoke in his characteristically measured tone. 'I think I understand sectarian issues better than you do. And I accord the same respect to other religions that I do to my own. I was speaking about the nature of our leaders. If all our leaders were like Gandhi or Nehru—'

The same angry voice again stopped the Baba in his tracks, 'Are you trying to say that your leaders are very nice and ours are bad? Let me tell you, Babaji, these Gandhi and Nehru that you have been touting don't even measure up to our Qaid-e-Azam's shoe. What do you rustic folk understand about political matters? Living within the confines of this village, what would you know about the real face of Gandhi and Nehru? They are the biggest agents of the British—'

'Munshi!' a worried Chaudhry Fazal Karim intervened this time. 'Stop it please. Let's bring an end to this useless discussion. We were all having such a lovely time until you brought up this pointless topic.'

'Pointless topic?' the Munshi flared up again instead of taking a step back. 'That reflects the ignorance of villagers like you. Sitting in your havelis, you can afford to make comments like this. Step outside and see the spectacle unfolding in the world around you. Take the trouble to read about the sacrifices of Hazrat Qaid-e-Azam, he who owns vast estates and yet toils day and night to serve his people. Why is he doing this? Not for any personal gain, I can assure you. He is doing this in the service of Islam.'

'But Munshiji,' Baba Deena replied, 'I hear the British rule is coming to an end and we will soon have our own government in the country.'

'Don't you remain under that illusion, Baba,' the Munshi retorted. 'It's going to be a jump from the frying pan into the fire. The British rule has had its own advantages. They've maintained peace between the communities. But mark my words carefully. The day these Congress party Hindus form the government, we Muslims will starve to death. The lives of Muslims will be safe only when we see the flag of Pakistan fly over these lands. Does anyone realize the existential danger that our religion faces at this point of time? It is easy to sit in your homes and gossip away over your hookahs but who is going to serve your community? And who ruled Hindustan till four hundred years ago? It was a Muslim nation and it was the flag of Islam that was seen flying high all the way from the east to the west of the country. And what's your position today? Think about it for a moment! Poverty and hunger are widespread across the community. You have become so used to being ruled by others that a slavish mentality has seeped into your lives. What's the point of living like this? Isn't it better to die?'

The Munshi's diatribe had a devastating effect on the congenial spirit of Lohri. The sense of joy and contentment evaporated from everyone's faces, replaced by lines of worry and a sense of emptiness. Several of them were upset over the Munshi's attitude and the blatant disrespect with which he had treated Baba Bhana. Chaudhry Fazal Karim sensed the mood and stepped in to restore the Baba's honor. 'You may be right, Munshiji, that an enslaved person has lost his self-esteem. But you can't disregard the Baba's words either. Isn't it true that Gandhi went on a fast-unto-death to protect the Muslims of Bihar? And what do you have to say about newspaper reports that Nehru threatened to rain bombs on the Hindu mobs in Bihar? Babaji was merely trying to say that if the Qaid-e-Azam or other leaders of the Muslim League had made a similar effort to stop the communal riots in their areas, our country might have been spared this calamity.'

'You really don't understand these matters, Chaudhryji,' the Munshi countered in the same belligerent tone. 'They shed these crocodile tears to fool the public. But their real motives are so complex that your simple brain can't even begin to comprehend them. Let's assume that Nehru really did threaten the Hindus. Does that explain why he went up to the Frontier areas to meet the tribal chiefs? He went with a devious message—that he would bring education to their people, wean them away from banditry, address their financial problems. But do you know his real intention? Like the British, he also wanted to bribe them so that they would turn against the Muslim League. That was his real motive. He thought he was being pretty smart but before our leaders, he is no more than a child. The Qaid-e-Azam spun such a web around him that Nehru had to return with his tail between his legs. He is lucky he came back alive after that hail of bullets aimed at his plane. Had Qaid-e-Azam not intervened in time to stop the firing, you wouldn't have found a trace of your Nehru! And those great supporters that he took with him, that Abdul Ghaffar and Doctor Khan ... they would have been reduced to chutney in the hills of Malakand if Qaid-e-Azam hadn't intervened to resolve matters.'

'Umm ... Where exactly was the Qaid-e-Azam at that point of time?' Boote Shah had barely raised this question to the Munshi when Baba Bhana caught hold of his arm to restrain him. 'Forgive me, Munshiji. You may have misunderstood me,' the Baba interjected. 'I never said that Hindu leaders are good or Muslim leaders are bad. All I meant was that if Gandhi and Nehru could intervene to stop the sectarian riots in Bihar, the Qaid-e-Azam could have done the same if he had wanted to halt this epidemic of violence in Muslim-dominated areas. Look at the way the situation has deteriorated in Hazara over the last month or so. Would it have continued for so long if an influential Muslim leader had stepped in to control it?'

'There is no point in trying to stop these things now,' the Munshi replied. 'Whether you listen from your right ear or from the left, let it be clear that this matter is headed for a decisive conclusion.'

'Decisive conclusion? What does that mean?' the Baba queried.

'It means that all Hindus and Sikhs should leave the Muslim areas and the Muslims should do the same from the Hindu areas. Last month, Hazrat Qaid-e-Azam had himself expounded on this issue. Since the Muslim and Hindu communities are intrinsically different, it is only natural that unless the populations of all the provinces are divided along religious lines, this kind of violence is bound to continue.'

'But Munshiji,' the Baba responded. 'An exchange of populations would be an expensive proposition for the Muslims. After all, you will end up with thirty crore Hindus on one side and only nine crore Muslims on the other. Wouldn't that make it difficult for the smaller nation to feel secure in the face of a much larger nation?'

'Difficult?' the Munshi sneered with renewed anger. 'Babaji, you are forgetting a very important fact. The Muslims will never again be dominated by anyone else. Once we are all together under the Pakistani flag, you will see what happens to your thirty crore Hindus. We will make sure that they end up missing the days of the British, I assure you.'

The Baba refrained from responding. He could see that the fanatical Munshi had decided to don the mantle of a religious crusader even before Pakistan came into existence.

The group sat around the Lohri bonfire a little while longer, but the conversation had petered out, replaced by a grim silence, almost like they wanted to speak but could think of nothing to say. Quite a few were wondering, 'From where did this inauspicious fellow land up in our midst? He's managed to wreck the charm of an occasion that we await the whole year.'

'Let's drop this subject, Munshiji,' Chaudhry Fazal Karim spoke with barely concealed irritation. Looking at the others, he said, 'I think it's time we headed home. The young boys and girls are also sitting quietly while we are around. Let them feel free to enjoy their evening.'

The group of elders started to abandon the bonfire and the gathering soon dispersed.

9

AS THE ELDERS left the scene, the boys saw that their own bonfire, sustained by the last few dung cakes and twigs, was on its last legs. They quickly moved across to capture the real estate vacated by the elders, whose bonfire was still going strong. As their conversation picked up, they were oblivious of the recent developments around that bonfire, unaware why their elders had come with so much joy and excitement but departed with twice the disappointment.

A mocking voice came from the girls' side, 'Look around, girls. The boys have retreated from their bonfire ... stolen goods, you know ... stolen stuff will never prosper ... look at our Lohri bonfire, in contrast ... if it doesn't continue till dawn, you can change my name.'

The girls had been speaking in subdued tones while the elders were around, and this was the first strong voice that had emerged from their section. Their timidity, it seemed, had left with the departing elders and they had rediscovered their voices.

The younger kids took advantage of the space vacated by the older boys to form their own little party. A few of the more enterprising ones managed to forage around for some dung cakes, twigs and just about anything else that could revive the fire. Satisfied that they now had a bit of their own bonfire going, they sat around it and started telling the kind of stories that kids love. One had started, 'And so the thief quietly returned home … He opened the sack he was carrying and spread out its contents before his wife. The thief's wife was flabbergasted. She had never seen so much jewellery, so many currency notes of twenty, forty and eighty-rupee denominations…'

As the story came to an end, another kid suggested, 'Let's play Cops and Robbers.' The others nodded in agreement and one of them offered to be the policeman. Soon, he was strutting around the group with a stick on his shoulder, stamping his feet on the ground as he circled the bonfire, shouting:

> Silent goes the night
> My gun's ready for a fight.
> Let the thief come, I say
> Bang, and a bullet goes his way!

As he spoke that last line, he brought the stick down from his shoulder, pointed it at an imaginary thief and shouted 'bang' at the top of his voice. The other kids reacted as if a gun had really gone off in their midst.

Meanwhile the older boys, mostly Muslims along with a handful of young Khatri lads, seemed to be getting bored of sitting around and chatting. Now that the elders had left, a few of them started getting devious ideas.

Tomfoolery and youthfulness tend to go together, one could even say that the process of growing up is incomplete if it doesn't include the occasional pranks. A couple of them turned their attention towards the rival camp and were stung by the sight of the girls' bonfire, its vibrant flames leaping towards the sky, making their own bonfire look even more anaemic. Roused by a sense of envy, one of them got up and yelled at his compatriots, 'He who doesn't bring firewood for our fire ... he ... he is the son of a pig!'

The gravity of that curse was enough to stir the somnolent group into action. They scooted out of the haveli and were seen returning in ones and twos a few minutes later. One had managed to pull three or four poles from a farmer's fence while a second had clambered onto a neighbour's terrace to retrieve a heap of dung cakes. Firewood, bamboo, dung cakes, twigs—they picked up anything they could gather and hauled it back to the haveli. One enterprising fellow who failed to find anything substantive snuck into a neighbour's courtyard and returned with two pieces of an old charkha, the frame of the wooden spinning wheel making a handy contribution to the kitty. None dared to return empty-handed and soon, the flames from their own bonfire were rising higher than the boundary wall of the haveli. Their rejuvenated fire infused a fresh burst of energy and a lusty voice started the first of several songs.

The girls' camp, in contrast, had a more subdued air about it. The vigour of the boys' bonfire had come as a rude shock. But there was another, possibly more potent reason. The girls were desperately waiting for the boys to leave so they could sing and dance without inhibition. The sight of the boys settling down for a session of their own was stretching their patience to its limits. The boys knew this well and felt that their own Lohri would be incomplete if they didn't have the chance to witness the girls dance with gleeful abandon.

The boys were under the impression that, as usual, the girls would break into song and dance soon after the departure of the elders. But the rivalry between the two camps this year had been a bit too intense for the girls to start their merriment while the boys were still around.

Let's start with our songs first, the boys reasoned. Maybe that will goad the girls into following suit. One said that he would try his hand at verse and began:

> *Those lovely eyes, I do submit*
> *Unleash arrows straight, my heart is hit…*

Others tried their hand at improvised verses of this kind for half an hour or so before someone suggested they move on to the more refined tones of the Urdu ghazal. One of them began:

> *To the killing fields she sauntered*
> *Deadly intent, and dagger in hand*
> *Ardent lovers dash ahead, gather in advance,*
> *Each ready with his head for a sacrifice grand.*
> *Lest stains of blood reveal her lover true,*
> *A layer of henna on her palms, she's planned.*

A few of the girls stole a glance towards the boys' camp, silently enjoying the ghazal. They kept their eyes lowered, careful to hide their emotions from their friends, putting on a show to the boys that they couldn't care less about their singing. A few, in fact, were whispering, 'Such louts … aren't they ashamed of themselves … utterly shameless … so cheap and inappropriate, their songs…'

The boys' ploy didn't work because the girls simply refused to respond. Desperate, they tried another gambit to lower their veil of reserve. Hoping that the girls would find it hard to resist the challenge of a tappa, the short verse that seeks a response from the rival team, one of the boys began:

Like the flower of a pomegranate,
I am most handsome among the boys.
Now, who's the loveliest among the maidens?

The tactic worked. Like an arrow that finds its target, the tappa created a stir in the girls' camp. The pent-up frustration of being unable to sing on the much-awaited occasion of Lohri was now threatening to explode. The challenge thrown at them so brazenly by the boys was the last straw. Angry eyes glared at one another, each trying to provoke the other to respond to the verse. The group was buzzing with a heated discussion, mostly conducted through impassioned whispers. Each one wanted to fire the gun from someone else's shoulder. One of the more brash girls turned to address the group, 'Didn't he say who is the most beautiful among us? So, let the fairest one respond?'

'You are right! Absolutely!' There was a tremor on many a lip, but their eyes had turned towards Naseem. It wasn't just her beauty that made her the obvious candidate to take up the challenge. She was also considered something of a wizard when it came to the back-and-forth banter of tappas.

'Come on, Seema,' their eyes seemed to implore. 'Our reputation now lies in your hands.'

The boys were also looking at them, eagerly awaiting a response to the arrow unleashed by them.

Tappas are quite popular across Punjab and are particularly delightful when one side poses a question and the other side sings its response. It takes both hands to clap, and the boys waited anxiously, their plans stuck until one of the girls picked up the baton.

The response finally came, but in a form that made it impossible to continue the chain. In fact, it made sure that the chain ended then and there. A melodious and somewhat nervous voice arose from the girls' camp. It overcame its initial diffidence and picked up strength as it travelled towards the boys.

> *Stand in the corner, miserable pervert*
> *I'm like your sister, don't forget*
> *Go find a harlot if you want to flirt!*

The boys were stunned into silence. It looked like someone had placed an invisible seal on their lips. They looked at each other, anxious eyes asking the same question, 'How do we get out of this predicament now?'

Weighed down by their own silence and tormented by the muffled sounds of victorious laughter from the other side, they pondered their next move. Finally, one of the smarter ones summoned the others close and whispered his plan. This brought back some cheer to their faces and one of them announced, 'Come on guys … it's pretty late now … time for us to be heading home.' The boys got up and started to leave the haveli.

Seeing that the field was now clear for them, the girls left their own diminishing bonfire and moved to the much larger ones the boys had vacated. As they gathered around it, they went up to compliment Naseem for her courage. She had managed to fell a powerful adversary with just one blow.

There was no stopping them now. The hours of restraint evaporated in seconds, and popular Lohri songs resonated across the haveli's courtyard. After a while, the songs gave way to tappas and after that, it was time for the giddha dance. Within minutes, dupattas were flying askew to reveal bare heads and the combined rhythm of the girls' feet was shaking the very foundations of the haveli. The rapid movements were also kicking up a fair bit of dust which had now blended with the smoke from the bonfire to create a pinkish cloud that hovered above their heads.

An hour went by, then another, and yet another as the girls danced the night away. Their legs were aching, and their tightly braided hair had shaken loose, swaying from the back to the shoulder and from the shoulder to the forehead as they danced to the rhythm of the claps. The faint twilight of dawn was making its appearance when one of the girls cried, 'Enough! I don't think I can lift my foot to take another step.' Other voices immediately rose in protest, 'Just one or two dances more, please. Lohri doesn't come every day. We waited a whole year for these moments.'

A new song started and the girls were getting ready for another dance when a deep voice intruded upon their merriment. The girls froze in their tracks, the words of the song stranded mid-sentence in their throats. Like a volley of bullets, a dozen or so boys shouted in unison, 'Assalamu alaikum!'

'A plague on all of you,' the embarrassed girls cried in dismay. 'So, you were hiding behind the wall to watch us, you rogues?'

'What else could we do?' the boys replied as they entered the courtyard and joined their group. 'You were refusing to sing and we didn't want to leave till we'd heard your songs.'

'Worthless rascals ... should be ashamed of the way you were spying on us...' the girls continued to curse the boys as they retreated towards their own bonfire.

'What's the problem?' one of the boys queried. 'You were listening to our songs and now we've heard yours. The skies haven't come crashing down on our heads, have they?'

'When did we listen to your songs?' one of the girls pouted in a patently fake display of anger that did little to conceal a mischievous smile.

'You had your ears turned towards us when we were singing, didn't you?' another one piped up.

'Okay, maybe we heard you,' another girl responded. 'But not like thieves hiding behind a wall.'

'There is no crime in stealing from a miser who wants to share nothing,' one of the boys responded.

'No crime in stealing, says he,' a diminutive girl pushed her way forward to confront him. 'And who are you to be issuing these fatwas?'

The arguments might well have continued for a while but the same melodious voice that had previously vanquished the foe rose once again to make its presence felt.

'*He leers at his own, the scoundrel's habit is bad.*'

The other girls quickly picked up Naseem's line and the chorus rose to a crescendo:

> *He leers at his own, the scoundrel's habit is bad.*
> *He leers at his own, the scoundrel's habit is bad.*

'Okay, sisters,' one of the more mature boys spoke in a respectful tone. 'The Lohri is over, so how about making peace now?'

'Make peace with my jutti,' the same diminutive girl shouted as she pointed at her foot. 'With Allah's blessings, we will get our revenge at next year's Lohri or you can change my name!'

Who could have known that an evil djinn had been secretly observing the revelries and getting infuriated? The girl's comment about getting 'revenge at next year's Lohri' was perhaps the last straw. The djinn told itself, 'How dare this girl make such brazen promises about the future? If I allow these people to stay together till next year, I don't deserve to be called a djinn.'

One of the girls had heard the djinn's ominous words. That same girl, the one who had been called the fairest one, the same gentle Seema. She stepped forward to restrain her aggressive compatriot and chided, 'Be quiet, Santo.' Turning towards the boys, she said, 'Let bygones be bygones, my brothers. Who knows which one of us dies and which one survives until next year's Lohri!'

Her measured words were spoken with a genuine warmth and the boys respectfully lowered their eyes. There was no trace of the mischief that they had displayed all evening.

As the two groups began to make their way out of the haveli, one of the boys—the same one who had initiated the tappa 'I am the most handsome...' turned around and shouted, 'Boys! Join me as I say, "May our sisters..."'

'Live forever...' roared the boys in unison.

Naseem responded with the call, 'And may our brothers...'

'Live forever...' cried the girls in one voice.

They exchanged cordial Lohri greetings and headed for their respective homes.

10

THE ADVENT OF the February–March month of Phagun is accompanied by an endearing mingling of mood, colour and fragrance. The vegetation starts to shake off the effects of autumn and winter to emerge with a youthful vigour. Colourful buds appear on branches that had become dry, lifeless twigs over the preceding months. The air around the trees is suffused with the delicate scents bursting forth from the buds.

The young boys and girls from villages in our countryside also draw inspiration from the rejuvenation taking place around them, creating a tumult of new desires, new aspirations. Acres of mustard fields acquire a golden hue and every nook and corner is resplendent with a riot of colours. The youth try to emulate these by making sure that the turbans sported by the boys and the dupattas donned by the girls are dyed in the brightest shades.

Phagun, it seems, is the month when Mother Nature and mankind walk shoulder to shoulder, each in sync with the other. The latter part of Phagun brings stronger winds that shake the branches and create a shower of fresh flowers as Nature starts to celebrate the colourful festival of Holi. Our people have taken their cue from Nature since time immemorial and their own celebrations of Holi during the last week of Phagun reflect their joy and anticipation over the imminent arrival of Spring. The hues of Nature are replicated in the heaps of coloured powders prepared for Holi. Young or old, everyone joins in the festivities and makes sure that a dab or two of colour is applied, if not sprinkled through a bottle of water, on anyone that they can catch.

It was now the latter part of the beautiful month of Phagun and who would have imagined that the blessings of Spring were about to be replaced by an unprecedented ordeal—that our Punjabi brethren would play Holi with blood and not with the floral shades of Nature. Who would have imagined that we Punjabis—known across the length and breadth of the country for our bravery, our generosity, our camaraderie and bonhomie—that *we* Punjabis would mark the end of Phagun by abandoning our humanity, taking on the form of the Devil himself?

It was during the second half of this ill-fated Phagun that the ominous clouds of communal strife first seen in the cities started to blow towards the peaceful countryside. Sectarian passions were being aroused among the guileless inhabitants of these villages.

Initially, it was the larger villages that fell prey to this deadly epidemic but it was only a matter of time before it started to envelop the smaller hamlets in its vicious embrace.

Chakri wasn't exactly a hamlet but neither did it fall in the category of the large villages. That could be one reason it hadn't fallen victim to the first wave of this epidemic of communal violence.

The strong bonds of kinship between the different communities in this village had been formed over the generations. Nor was this unique to Chakri. It could, in fact, be described as one of the defining characteristics of the entire Pothohar region. Each person depended on the other for their well-being. They were tied to each other by their shared interests. Each community followed its own religious practices and rituals and there was never a trace of prejudice amongst any of them. The occasional attempt by some overzealous soul to create friction was quickly snuffed out to restore the same spirit of fraternal amity with which they had lived over the centuries.

That spirit stayed intact in Chakri even when they started to receive news reports about the outbreak of sectarian strife in several nearby cities. They failed to stir any communal passions as long as they were read out merely as 'reports'. But that started to change when Munshi Abdul Rahman and some of his acolytes took to spicing up the reports with their own toxic assertions before spreading them among the unsuspecting villagers. His campaign sent a wave of anxiety through the Khatri community, particularly when they saw him draw the allegiance of some of the young hotheads of the village. The Munshi's message carried a certain appeal for these youngsters and they secretly attended his meetings, though none of them would have dared say as much in the presence of their elders. They knew that the elders were keeping a watchful eye and there was an uproar in the family whenever a youngster was seen associating with the Munshi's agenda.

The wave of sectarian violence that had started in Rawalpindi was inexorably making its way towards Chakri. The residents of the village could sense its approach and were on the alert. The elders of the Muslim community saw the danger and called for an urgent meeting that was attended by virtually anyone of standing. One by one, they placed their hand on the holy Quran and solemnly swore they would protect the Khatris of the village to their last breath, that they would be ready to shed their last drop of blood to ensure the safety of their non-Muslim brethren. But they were also increasingly mindful of a threat from within, the fact that many of their own youth could be seen hanging around Munshi Abdul Rahman. The danger from that threat seemed to multiply overnight when a scrawny, unkempt sort of Moulvi appeared out of nowhere and became a constant presence by the Munshi's side.

The Khatris of the village were living through a perilous phase. If they saw any silver lining during these grim times, it came from the robust defiance of their Muslim neighbours who often showed their machismo by thumping their chests and asserting, 'Brothers! Please stop worrying. No one is going to touch you. To reach you, they will have to cross our dead bodies first.'

The Khatris initially sought solace in the unequivocal assurances given by the elders of the village who had taken the onus of protecting their non-Muslim neighbours. But news trickling in from other villages soon started to erode their confidence. Until now, the looting of Khatri properties in other villages of their region had been attributed to bands of plunderers who had drifted in from other areas. There was the occasional incident where some Muslim residents of the village also joined in the plunder, but such cases were few and far between. By and large, the Muslim communities stood by their Khatri brothers and made a valiant endeavour to protect their lives and properties. But the bands were becoming larger and more violent, and the locals often found themselves powerless to protect their wards. There were times when they found it prudent to step out of the way and avoid the wrath of the marauding hordes. And then there were those whose avarice got the better of their morality. If some Khatris had abandoned their homes and fled to escape the marauders, these worthy locals would quickly reach the houses ahead of the horde to sneak away with the more expensive possessions. This wasn't motivated by any sense of antagonism towards their neighbours. They were simply driven by the logic that if outsiders were going to help themselves to gold, jewellery and other valuables worth tens of thousands of rupees, why should they deny themselves the rare opportunity to acquire instant prosperity. This is quite a normal human impulse and should be understood for what it is.

As the Khatris of Chakri heard these tales from nearby villages, their anxiety about the future grew. Would their Muslim brothers actually sacrifice their own lives to protect them? Maybe not, they worried. But even in these tumultuous times, there was one house in Chakri that maintained its equanimity. Each time a group of Khatris approached Baba Bhana and argued that it was time to leave their beloved village, he would respond, 'Friends! There is no point in arguing with Fate. We cannot change what the Lord has written.'

11

IT WAS AROUND seven in the evening. The expanding shadows of the night appeared to have strangled the vibrant energy of the village. The stench of fear was all pervasive and the gentle evening breeze seemed much too feeble to blow it away.

Boote Shah was trudging back towards the village from his fields. The listless expression on his face suggested that his legs had no vitality of their own, that they were being forced to carry him towards his destination.

The lanes and by-lanes of the village already wore a deserted look and scarcely a sound emerged from any of the houses. Every few minutes, the silence was broken by the menacing shrieks emanating from a colony of bats that lived in the ample branches of the old peepul tree. Or it was the pulsating sound from the group of vultures ominously circling above the village, their heavy wings flapping to create their own dirge in the background.

Boota Shah's steps slowed involuntarily as he approached the Haveli of the Anands. He stole a quick glance over the crumbling wall and its old Nanakshahi bricks, heaving a deep sigh as he recalled scenes from a year ago. It was the first day of Holi and the festivities had continued late into the night. The Muslim and Khatri youth of

125

the village had excelled themselves in putting on their one-act plays and performances of mimicry which had the audience in splits. The young fellows must have collected well over a hundred rupees that night as the elders of the village showered them with cash and appreciation. To be fair, it was Chaudhry Fazal Karim who set the ball rolling when he announced a prize of ten rupees for the actor who did the best impersonation. This was quite a large incentive and the young performers truly surpassed themselves as they vied for the award. The honour eventually went to Naseem's older brother Aziz who pulled off a remarkable impersonation of an ascetic fakir who often passed through the village.

An ache went through Boote Shah's heart as he recalled the merriment from the previous year. This, too, was the first day of Holi but the village seemed completely oblivious of the festive occasion. The unending reports of plunder and killings had cast a pall of gloom over the village, making the festivities of yore a distant dream that seemed to have died forever.

As he left the Haveli of the Anands and headed towards his own place, his mind was burdened by another thought that only added to his melancholy. He was getting genuinely worried about Naseem. He felt his heart sink each time he looked at her face these days.

Naseem had stopped smiling. It was always her smile that Boote Shah found most endearing. A demure, shy kind of smile that often seemed to conceal a deeper emotion. It was rarely on display since that unfortunate incident with Yusuf but the incessant reports about communal violence and pillage over the last few weeks seemed to have taken a further toll on her. Looking at Naseem's face, Boote Shah felt that her fair countenance had been drained of all blood, leaving a pallid imitation in its wake. Her large and expressive eyes now seemed to convey a sense of deep and unrelenting disillusionment.

Each time he looked at her, he felt that she was sinking under some insurmountable burden that may soon crush her heart into tiny fragments.

For several days now, he had reflected on the merits of going to Naseem's place for a heart-to-heart, possibly to pick at some of her recent scabs and see what was going on in her heart. Or maybe to create an opportunity for a cathartic outpouring that could ease her burden. But he hadn't been able to do that.

As he approached his place today, a fresh idea crossed his mind. I should have assigned this task to Rukman, he reasoned. She should go and have a chat with Naseem.

Endowed with a stout frame and delicate features, Rukman always had an aura of serenity about her. Her broad forehead and open smile were, perhaps, an indication of her large-hearted persona. She couldn't be much older than twenty-five or twenty-six and had already been married for a decade or so. She had managed to look youthful despite these years of marriage, possibly because she had not borne any children. But that inability to bear a child also had another side to it, one that could be discerned in that resigned expression that lingered beneath her cheerful countenance. She tried to keep it hidden, and was seen as a jovial soul in her neighbourhood— someone who could share a hearty laugh with the young girls as easily as she could share confidences with the older women. That somewhat contrived facade helped her cope with her underlying sadness, keeping her distracted from her own sense of inadequacy.

Boote Shah went to the kitchen and sat down for his meal but got up after eating just a handful or two. He took some water to rinse his mouth, and wiped his hands dry with the small towel as Rukman turned towards him enquiring, 'What happened? You left most of your food on the plate!'

'Nothing! I wasn't too hungry today.'

'No! That's not true. Your face tells me straight away that you are disturbed about something.'

Boote Shah sat down and explained that the reason for his gloom was no different from that of everyone else's in the village. It was the imminent danger of sectarian violence consuming their lives. Rukman responded by repeating Baba Bhana's sage advice about accepting the will of the Lord and keeping morale high during any adversity. Boote Shah heard her out but decided to change the subject. 'You are right that we should have faith in the Lord and we should readily submit to His will … but there is also another matter that has been driving me sick with worry.'

'And what's that?' Rukman asked anxiously.

'Have you noticed Seema's appearance lately?'

'Of course, I've noticed. God alone knows what's happening to that girl. She seems to be withering by the day. Her banter, her comments, her laughter used to light up this home the moment she entered. But these days, she seems to have lost her tongue.'

'So, wasn't it your responsibility to check on her and find out if she is facing any particular problem, my dear woman?'

'I've asked her often but she always finds a way to evade the subject. Each time I raise the subject with her, she has this stock response, "There's nothing wrong with me, Bhabi. This is all a figment of your imagination."'

'I believe something serious is going on, otherwise…' He heard someone call his name and went outside to check.

A group of four men were standing in the courtyard—Munshi Abdul Rahman from the school, a youngish man with a mature beard typical of a Moulvi, the cobbler Hidayat's son Inayat, and the butcher Nabiya's son Illamdin.

'Welcome! Please come inside,' Boote Shah smiled with his usual courtesy.

'We've come to see the Taya,' Inayat responded.

'He is resting in the living room. Come with me,' Boote Shah escorted them inside the house. The door of the living room was closed but an old man's melancholy tones could be heard chanting:

Recite the name of Lord Ram and keep your mind at peace,
He will solve your troubles, our Lord Ram Chandra Raghubir...

'Greetings, Taya,' Inayat stepped forward and addressed the Baba. The Baba peered through the thick lenses of his spectacles but failed to recognize the young man until he recognized the voice. 'God bless, Inayat,' he replied as he tried to discern the faces of his companions. 'And who are these gentlemen with you?'

Inayat introduced the team to the Baba, who graciously moved to the corner of his couch and invited them to sit beside him. Boote Shah walked across to a stool and turned up the wick of the lantern to light up the room.

'So what brings you this way?' Baba Bhana smiled gently as he twirled his greying moustache.

'Nothing particularly important, Taya,' Illamdin replied. 'We were passing this way and thought we would look you up.'

There was something about the way Ilamdin said 'nothing particularly important' that told the Baba that something serious was afoot.

'Anyway, let's do the important stuff first. Will you have a cup of fresh milk?'

'No thanks, Taya. We had our meal before coming to your place,' Inayat said before adding, 'actually our Munshiji and the Moulviji wanted to discuss something with you, and I volunteered to bring them across.'

'By all means,' the Baba turned his head towards them as he spoke. 'Tell me, Moulviji,' he blinked behind his glasses as he looked at the Munshi and the Moulvi.

The Moulvi had a dark but sallow sort of complexion. His gaunt frame made him appear taller than he was but the sunken cheeks, eyes set deep in their sockets, and lips that seemed more a shade of black than purple, added to the image of a man who was either an opium addict or perhaps one suffering from a protracted ailment. He wore a pair of tight churidar pyjamas that looked oddly loose and ill-fitting on his spindly legs. His long achkan-style coat extended a couple of inches below his knees, making an unsuccessful attempt to give some kind of shape to his emaciated body. The achkan was visibly dirty, and the presence of some prominent grease stains suggested that a proper cleaning of the fabric was overdue. His beard essentially flowed down from his chin, making his cheeks look like a rough, unfinished piece of leather. A few scabs could be seen on the sides of his elongated neck, possibly an outcome of his efforts to ensure that the beard retained a monopoly on all facial hair. His Adam's Apple appeared twice the normal size, often moving visibly as he spoke.

'I wanted to say—' the Moulvi had just started to speak when the Munshi intervened. 'We have caused you this inconvenience tonight, Babaji, only because we wanted to apprise you of the deteriorating situation and of some of the emerging dangers. You are fully aware of the communal tensions around us and the fact that these are getting more and more ominous with every passing day.'

The Baba was listening attentively. Maybe the rumours that he had heard over the last few weeks were baseless, he thought. He had been informed that the school munshi had enlisted the help of an unknown Moulvi to vitiate the atmosphere in the village. But what he was witnessing today seemed to run counter to those impressions. If the Munshi and the Moulvi had indeed come to his home to apprise him of imminent dangers, they deserved his gratitude. He sighed deeply before lifting his eyes to see them from this new perspective.

'That's very gracious of you, Munshiji,' the Baba looked at them with genuine appreciation. 'But I've always been one hundred per cent sure that no matter what the challenge, our village will be able to weather these storms and maintain its amity. And with caring folks like you around us, we can afford to have our nightly glass of milk and sleep soundly in our beds.'

'You are right, Babaji,' said the Munshi as he pulled out a yellow pencil from the upper pocket of his jacket and started to scratch its tip with his nails. 'But you must also be aware that these communal issues can be quite sensitive and even the slightest mistake can result in irreparable damage.'

'What are you trying to say? I'm afraid I don't understand,' the Baba said with a hint of irritation.

'What he is saying is quite clear, Taya,' Illamdin hurried to intervene. 'Munshiji wanted to have a word with you about Sugara Maasi's daughter.'

Baba Bhana reacted like he had bitten on a pebble while chewing his food, his expression revealing a mix of shock and revulsion. 'About Seema?' he asked.

'Indeed,' Inayat responded as he poked his little finger into his right ear to deal with some nagging itch. 'Babaji, the whole village knows that you have raised their family as your own but surely you agree that when it comes to matters of religion, you must go your way and they have to go theirs. Because adherence to our faith and religion is vital for all of us.'

The impact that the Munshi's initial statements had made on the Baba was wearing off quite rapidly. But what were they getting at? He still wasn't able to fathom it. He wanted his uninvited guests to reveal their true intent as quickly as possible.

The Munshi stepped in to clarify before the Baba could voice his query. 'You see, the girl is now at an age where she would be better off if she is in the care of persons from her own faith. I know that you have looked after the family from every respect, but Babaji … you can't stop tongues from wagging, can you? It might be a minor matter but people will add ten other titbits to make it a big story. So, we've come to request you that you ask the mother and daughter to return to their own house. How much longer can we place their burden on your shoulders?'

'A burden on my shoulders?' the Baba's mouth remained open in astonishment as he repeated the question.

'Of course, Babaji,' the Moulvi interjected. 'Munshiji is absolutely right. Besides, why should you continue along a path that will only bring you disrepute?'

'Disrepute? Disrepute to me?' the Baba's breathing quickened as he spoke.

'Isn't it bad enough, the stuff that people are already saying?' Illamdin demanded, biting the nail of his thumb as he spoke. 'The village has had to hang its head in shame because of the actions of this girl.'

'But,' the Baba replied in a worried tone. 'It wasn't the girl's fault, nor was it mine…'

'Let's not get into the matter of whose fault it was, Babaji,' Inayat butted in. 'The matter was quietly buried because of your stature.

Otherwise, your son…' Inayat turned around to glare at Boote Shah with unbridled hatred as he spoke.

'Which son of a—' the abuse was still in Boote Shah's throat when the Baba scowled at him and warned, 'Be quiet, young man. This doesn't concern you. Go ahead and attend to your errands.'

Boote Shah swallowed the Baba's insult along with his own anger, as though he'd been asked to drink a cup of poison, and quickly left the room.

The Baba could feel his temper rising but a regard for his own age and a certain latitude for the youth of the visitors helped him keep it under check. Changing his tone to indicate that he wanted to bring the discussion to an end, he said, 'Alright, let's accept that it's all my fault, or my son's. But can you please tell me what exactly has brought you here tonight?' The Baba's eyes were showing a tinge of red as he spoke. He was worried that he might insult his guests by saying something inappropriate.

'We want just two things, Taya,' Illamdin responded. 'First, please ask the two of them to leave this house and return to their own home at the earliest. Second, please get Naseem's consent for the nikah.'

That first demand, on its own, would have been enough to infuriate the Baba. But it was the second one that really got him going.

Heaving a deep sigh that tried to conceal his anger and disgust, he replied, 'Alright, young man. Let's say I agree with your demand and ask them to return to their old house just to satisfy you. But what do I do about your second demand to get her consent for nikah? How am I supposed to do that if I have no relationship with them? I'll leave it to you folks to sort out the matter of the nikah.'

'That's not how it works, Taya,' Inayat answered. 'It doesn't matter whether you are related to them or not. We know that the nikah can't be done without your approval.'

'And what does that mean?' the Baba asked in yet another desperate attempt to keep his anger in check.

'What it means,' the Munshi interposed, 'is that we have already explored the topic with Sugara bibi.'

'And what was her response to you?'

'She said that this matter is entirely up to the Baba. She will not act on this without getting a nod from you.'

'Fine,' the Baba countered. 'I agree that I am also keen to see Naseem married soon. I lie awake at night worrying about this girl's marriage because it is a promise that I had made to her father. I've been searching for the right person so that I can relieve myself of this responsibility but...'

'You don't have to worry about that, Taya,' Illamdin butted in. 'We've found the right boy for her. We just need you to say yes.'

The Baba tried to calm himself down as he spoke, 'If you are so keen to get my consent, please bring the boy over so that I can see him. Surely, I have the right to meet him, to know him and his background.'

'See him by all means,' the Munshi replied enthusiastically. 'You can see him right away. Here he is, Babaji.' He turned to point at the Moulvi, who was busy scratching the side of his neck, his fingernails leaving little tracks along their arid pathway.

'By the grace of Allah,' Inayat added. 'He comes from a very affluent family, our Moulvi. He is well-educated too. If you ask me, he is the perfect candidate in every respect.'

Seeing the Baba sink into a deep silence, Illamdin asked, 'So what do you think, Taya?'

The Baba seemed to be paralysed. Speaking with a great deal of effort, he replied, 'Okay, let me think about it.'

'What's there to think about, Babaji?' the Munshi asked with a tone of humility. 'Grant your consent now and do a noble deed at the same time. Say yes and let's close this discussion.'

'Munshiji!' the Baba spoke with exasperation. 'We are talking about the life of a young girl, not bargaining at the grocer's for flour and lentils. Let me think this matter through. I also want to consult the other elders of the village in this matter.'

'Elders of the village?' the Munshi laughed sarcastically. 'Forget about those old-fashioned fellows, Babaji.'

'But I am also one of those old-fashioned fellows, Munshiji. In fact, I am probably the most old-fashioned of the lot simply because I am the oldest one in the village.'

'So should we conclude,' Inayat started heatedly, 'that you are refusing to provide your consent?'

That was the last straw for the Baba. He could no longer control his anger. He had done his best to maintain the dignity of his guests and he still didn't want to say anything that would cause offense to the Munshi or the Moulvi. But the other two were youngsters from his own village, boys that he had slapped when they had misbehaved. The way they had behaved today had breached every norm of respectful conduct. Eyes blazing as he looked at them, the Baba hissed, 'Listen, you ruffians! You seem to have forgotten who you are addressing. One tight slap from me and your face will be twisted around to stop you from jabbering like this. Why don't you tell me about yourself? Was your marriage decided by you alone? And your sister Fajjan who got married last year. Was her nikah read out without the consent of her family? You wanted to hear from me so here it is. I will not provide my consent for Naseem's nikah. You can do what you like. I will call the panchayat tomorrow and place this matter before the elders of the village, so get ready to face the consequences. You were born in our hands and now you want to turn around and give orders to us? Get lost or else...' The Baba's voice was choking with rage, and it took a while before his coughing stopped and he was again in a position to speak.

The Munshi and the Moulvi were under the impression that the two youngsters would react violently to the insult heaped upon them by the Baba but they remained frozen. And while the Baba had directed his tirade at Inayat, he left these two in no doubt that they were the real targets of his attack. They were seething over the unexpected humiliation at the hands of the old man.

'Come on, Illamdinji. Come on, Inayat Khanji. Let's go,' the Moulvi lifted his gangly frame from the bed and swayed out of the room. The other three followed suit.

Inayat didn't have the courage to look the Baba in the eye and respond but he chose to deliver a parting shot as they left. 'Fine. You'll see what happens now,' he warned.

The Baba remained silent.

12

THE FIRE BURNING in a kiln has the ability to transform soft clay into hard ceramic but if the same fire burns in the kiln of the human mind, its heat can weaken the defences of the mind to a point that they start crumbling. Can you imagine the condition of a person whose mind is being subjected to the intense heat of not one but several fires burning at the same time? Perhaps a look at Naseem's face would give you an idea. Her gentle mind, a mind so sensitive that it gets singed by the heat of the slightest friction, finds itself facing the ordeal of multiple fires. It must be a testament to her resilience that she is still alive.

She recalled those days when they were little children playing their innocent little games, oblivious of the strands of love that were pulling them closer to each other. Over the years, those strands had grown into an unbreakable cord that bound them. This was a new feeling for Naseem, one that often left her wondering about it. How did it happen? A wayward and stubborn lad whose failings far outweighed his virtues had become such an integral part of her consciousness! They were just a couple of kids playing hide-and-seek and messing around in the mud. When did this lovebug decide to establish its permanent residence in her heart?

When did this Yusuf become such a central pearl in my necklace of memories, she pondered. What exactly did I see in him? The fact that he was willing to go to any lengths to please me? That he was ready to steal stuff that I liked? That he would beat up other boys and girls if I had teased him? That he would even beat me up without any rhyme or reason?

The more she thought of him, the more she came around to the recognition that perhaps his only saving grace was his willingness to comply with whatever she asked of him. If she advised him to follow a particular path, he would readily change track and obey her instruction. If she told him to desist from engaging in some odious activity, he would immediately acknowledge his mistake and swear that he would never do so again. But how long would these pledges last? His mind was like a leaky vessel. Naseem would pour her advice into it and it would stay for a while before it started to drip away. Before you knew it, he was back to his old antics.

Naseem remembered the times when the indiscretions of her wilful companion had brought her to the verge of tears. She would yell at him, he would see her tears and proffer an unqualified apology, and they would make up. But it was all so transient, a lull before the next storm.

'Yusuf is a terrible fellow … Yusuf is a thief … Yusuf is a rascal…' Naseem had often heard these phrases in the village, from young and old folks alike. She'd recoil each time, as though every abuse was a blow to her own self. There were times when she wanted to confront Yusuf, to pick up a heavy stone and smash it on her own head. Or to bang her head against a wall to make him feel the hurt his actions were causing. But she was being naive if she believed that this would really get him to mend his ways.

As adolescence gave way to adulthood, Naseem found herself marvelling at the way her mind was crafting a gentle, charming image of Yusuf. She had always wanted him to transform himself from a scoundrel into a decent human being. But over the years, her ambition had grown and she dreamed of Yusuf evolving into some kind of an angel. And as for Yusuf? Well, he was like the proverbial dog's tail that can't be straightened by wishes alone. He remained the same rash, irresponsible Yusuf that she had always known. But even by his own standards, the way he had molested her during their last encounter was the last straw. He had slapped her, violated her dignity, broken her bangles and forced her to escape from his clutches. It was more than enough to ensure that his name would soon be erased from her heart. As days passed into weeks, Naseem felt that she had finally been able to expel him from her life.

But that letter! Those three pages had managed to turn everything upside down. The dormant emotions she had hoped to bury for good were getting animated once more. Not only had the letter rejuvenated her love for him; it had also brought to fore a dread about his well-being. She could hear a cacophony of cries rising from within and crashing against her eardrums. 'What if he's consumed some poison and killed himself? What if he's gone to some distant land to escape the opprobrium? What if … what if…?' Soon, the voices were accompanied by nightmares that haunted her for days on end. Of Yusuf's body being washed up along the banks of the river; of Yusuf getting decapitated under the wheels of a speeding train; of Yusuf locked up in some dingy cell inside a prison…

That letter had left her in a constant state of agitation, distraught and anxious to learn about Yusuf's well-being. She thought long and hard about it and each path seemed to lead her deeper into a maze. She felt imprisoned by an insurmountable wall that she could neither break nor leap across. Each time she pulled Yusuf's letter out of the trunk to read it yet another time, she found tears flowing down her face.

There were times that Naseem chafed at the restriction imposed by the Baba, but her abiding respect for him kept her from taking the matter into her own hands. Not that she didn't think about it. But it was always accompanied by the reservation, 'No! How can I violate Babaji's instructions? We've seen over the years that his judgement is impeccable. He would have taken into account the interest of both sides.'

The kiln inside Naseem's tender heart was stoking three separate fires at the same time—of love, of the grief of separation from her lover, and of a deep anxiety about her lover's fate. And if that wasn't enough, there was yet another fear that had cast a pall of gloom over her. She worried day and night about the safety of her foster father and his family. Rumours about the spread of communal violence were pouring unabated into their village. Who knew which way the blood-thirsty tempest would turn, which village would become the next target of its frenzy? Who hadn't heard about the village where Khatri homes had been looted, or the one where many residents had been slaughtered, or the one where young girls had been abducted? Naseem winced each time she heard a fresh rumour; every new report seemed to draw another sip or two of blood from her frail body.

Naseem had also observed the arrival of a new virus in the village in the form of the Moulvi. He seemed hellbent on spreading the infection of communal discord amongst people who had lived in harmony for generations. Watching his actions, Naseem was convinced that it was only a matter of time before the Khatri community was scorched in the flames of his incendiary rhetoric.

She'd spotted the Moulvi in her neighbourhood a few times, usually accompanied by that Munshi from the madrasa. A mere glance at their godforsaken shadows was enough to send a surge of fury through her body. She wanted to lash out at them, gouge their faces and make them pay for the havoc they had unleashed on her happy little village. So when she had seen their wretched souls saunter into her own courtyard the previous afternoon, she felt like a handful of salt had been rubbed into a gaping wound.

The Moulvi was accompanied by the Munshi and a couple of other young men. Naseem's mother was lying on a cot in the courtyard, gasping for breath as she battled a fresh attack of asthma. The local lads greeted her and unceremoniously perched themselves on the side of her cot.

Naseem stayed indoors, carefully listening to every word of the conversation. They must have spent half an hour or so before leaving in a huff. Naseem could see that they were angry and muttering something as they left. She wanted to pick up some scalding pieces of coals from the hearth in the kitchen and hurl them at that moth-eaten Majnu of a Moulvi. Didn't she have enough troubles already? And now this new problem had landed on her doorstep. She had heard her mother's firm rejection of their proposition. She had also seen their sullen faces as they withdrew. This isn't over yet, she told herself. She had seen the wrath on Munshi Abdul Rahman's face, heard him mumbling in rage, 'We'll see that old codger and find out how brave he really is.'

Naseem found it hard to sleep that night. Her mind was in turmoil as she grappled with one challenge after another. To make matters worse, her mother's asthma was giving her a hard time. Naseem got up every couple of hours to prepare a brew that would give her mother some relief, keeping the fire in the hearth going right through the night. Rukman came over for a while and sat by Sugara's side, insisting that she could stay the night and help. But Naseem would hear none of it. Rukman, after all, was also responsible for a bunch of chores for Babaji and she couldn't keep her away from those.

Compared to other girls her age, Naseem was pretty tough and resilient. She had grown up dealing with adversities big and small, and could take quite a lot in her stride. But tonight was different. This tidal wave of difficulties was enough to knock her off her feet and carry her into a bottomless abyss. She broke down and wept, a flood of tears streaming down her face as she sobbed, alone and overwhelmed. Her thoughts turned to her brother Aziz and the numerous letters that she had written. 'I'll come in a few days,' was the response she got for each desperate appeal. How could he be so heartless, she wondered. And the rivulet of tears grew as she thought of him, and of her mother who had urged, 'I suggest you send a telegram to Aziz tomorrow and ask him to come immediately. Who knows…?' Was her mother suggesting that her own end was near, she wailed in silence.

Naseem also had another reason for sending letter after letter to Aziz. The epidemic of communal violence was spreading everywhere, and she feared for the Baba and his family. She needed Aziz so that they could work out a plan for the family's safety.

Fear of death is a fairly universal ocurrence. Even the bravest of men can quiver in their shoes when they come face to face with it. And yet, there are times when that same fear of death vanishes, when we almost plead for it to come to us and take us away. At times like these, we see death as a saviour. Today we see our young girl, one who is yet to enjoy her life in this world, calling for Death to save her from her troubles.

That night finally gave way to dawn but Naseem hadn't slept a wink. Instead of sleep, her eyes were still brimming with tears that flowed at the slightest pretext. Her pillow drenched from the incessant stream, she raised her head to flip it around when she heard her mother gasping for breath. Throwing her quilt aside, she hurried towards her mother's bed and bent over to take a closer look. The wheezing from her chest was clearly audible, as was the rasping sound of phlegm. The effect of the medicine had worn off. Naseem went across to the kitchen to heat a pot of water on the hearth. A fresh hot brew ought to soothe the system for a while.

Naseem's eyes were swollen from lack of sleep and the incessant crying. Her head felt heavy as she sat in front of the hearth and used the iron tongs to turn a sturdy log and stoke the fire. There was a loud hiss and crackle, possibly from a damp section of the log. She could also see some reddish resin seep onto the floor. It smelled like cheap liquor, and as she sniffed it, she felt a similar odour wafting towards her from the pan as the water began to boil. She shuffled back and craned her neck away from the hearth to escape the odour, her face turning towards the door that opened into the courtyard.

The early light of dawn was starting to filter into the courtyard behind her. The cheerful chirping of morning birds could be heard from where Naseem was sitting in the kitchen. Gentle gusts of a cool breeze drifted through the courtyard, adding their own touch to the pleasant ambience. Naseem, however, was lost in her own world, one where everything had a dark and sepulchral hue. The brew was bubbling away on the hearth, but Naseem's attention was focused on the mango tree in the courtyard. Its golden leaves were heavy with the night's dew and little droplets were tumbling towards the ground. Each leaf appeared to express an unspoken anguish through these tears.

Naseem moved her gaze away from the tree, only to discover that her own eyes were shedding similar droplets. She wiped them away with the corner of her dupatta and picked up the ladle to stir the brew as she tried to focus on the pot. Her hand was moving the ladle while her mind was heading towards a decision that was dangerous but also strangely reassuring. Death! That was the only solution! Now, what would be the best way to make sure that she could take her own life without too much pain or suffering? Her mind started to explore the options.

The part of the log that was previously dripping some resin had now made its way into the hearth and was burning away at a furious pace. The brew was frothing at the surface as it continued to boil, but Naseem felt that it needed a few more minutes before it was ready.

She got up from the hearth and walked towards the mango tree, standing before it to stare at the fat drops of dew that were still rolling down from the leaves. Chapter by chapter, the entire history of that tree was unfolding before her eyes. She could still feel the shape of that slender pit in her palm. Lingering a little while longer, she let out a painful sigh and wiped a tear with her forefinger before turning towards the kitchen. Her ears perked up as she heard an unusual sound. A melodious voice was singing some soulful verses in the distinctive notes of Raag Asa.

Instead of going to the kitchen, she headed for the door that opened into the street. The voice was now becoming clearer:

> *Let Allah o Allah be your song*
> *And leave those sighs so painful and long…*

As she opened the door, she could hear the approaching steps of the singer and his verse:

> *The Creator resides within you*
> *Submit to the Lord, whatever you do…*

She poked her head outside the door and saw an old fakir, his slender frame wrapped in a coarse black shawl. He was lost in his own rhythm, his bald head swaying gently as he sang:

> *Let Allah o Allah be your song*
> *And leave those sighs so painful and long...*

The words were like a soothing balm on her battered core. The fakir may have had the good Lord in mind as he sang these verses, but Naseem saw in them another dimension. In these early moments of dawn, the Lord had sent His own messenger from the heavens to relay these words to her.

The fakir continued with his melody as he passed her door, oblivious that a young lady was hanging on to each word with rapt attention.

'O noble Saain!' Naseem called as he advanced half a dozen paces beyond her house.

The fakir turned around and asked, 'What's the matter, my child?'

'Saainji', Naseem lowered her head to pay her respects as she spoke. 'Can you please sing the remaining verses of this hymn for me? I'll be truly obliged.'

The fakir heard her request with a smile and started without hesitation:

> *Still far away, that destination of yours*
> *Why sit down in such despair.*
> *Just rise and return, to that path of yours*
> *Don't die in misery, without a prayer.*
> *Let Allah o Allah be your song*
> *And leave those sighs so painful and long.*
> *Wasting away those tears of yours*

> *Pearls ripped away from necklace dear.*
> *Grief that lies in this heart of yours*
> *Just let it be and have no fear.*
> *Let Allah o Allah be your song*
> *And leave those sighs so painful and long.*
> *Will pull you down, this sorrow of yours*
> *And drown you in its deathly wave.*
> *Like a boat so frail, these eyes of yours*
> *Filled to the brim, pose danger grave.*
> *Let Allah o Allah be your song*
> *And leave those sighs so painful and long.*

The fakir completed his hymn and looked at his audience. Contrary to expectation, he found tears rolling down the girl's eyes, she was sobbing as she tried to regain some control over her emotions. She felt like she had come awake from a deep slumber.

She quickly slipped inside the kitchen to offer the customary alms of some flour and lentils to the fakir. She heard him calling after her, 'Allah's child! Blessings! Keep Allah's name on your lips.'

As she returned with the flour and lentils, she could see that the fakir had already moved a fair distance beyond her door. He was again swaying with the rhythm of his melody as he walked, singing:

> *Let Allah o Allah be your song*
> *And leave those sighs so painful and long.*

Naseem didn't have the heart to shout after him yet another time. She went back to the kitchen with a feeling of lightness, the sense that an immense weight had been lifted off her shoulders. The fakir's hymn kept echoing in her mind.

13

'SEEMA!' WHAT'S HAPPENED to you, sister? You've become thin as a reed!' Aziz exclaimed with concern as he entered the house around sunset.

'Nothing much, Bhaaji' Naseem mumbled to reassure her brother. 'It's only a bit of … a bit of…,' she trailed off as she searched for a persuasive reason. She thought of saying that she had been suffering from regular headaches, or from intermittent fever but it seemed so contrived. A headache can't make a person so frail. And Aziz knew that she had never had any kind of fever in her life. How could she tell such a lie to her brother?

'Really, Ma!' Aziz continued as he sat beside Sugara on her bed. 'I can understand that you look quite weak because you've been sick for a while, but what's happened to her? She was fine when I left this place. What's happened to her happy, chubby little face? She's reduced herself to a miserable skeleton.'

Aziz was three or four years older than Naseem and had grown up into a fine young man. Like his sister, he also had a light complexion and a handsome face, further embellished by a fine moustache. His eyes reflected a blend of humility and masculine confidence. His broad forehead suggested an honest character.

Aziz hadn't progressed very far in terms of formal schooling. He had left home to work in Rawalpindi at a fairly young age and didn't spend very many years in the madrassa. But he was fortunate to befriend some respectable folks and their company had not only polished his rustic language, but also given him an air of sophistication that belied his lack of education. He was dressed in immaculate khaki shorts, brown sandals, a burgundy-coloured serge jacket and a fine muslin turban, with the tail of its fabric draping proudly across his shoulder.

Naseem marvelled at the turn of events in such a short span of time. She had started the day with her early morning interlude with a carefree fakir who had miraculously lifted her sinking spirits, whose verses had continued to echo within her long after he had left. And before dusk on the same day, she had seen Aziz arrive at their doorstep.

'Seema!' Sugara called her with the intention of sending her off so that she could speak privately with Aziz. 'Why don't you go make some tea for your brother?'

Sugara started as soon as Naseem had entered the kitchen, giving him a full and unvarnished account of everything that had transpired. She thought briefly about leaving out the bits about Yusuf but decided against it. It was best that he heard the facts from her than receive lurid accounts from some of his friends in the village. Fearful that Aziz might fly into a rage and do something violent, she gently walked him through the entire episode.

Aziz felt his body tingling with fury as he heard the details from his mother. He wanted to rush out and do something but kept his cool. There was much that he still had to hear from his mother. She paused to clear her throat before describing the Moulvi's activities in the village and his visit to their home. He had come the previous day with some of his compatriots and had threatened them with consequences if they didn't leave Bhane Shah's house.

Her narrative produced a deep sense of concern in Aziz. He understood the worries lying behind Naseem's pallid face. But his thoughts had already turned to a more pressing matter. The ill winds of communal violence were approaching their village and he had to make arrangements for the safety of Bhane Shah and his family.

He also heard with growing disquiet as his mother recounted additional details about the Moulvi's collaboration with the school's Munshi and their malign influence on some of the local youth. For a while, his anxiety over his mother's health was set aside. His own anger over the Moulvi's offensive behaviour in asking for his sister's hand and the obnoxious manner in which they had threatened his mother would also have to wait, as would his concern over his sister's future. Moving Baba Bhana and his family out of the village and taking them to a safe location was the first priority.

'May we be cursed forever,' the young man spoke in anguish, 'if this family comes to any harm while we are alive. I have an idea, Ma. Let's all move to Rawalpindi for some time. I will go across to Bapuji and ask him to quickly pack a few things. Honestly, Ma, we can't afford to delay this a minute longer. I know that Rawalpindi, too, isn't immune to this virus of communal violence. But I have a plan. Nobody knows the three of them in Rawalpindi. If we get them to don Muslim attire and accompany us, they will be safe. They can stay with us as long as they want and none will be any wiser.'

'May you live long, my son,' his mother spoke with pride. 'I'll ask for nothing more if you can take this huge responsibility on your shoulders.'

'Fine! So I am going across to the haveli,' he said as he left her bed and started to head towards the door.

'Hold on for a minute,' she called. 'You must be tired from the journey. Have some tea before you go.'

'Don't worry, Ma. The tea isn't going to run away.' He had barely taken a couple of steps towards the haveli when he saw the Baba approaching. He was treading gingerly, exploring the ground with his walking stick as he advanced towards them.

'Salaam, Bapuji!' Aziz exclaimed as he flew towards the old man and clasped him in a warm embrace.

'Who? Is that Aziz—my son?' The Baba's trembling arms went around him as he kissed the young man's forehead and stroked his back. 'So you finally found the time to come, you good-for-nothing lout? All those letters…'

'What could I do, Bapuji?' Aziz was still soaking in the warmth of the old man's embrace as he spoke. 'My work just wouldn't let me…'

'Work? What kind of work is that, you idiot?' The Baba's cloudy eyes exuded affection as he gazed at the young man's face. 'The hell with your work! We are all praying for his mother's health and this joker is going on about his work. Anyway, thank God that you are finally here.'

Aziz held the Baba's arm as he entered the house. Sugara lowered her dupatta over her face in deference as she greeted him, 'Please come inside, Bhaiyyaji. May you live long.'

'How are you doing?' the Baba asked before adding, 'I must confess that I've become pretty useless of late. I am mostly stuck indoors and find it difficult to even come to this place. These eyes of mine have simply given up on me! They've really put me in a tough spot.'

'You shouldn't have bothered, Bhayyiaji,' Sugara spoke with reverence. 'Aziz was in fact heading to your place. To be honest, there is nothing that we ever need to ask while you are around, Bhaiyyaji. Rukman dear has been sitting by my side past midnight every night.

If I experience even the slightest discomfort, I discover her standing right beside me ready to help.'

'Hare Ram! Hare Ram!' the Baba intoned as he changed the subject. 'So the boy's come! Thank God for that. I feel like giving the rascal a sound thrashing but I'll let it pass. You know these youngsters don't care a fig for their parents these days. Your mother is so ill and you are obsessed with your work, one may ask?'

Aziz smiled at the affection hidden behind the reprimand and looked at the Baba with respect as he spoke, 'Forgive me this one time, Bapuji. I'll make sure it doesn't happen again.'

'So where's Seema today?' the Baba looked at Sugara as he spoke.

'She's in the kitchen. Should I call her?' Aziz replied before his mother could speak.

The kitchen was close enough for Naseem to hear the conversation. The pan for brewing the tea was already on the hearth and the fire had come alive. She was on the verge of getting up to meet the Baba when she heard her name being said. She sat back on her haunches and decided to wait.

'What's the matter, Bhayyiaji?' Sugara coughed laboriously as she spoke. 'Did you want to say something about Seema?'

'Indeed,' the Baba coughed to clear his throat before speaking. 'I wanted to come last night itself but these damn eyes. They refuse to cooperate.'

'You should have called me over instead of putting yourself to such inconvenience.'

'Don't be silly,' the Baba growled. 'Are you in any condition to leave this place?'

Coming back to the subject, he began, 'He also came to your place last night, didn't he? That fellow, what's his name…?'

'They came,' Sugara hissed. 'Those damned thugs…'

Aziz didn't see the need to enquire. He had already heard the whole story.

'Calm down, girl!' the Baba admonished. 'They also came to see me.'

'What did they say?' Sugara's lip quivered in anger as she enquired.

'Pretty much the same thing they said to you. Plus a few threats too.'

'Threats?' Aziz bristled. 'What kind of threats, Bapuji?'

'Why don't you sit quietly, boy. Another word out of you and I'll ask you to leave,' the Baba cautioned the young man to nip his anger in the bud.

'So?' Sugara asked breathlessly. 'What did they say?'

The Baba gave them a blow-by-blow account of his exchange with the four men.

'Who do they think they are, these bastards, throwing their weight around?' Aziz grimaced, failing completely in his effort to restrain himself. A withering look from the Baba forced him back into silence.

'Wretched busybodies, if you ask me,' Sugara wheezed. 'Came to tell us how much they cared for our welfare! Nobody showed up all these years to ask about us. Now they see a young girl and they want to say they care about us. Aren't they aware that the girl has parents who can look after her? And behold that fellow they brought along to propose. Utterly bereft of looks. Neither a face nor a frame. To be honest, Bhayyiaji, I wanted to give them a piece of my mind. But then I told myself let these blind dogs bark at the wind. How does it affect me? But you had to see the way they came, Bhayyiaji. Like they had come with a personal message from the Nawab. And the threats? If you don't agree we'll do this, we'll do that. I say...'

'How dare they?' Aziz spluttered, his carefully nursed bundle of patience unravelling as he heard his mother. It took a long look from the Baba before he regained his composure.

'Okay that's enough about their nonsense,' the Baba turned serious as he spoke. 'Let's turn to the other matter that they brought up, the one about leaving this house. I've been at sixes and sevens since I heard that. God alone knows why they are so irked by me. Not that I care too much about what people say. I've come to share something more personal. You see, this matter of religion that they brought up … I feel that it is really up to each one of us to follow our religion the way we want. So let's put this factor aside. More important than religion is the nature of our relationship. So please listen carefully, my dear girl. Rahim Baksh passed away years ago and who knows how long I'll be around. But he said something to me before he died and those words of his will stay with me as long as I am alive. And after me, I am sure that Boota, if he is his father's son, will also honour my word. As far as this house is concerned, anyone who says that it belongs to Bhana is sadly mistaken. This house is yours and you are its owner. If you don't believe me, you can take a look at this.' The Baba reached into a deep pocket of his waistcoat to fish out an oldish parchment and handed it to Sugara.

'What is this, Bhaiyyaji?' she gave the document a cursory glance and asked without making any effort to open it.

'This is the registration document for this house. I had the papers transferred to Aziz's name a couple of months after Rahim Baksh died. This life of ours is so fraught with uncertainty. I thought it's best that I put this matter to rest while I am still around. Rahim Baksh, God bless his noble soul, was like a real brother to me even though he was a fair bit younger. I know that there isn't very much that I can do for anyone but I wanted to make sure that my friend's family would always have a roof over their head.'

Sugara was stunned. An act of such enormous generosity? And done ever so quietly, without a word to anyone? Her eyes became moist with gratitude. Aziz also gulped a couple of times to keep his emotions in check.

'I had no intention of bringing up this matter of transfer of property,' the Baba continued. 'Because I do understand that by sharing this information with you, I could create a sense of undue obligation. I had to bring this up today, my dear girl, only because I don't want people to think that your children don't live in their own house, that they are dependent on someone. That's why I have declared explicitly in these papers that I have received the full price of this house. Frankly, I was stung by the language used by those boys last night. How dare anyone suggest that Rahim Baksh's kids are deprived of such a basic necessity! And let me tell you another thing, my dear girl. I still haven't cleared my debt to Rahim Baksh. That will only happen the day that we can send off a happily married Naseem in her wedding palanquin and the day this foolish boy sits astride a horse to attend his own wedding festivities.'

A kindly smile accompanied the Baba's reference to the 'foolish boy'. Aziz smiled for a brief moment before lowering his eyes in respect.

Sugara tried to say something but couldn't. The tears running down her cheeks were saying what her lips couldn't. Each droplet was an expression of her gratitude and respect.

'Bhayyiaji,' she finally spoke as she attempted to hand the papers back to the Baba. 'Most people try to make a distinction between who is family and who isn't. But I want to say that for me, there's my Allah, and there's...'

The Baba quickly interrupted her before she could complete. 'So, what was I saying?' he continued. 'I meant that if you want to move into your old house to assuage these people, I won't come in your way. Both houses are yours and you are free to stay in either one. And if you do want to consider a move, I can send a couple of workers to fix up that place.'

'Please don't say such a thing, Bhayyiaji,' Sugara pleaded with a tremor in her voice. 'Those people can do what they like. But you have given us shelter here. Don't push us out of here. As for me, I wouldn't want to leave this abode even if someone opened the doors to paradise itself. May Allah give my remaining days to you so that you can get these kids settled.'

'Bapuji,' Aziz jumped to take advantage of a brief pause in the conversation. 'There were a couple of other things that I wanted to discuss with you.'

'You too? Okay, go ahead and get it out of your system if you are in such a rush,' the Baba smiled at him.

'Bapuji!' Aziz started in a deferential tone. 'You've never turned down any request of mine, right? So I have one specific request today that I want you to accept.'

'Why wouldn't I accept it if it deserves to be accepted?' Baba looked at him closely as he replied.

'I want to suggest that we should all head to Rawalpindi for a few days.'

'Certainly, if you have the funds to support both of them. But I know that you get a fairly modest wage. Will you be able to manage?'

'Not just the two of us,' Aziz clarified. 'I meant all of us, including you.'

'Including me?' the Baba appeared a trifle nonplussed.

'Absolutely. You, Bhaaji and Bhabiji too.'

'Don't be silly,' the Baba chided him. 'Are you assembling a platoon or something?'

'Bapuji,' Aziz implored. 'Please don't say no to me. There's no way I'll let you stay here. The communal riots have spread to the villages and who knows when our Chakri gets caught up in the frenzy. You'll have to leave this place with me, Bapuji. And we'll have to do it as soon as possible. I know quite a few people in 'Pindi and I promise you that you won't face any problems. We'll dress you up in Muslim attire when we leave this place.'

'May you live long, my son,' the Baba stroked Aziz's back affectionately as he spoke. 'It is youngsters like you who now have to look after old folks like us. Who else will care for us if you won't? But listen to me, son. What has been written in our destiny is immutable. If it has to happen, it will happen. I am touched by your concern but you do know, my son, that it isn't easy to drag these old bones of mine very far. As far as your brother and bhabi are concerned, I agree with you. Let them go with you for a few days. And you can also give a flavour of city life to Naseem and your mother.'

'And you, Bhayyiaji?' Sugara mumbled, recoiling as if someone had struck a savage blow.

'Let me be, my dear girl,' the Baba replied with absolute assurance. 'I don't have a lot of time left, and I would much rather spend my remaining days here. I was born in this village and I want my funeral procession to leave from here too. That's something I've always wished for.'

'We would prefer to drown with shame,' Sugara cried. 'To go without the patron of this home? Then what's the point of us going anywhere? Come on, Bhayyiaji. You have to be reasonable...'

Their discussion might have continued for a lot longer and who knows where it would have concluded, but their attention was abruptly drawn to voices from the street. A few could be heard shouting, 'Attacks on the neighbouring village ... murders, looting...'

Sugara, already in a bad shape from relentless attacks of asthma, found herself gasping for breath. She made space for herself in a corner of the bed to lie down. Aziz and Naseem ran towards the street to check. Baba Bhana followed them at an unhurried pace, his lips gently humming, 'O Saviour Lord, save us and take us across...'

14

FEBRUARY WAS COMING to a depressing culmination and the Khatri families of the area had started to have sleepless nights. Those who had the resources were packing up and leaving, heading for anywhere that gave them a sense of security. The ones who had chosen to stay back were now stuck between a rock and a hard place. Reports of pillage and murder were flowing in from just about everywhere. Roads connecting the villages with major cities were deemed perilous and safe havens were few and far between. In Chakri, most Khatri families thought it wise to pack their valuables and seek refuge in Gurudwara Gulab Singh that was located right in the centre of the village.

The mobs responsible for their plight, it seemed, were following a carefully chalked out plan. The size of the marauders' horde could range anywhere from about fifty to as many as two thousand, most of them armed with some kind of weapon. They would pick a particular part of the countryside and descend on a vulnerable village, followed by a second and a third. They roamed the area with absolute immunity, acting like they had the reins of the government in one hand and the judiciary in the other.

The various cogs in the machinery of the British government often worked hand in glove with the looters, starting with the village clerk to the magistrate in the court, from the lowly office boy to the police inspector. The police force in these parts was almost entirely Muslim and its members could often be seen not merely encouraging the looters but actively joining the mobs on their murderous rampage.

Before embarking on their raids, the leaders of the mobs had precise intelligence about the number of Hindu or Sikh homes in a particular village. They knew the neighbourhoods in which those homes were located and went after their targets with the certainty of one who has a detailed map of the village.

The misery of the victims had to be seen to be believed. Young and old alike were being butchered to death. Imagine the plight of parents seeing their young daughters being brutally raped before their own eyes, of husbands seeing their wives being dishonoured in their presence and brothers watching their sisters being violated or abducted while they could only stand and watch. Hundreds of girls and young women tried to escape this fate by jumping into the nearest well, by taking an overdose of opium or even by setting themselves on fire. They preferred death over dishonour.

These abominations gathered momentum in the Pothohar region in the first week of March and came in repeated waves. There were periods of brief respite when the violence ebbed. But any relief was short-lived because the mobs always returned with a renewed venom. And it went on and on. Until there was hardly a single Hindu or Sikh family left in all of Pothohar.

There was a distinct pattern in the modus operandi of the Muslim mobs. As they approached a village, they would split up into two groups. One would focus on the task of looting anything of value and carrying it out of the village. The other would round up all non-Muslim families and gather them at one location.

There were times when a wealthy family thought they would save themselves by voluntarily handing over their cash to the looters. The amounts could range from a thousand or two to upwards of a hundred thousand rupees. But the outcome was no different. The looters would lure the family into surrendering all their cash and jewellery, after which then they would go ahead and plunder everything else that was of value. Once they had taken what they wanted, they would often burn down the house, murder the men, and make off with the women.

In some cases, the hapless victims were offered a choice. They could convert to Islam and survive. But the choice was loaded with all sorts of riders, some of them so humiliating that the victims preferred to die rather than live with those terms. Here's a sampling of the riders that had to be accepted *after* conversion to Islam:

1. After conversion, the man would have no claim on his wife. He would be obliged to divorce her and she would have to agree to be settled in a Muslim home.

2. All unmarried women in the man's home, the young or the not so young, would be expected to marry Muslim men in accordance with Islamic customs.

3. The man's property would remain in the custody of Muslims until he had provided sufficient evidence of his fidelity to Islam and Muslims were satisfied that he would not turn an apostate.

4. If the newly converted Muslim was seen to violate any of the above conditions, he would be put to death and all his property and assets would be confiscated.

If the first three clauses appeared too onerous, it was the compliance needed under the fourth that turned out to be the last straw. Who would want to live a life of such abject dishonour with the Sword of Damocles hanging over their heads? Was that really a life worth living?

Some tried to find a way that could save their lives and also help them retain their religion. The method appeared simple. They would agree to convert to Islam since that was the only way to stay alive. Having averted the immediate threat, they would seek protection from the army and once they had been taken to a secure location, they would return to their original faith. The ruse worked for a while and quite a few Hindus and Sikhs lived to tell their tale. But it didn't last too long. The marauders soon got wise to this survival strategy and returned with greater vengeance. The window allowing converts to stay alive was slammed shut and a new wave of terror was unleashed. Virtually every non-Muslim male, young or old, active or infirm, was fair game in the slaughter. Young women were taken into captivity and packed off to distant locations so that the perpetrators could claim innocence. Some of their compatriots had earlier been arrested when the army or police raided their homes and found the abducted women. There was neither respite nor any recourse to escaping this latest round of carnage. The marauders' methods were well-established by now: loot anything of value, burn down the house, kill the men and abduct the women. Week after gruesome week, the same sequence played out in one village after the other.

But the Lord operates in mysterious ways. Our scientists and intellectuals would, of course aver that there is no such thing as a Miracle of Nature. There is an event, they argue, and there is a rational explanation for that event. Just like in arithmetic, where a question is posed and there is an answer for the question. And yet, we come across miracles for which the human mind—no matter how clever—has no real explanation.

One such miracle was unfolding before our eyes. We were seeing it happen, but the answer was beyond our ken. On one hand were the Muslims carrying out such a brutal massacre of Hindus and Sikhs, a bloodbath that threatened to turn our hallowed lands crimson with our own blood. We could see those heartless gangs descend on a village and turn prosperous homes to ash in a matter of minutes. Vibrant, living men being reduced to corpses. Wealth accumulated over generations being looted in seconds and precious heirlooms burnt without a thought. Wailing mothers saw infants being ripped from their arms and slammed mercilessly against walls till they were reduced to pulp. Young women being tied up like cattle and carted off into the unknown. But at the same time, on the same land and under the same sky, we were able to witness events that were nothing short of a miracle. Muslim families, firmly believing in the same God as the marauders, had taken it upon themselves to provide succour to their non-Muslim friends, often guarding them with the ardour with which a hen protects her flock of chicks.

Incidents like these weren't confined to a village or two. Every village in the area had its own story of Muslims who provided shelter to Hindu and Sikh families and either saved them from certain death or tried valiantly to shield them. Isn't it truly a miracle of the Creator that these two streams emerge from the same natural spring? One is laced with deadly poison and the other provides the water of life itself. How can the human mind fathom this mystery?

A miracle on very similar lines was also being revealed in our small village called Chakri where agitation was writ large on the faces of some seven or eight Muslim elders as they hurried towards Baba Bhana's haveli. On reaching the haveli, they learned that the Baba had gone to see Sugara. A couple of members of the group were asked to stay back at the haveli while the others made haste towards Naseem's place.

They had barely reached the door when they were joined by a distraught group of three or four men. In voices muffled by fear, they announced, 'The entire Khatri quarter of Neela village has been burnt to ashes.'

The news sent a shiver through Chaudhry Fazal Karim's group. Neela village wasn't too far from Chakri. If the communal inferno had reached Neela, it wouldn't take long before it arrived at Chakri's doorstep. There was a renewed urgency in their steps as they entered Naseem's courtyard. Their eyes first fell on Aziz and Naseem before moving on to Baba Bhana who was a few yards behind and heading towards them.

'Babaji!' the Chaudhry exclaimed. 'You are sitting here without a care in the world while the marauders have already reached Neela!'

The Baba's worried face showed a rare moment of annoyance before he regained his composure and replied, 'Chaudhryji! If that is indeed the Lord's wish, who are we mere mortals to be naysayers?'

'This is no time for philosophical discourse, Babaji,' one of the Chaudhry's companions interjected. 'It is best to move away from a blaze heading towards you. Come on, let's get moving.'

'Where to?' the Baba asked in astonishment. Wide-eyed with fear, Naseem and Aziz looked at the visitors before turning towards the Baba.

'There's no time to discuss,' the Chaudhry responded firmly. Looking at Aziz, he fired, 'Listen, young man! Are you well? When did you arrive?'

Without waiting for a reply to his queries, he ordered, 'Go across to the Baba's place and help Boote Shah pack the valuables. I've left a couple of guys there to help.'

Still barefoot, Aziz rushed off to the haveli. The Baba arrived a few minutes later to see that some of their precious stuff had already been packed. Boote Shah and Rukman were fetching their jewellery and other belongings from inside while the Chaudhry's men wrapped them in cloth to make small parcels, some of which were placed inside a metal trunk and others dropped into a couple of gunny bags. Aziz's hands seemed to move at the speed of lightning as he helped with the packing.

Overnight, virtually everything of value was packed and moved to a store room at the rear of Chaudhry Fazal Karim's sprawling house. This cleared the way for a lengthy and often heated discussion on the next big decision. The Chaudhry was insistent that the Baba and his family should stay at his home. Protecting them was a matter of honour and they would happily shed their own blood before anyone could touch them. Aziz, on the other hand, asserted that they would be safest in Rawalpindi and that he would quickly make the necessary arrangements for their move. Each side argued its case passionately. Aziz, as the younger party, had to speak with due deference to the Chaudhry, but his arguments couldn't be dismissed out of hand. After they had gone back and forth a few times, Aziz summed up his position, 'Chachaji! You are absolutely right when you say that anyone threatening Bapuji will have to kill you first. And I know that no one from our own village would dare to cross a line that you have drawn. Indeed, I wouldn't be worrying at all if that were the case. But the real danger is not from our own village but from outside. What will we do if a mob of a thousand or so bandits descends on us? How will you protect Bapuji from them? In fact, there is every possibility that you will also lose your own lives.'

The young man's logic was sound and for a moment, everyone fell silent to reflect on his words. An understanding was soon reached that the Baba and his family would first move to the safety of the Chaudhry's home. They would deliberate some more on the issue and if Aziz's plan was feasible, they would act upon it.

Next morning, the Baba, accompanied by Boote Shah and Rukman shifted to the Chaudhry's place. They were followed a little while later by Sugara, Aziz and Naseem who also packed their relatively meagre belongings and brought them over. Each one of them volunteered to stay back and look after the house, insisting that being Muslims, they would be safe. But there was no agreement on who would be the one to stay back. Eventually, all three swore on the Quran that they would stay together wherever they went.

15

OVERNIGHT, THIS IDYLLIC little village on the banks of the Soan had taken the shape of a small refugee camp. Even as the Baba's belongings were being moved to the Chaudhry's home, groups of Khatri families from several small villages near Chakri were heading for Gurudwara Gulab Singh to seek refuge. The gurudwara had a fair-sized sarai to accommodate pilgrims and the lodgings became a magnet for families fleeing from their own homes. The gurudwara's proximity to a main road provided hope that some army lorries might pass that way and carry them to safety. Moreover, the gurudwara was a sturdy, two-storied structure with doors that wouldn't succumb easily to an assault. The stone construction of the gurudwara also meant that it would be less vulnerable to the kind of arson attacks that had become so commonplace. But perhaps the best feature of the gurudwara was that its high rooftop provided an unimpeded view of the surrounding plains. A hostile group moving towards the gurudwara could be spotted from a distance. Beyond these physical advantages of the gurudwara, there was a less tangible but equally important factor. The Muslim population of Chakri was widely regarded as the most tolerant and trustworthy in this part of Pothohar.

By next morning, the gurudwara complex had become a temporary abode for a total group of around two hundred that included residents of Chakri itself and those who had streamed in from neighbouring villages.

Hearing about the influx of refugees, Baba Bhana and Boote Shah, accompanied by a few of their Muslim neighbours, rushed towards the gurudwara. Chaudhry Fazal Karim, meanwhile, had converted his spacious courtyard into a makeshift kitchen. The household's largest pots and pans were pulled out and a clutch of mostly Muslim men and women had set about in earnest to feed the refugees. Some of the women were kneading dough and making chapatis while the men busied themselves ferrying the materials and stirring the pots with large ladles.

Upon entering the gurudwara premises, the Baba and his team observed that the refugees were still in a state of shock. They stared wide-eyed at the gurudwara's gates, apprehensive that Death itself could arrive any moment. The state of parents with young daughters was especially woeful, their faces contorted with terror and their eyes fearful of some unknown catastrophe that was lurking around the corner.

It was about mid-day when the village received reports that the army had established a new camp in Chakwal from where lorries were being dispatched to riot-affected areas to bring refugees to safety. Chaudhry Fazal Karim heard the news and immediately ordered his son Fatta to take their best horse and head for the camp. Chakwal was around twenty miles from Chakri and his departure created a buzz around the gurudwara. God willing, Fatta would succeed in his mission and they might even see an army truck reach the gurudwara by nightfall.

The rest of the day was spent counting the minutes while the refugees waited for the army to come to their rescue. That embryonic sense of hope, however, was tinged with a foreboding that the marauders would arrive before the army and they would all be slaughtered. Their misgivings, it must be said, weren't entirely unfounded. Over the course of the day, rumours had started to trickle into the gurudwara about suspicious goings on involving some Muslim youth from Chakri itself. It was said that they were hatching some nasty plot but nobody seemed to know what exactly was afoot.

The Baba and his compatriots went around the gurudwara, meeting each one of the new arrivals and reassuring them that they would be safe. They recounted their nightmares and listened patiently to his counsel. The conversations would usually end with the refrain, 'Babaji! Why should we be afraid while you are around?' But those words … they were mere words. The despair that had seeped into the very depths of their hearts was another matter.

When the refugees arrived at the gurudwara, they weren't exactly empty-handed. Nor did they come laden with everything they had. A majority of them were carrying one or two trunks, a bedroll and the occasional bundle that often looked like some odds and ends had been rolled into a bedsheet. A few of them were also carrying some cash and jewellery, usually hidden within folds of clothing or inside a pillow or perhaps somewhere on their person.

The condition of Naseem's mother, meanwhile, was deteriorating rapidly. As a result, Naseem had one leg at home to keep an eye on her mother and the other complying with the Baba's instructions. Along with Aziz and Boote Shah, she was also volunteering at the gurudwara to serve food to the refugees. As for the Baba, he had taken it upon himself to provide solace to the poor souls, counselling fortitude and even providing a dose of religious and spiritual guidance which would be valuable if Death did come knocking on their doors.

Morning gave way to noon, then evening arrived and thereafter, night. But no sound of any approaching truck or lorry. A few persons had gone to the roof of the gurudwara, their eyes trained in the direction of the road as they hid behind the parapet. The only thing they could see was the shimmering ribbon of Soan as the river meandered around the village. Nothing else.

In the last few hours, there were reports that a very large horde of marauders was heading in their direction from Dadhiyal. If the mob reached the gurudwara before the army, nobody would be able to save its occupants. Not the resolute men from the village, nor anyone else. You could almost smell the ominous scent of fear within the walls of the gurudwara.

The Baba, Boote Shah and Aziz stayed in the gurudwara as the two younger men served meals to the refugees. Sugara was getting worse by the hour and Rukman had joined Naseem in tending to her at the Chaudhry's place. Hearing about Sugara's condition, the three of them decided to leave the gurudwara and check on her.

The family found it impossible to get any sleep that night. Sugara needed constant attention, and there was too much going on in the village. Around fifty or sixty of the village's Muslim residents took the responsibility to stand guard outside the gurudwara and patrol up and down the Khatri neighbourhood.

Fortunately, the night passed peacefully and the advent of dawn brought the welcome sounds that the gurdwara's inhabitants had yearned for all night—the purring of a lorry motor could be heard in the distance, heading towards their own village. Within minutes, virtually the entire village—Khatri and Muslim alike—was rushing towards the road. They saw two army lorries standing near the banks of the Soan.

A group of four soldiers, each armed with a Sten gun, stood outside their respective lorry while a lieutenant shouted instructions. 'Get into these trucks as quickly as possible. We will take as many as we can fit into these vehicles.'

His words triggered something of a pandemonium in the gurudwara. The bedrolls were packed and trunks and sundry packages were being gathered along with other belongings. A similar scene could also be witnessed at Chaudhry Fazal Karim's house. Most of the Baba's stuff was still packed the way they had brought it from his place. The Chaudhry and a couple of his compatriots started to haul it out of the storeroom. They were on the verge of leaving for the road when the Baba emerged after administering some medicine to Sugara. He beckoned them to stop immediately and keep his baggage back in the storeroom.

'Why, Babaji?' the Chaudhry asked sharply. 'Why on earth did you stop them from taking your baggage to the lorry? We'll lose your place in the lorries if we don't hurry.'

'Chaudhryji, let all the others secure their place first. We will see after that,' he replied with his usual composure.

'What nonsense is that, Babaji?' the Chaudhry retorted with barely concealed irritation. 'Do you really think that the two lorries can carry everyone?'

'In that case, we'll have to stay put.'

'And why is that, Babaji?

'Because no one from our family will leave till everyone else has left. I suggest, Chaudhryji, that you tell these boys to run across to the gurudwara to help the others. You and I can follow them and assist where we can. We must ensure that we can get the largest number into those trucks.'

The Chaudhry tried his best to reason with the Baba. His compatriots also joined in but the Baba would hear none of it. They had little option but to give in and reluctantly carried his belongings back to the storeroom before leaving for the gurudwara.

On reaching the gurudwara, they saw that Aziz, Boote Shah and Fatta were already helping the refugees carry their baggage to the trucks. Within minutes, both trucks were packed to the rafters. The trunks, bedrolls and other packages were spread along the floor of the truck with the refugees, young and old, perched gingerly on top. A few of the sturdier young men even managed to secure a foothold of sorts on the mudguards, dangling precariously from anything that might offer a semblance of support. There was no way that the entire lot of two hundred odd souls could be packed into the two vehicles and the fact that only forty or so remained was no small feat. But the desperation with which the last few families tried to squeeze themselves into a non-existent space finally provoked a sharp reprimand from the lieutenant. Two more trucks were going to follow these, he assured everyone. They should be here in the next couple of hours. But who among this stricken lot had the appetite for these promises? Who knew what calamity might fall upon them during those hours? Finally, the two trucks had to leave and the ones who couldn't find a place trudged wearily back to the four walls of the gurudwara.

16

IT WAS THE ninth of March, the twenty-fourth day of Phagun. The two trucks had left and Baba Bhana's family, along with the remaining contingent of refugees, spent the day waiting for the army to bring the other truck. The clock was ticking and every hour brought in alarming reports that trouble was lurking round the corner. One said that a large mob had gathered at Bhunder and was preparing to move towards Chakri. Another said that the Muslims of Kamdiala were hand in glove with some army personnel and were using them as a cover to plunder village after village. A third report was even more worrisome. It suggested that army man Subedar Rustam Khan, a man who belonged to Chakri but now lived in Rawalpindi had rustled up a posse of armed gangsters from the city. They had allegedly commandeered a jeep and a lorry and were heading in their direction.

While none of the reports was confirmed, each appeared more frightening than the other. The Baba worked with the Chaudhry to ensure that sufficient food and water was stocked inside the gurudwara before its massive gates were firmly bolted from within. Within the gurudwara, the locals made an earnest effort to hide the refugees in areas that would be hard to reach. The fact that they still had a sizeable group of young women amongst the refugees was an additional headache.

A very different scene was unfolding at the Chaudhry's house. The argument that had started even before the Baba and his family moved in was now gathering steam. Aziz remained insistent that all three members of the Baba's family must be escorted to Rawalpindi under the cover of night and that they should leave without further delay. But the Chaudhry and his family saw it as a foolhardy proposition. First, they still remained hopeful that a rescue by the army was imminent. And second, they were openly sceptical that the Baba could make such an arduous journey during the night, considering that he was near-sighted at the best of times. Making the journey during the day was ruled out because he was quite well-known in these parts and would be an easy target. Using a horse to carry him was also ruled out because the hills surrounding the village were quite rocky and the sound of hooves would travel for miles.

This wasn't the only argument that they were trying to resolve. There was a smaller debate that was taking place within the larger discussion. Naseem was absolutely unrelenting in her decision to stay with the Baba until he and his family reached a secure destination. She acknowledged that her own mother was on the deathbed and may not live very long, but insisted that this would have no effect on her resolve to stay by the Baba's side. The balance of that particular debate tilted when Aziz took his sister's side and stated that neither of them would countenance leaving the Baba.

After much discussion, it was agreed that they would wait another day or so to see if the army arrived with its lorries. If that didn't happen, they would go along with Aziz's plan.

Naseem, meanwhile, had mentally prepared herself that she would stay with the Baba's family wherever fate took them. The decision wasn't taken out of any sense of obligation, nor a desire to repay a debt that she and her family owed to the Baba. She had this feeling in her bones that she wouldn't be able to survive any kind of separation from her foster father. She also knew that the Baba and his family would have to leave the village sooner rather than later. Under the prevailing uncertainties, who knew where they would eventually land up.

Knowing that the inevitable was around the corner, Naseem started to pack the odds and ends that she needed for their journey. Her meagre personal effects had already been sorted but she felt that some unseen shackles were still trying to tie her down to her home. Memories of Yusuf had returned in a flood that threatened to carry her in its flow. Her mind kept hovering around the thought, 'I haven't heard from him for so long. Could he really have gone down the path he'd hinted at in his letter? Could he really have taken his own life? Can I believe that he has simply vanished from this earth? But if that were the case, why does my heart keep saying that he is very much alive? Could that be true? That he is still alive...?'

She was still engrossed in these thoughts when her mind stumbled upon a plan. She wasn't sure if it was far-sighted or foolish but there was a distinct spring in her step as she walked across to the room at the rear of the house and collected some paper, a pen and an inkpot. Sitting quietly in a corner, she started to write a letter. Once she had finished, she folded another paper into a small envelope, pushed the letter into it and sealed it with some glue.

She had quite a few friends in the village but Jeeva was the one she could trust the most. The two girls had often shared their deepest secrets and Jeeva also happened to be a cousin of Yusuf's. Naseem walked to Jeeva's place and spoke in a voice that conveyed the depths of her anguish. 'Jeeva! I'll be leaving this place soon. If I am lucky, I will come back some day but who knows? But there is something important that you must do for me. If Yusuf ever returns to this place, you must give him my letter. And you must swear on Allah that nobody else will ever get to know about this matter.'

Having assigned this responsibility to Jeeva, Naseem felt that a huge burden had been lifted from her heart.

And what about the Baba? He seemed to have entered a state where he was neither angry nor sad. The only visible change was the fact that he could often be heard singing these verses from the Sikh scriptures:

> O Savior Lord, save us and take us across.
> We fall at the Guru's feet, our work is done
> You are merciful, keep You in our minds we must.

Or he would switch to these verses from Ramcharitmanas:

> Keep chanting the name of Lord Ram
> Keep patience in your heart
> He Himself will resolve your tasks
> He, Lord Ramchandra, Raghubir.

He had the calm demeanour of one who has elevated himself above the affairs of this world and entered some entirely different realm. But despite this impression of detachment from his surroundings, the Baba was observed doing something that seemed completely out of character. He had taken out an ancient dagger, its sheath almost threadbare at places. And he spent hours working on sharpening it with a rock before placing it back in its sheath and tucking it into the folds of his dhoti.

The sun was setting on another tension-filled day. Patrolling in the Khatri neighbourhoods was stepped up a notch as night fell, with a total of sixty or seventy Muslim men making the rounds between the gurudwara and the Khatri houses.

That night also passed peacefully and all the rumours started to appear baseless. There was a feeling in the village that maybe, just maybe, the worst was over and they could breathe a little easier. The doors of the gurudwara, however, remained firmly closed.

Next morning, a couple of strangers were seen ambling through the village. There was something suspicious about the way they looked around as they walked. Upon being accosted by the wary residents, they gave some roundabout answers which didn't quite add up. Their interlocutors were left with the nagging doubt that something was seriously amiss. The village would continue to remain on guard, it was decided.

That evening, just as the sun was getting ready to disappear behind the horizon, clouds of dust could be seen billowing from the nearby village of Holiaan. Hearts pounding in their chests, people ran up to their rooftops to get a glimpse of the heart-rending sight. Some people were reporting that it was a gang led by Munshi Abdul Rahman which was wreaking havoc in the Khatri areas of Holiaan.

Naseem felt her heart sinking as she tended to her ailing mother. It seemed that some invisible force was holding her up, preventing her from collapsing in a heap. She held the verses of the old fakir in her heart and the words seemed to come straight from her soul as she hummed,

> *Let Allah o Allah be your song*
> *And leave those sighs so painful and long…*

By nightfall, every passing moment seemed to add to the trepidation of the group that had taken refuge in the Chaudhry's home. The small family of Khatris felt like they were on a tiny raft, trying to stay afloat in a vast ocean of death, aware that a single powerful wave would spell their doom.

A voice outside the Chaudhury's house shouted, 'Look! You can see smoke rising from Dheri village ... Did you hear those gunshots from somewhere in the west?'

Boote Shah instinctively picked up his staff for protection as he headed for the rooftop. Aziz had taken an old axe, sharpened its blade and fixed it on a long staff to fashion a lethal-looking weapon. Naseem's face was a picture of despair as she paced up and down with no apparent purpose. Her lips looked colourless and dry as a twig. Maybe the moisture had all flown towards her eyes, from where it was dripping relentlessly. Her throat felt so parched that she found it hard to utter a sound.

The Baba seemed to be the only one who sat unperturbed, a light blanket draped around his shoulders as he sang with full concentration:

> O Saviour Lord, save us and take us across
> We fall at the Guru's feet, our work is done
> You are merciful, keep You in our minds we must.

A cloud of fear hung over the house. Sugara, lying in the bed next to the Baba, turned her head in his direction every few minutes to ask in a barely audible voice, 'Bhaiyyaji! What's going to happen?' And the Baba would reply with complete equanimity, 'Turn your thoughts towards the Lord, my dear! Set these worries aside.' Having admonished her gently, he would resume, 'O Saviour Lord, save us and take us across...'

That night appeared to stretch endlessly, every passing hour seemingly bringing some unseen danger closer to their doorstep. The Chaudhry, along with a dozen or so other large hearted Muslim men, had picked up sturdy six-feet-long staffs and taken it upon themselves to monitor the Khatri neighbourhood. After every couple of rounds, they would come back to the Baba and assure his family, 'Stay strong, everyone. Don't lose heart! They will have to kill us before they can harm a hair on your heads.'

An eerie silence had descended over the village. Everyone seemed to be wide awake, ears straining to pick up any unusual sound. The six men who were trying to sleep inside the Chaudhry's house would spring up at the slightest noise, even though they knew that the Chaudhry and his team were patrolling outside.

Aziz had deliberately left the gate of the courtyard ajar so that he could maintain contact with some of the young men who were making the rounds and pick up the latest reports from them. The occupants of the room adjoining the courtyard sat like statues on their respective beds, silent and motionless. Aziz and Boote Shah, armed with their axe and staff, sat on the floor along with a couple of other young men. Aziz would get up every few minutes urging, 'Bapuji, why don't you sleep for a while … Seema, you are going to tire yourself if you keep sitting in this position … Ma, why don't you take a short nap. You'll feel better … Rukman bhabi, why are you looking so pensive? Allah will look after everyone…' But sleep isn't something one can always control. Especially under such circumstances!

The Baba, meanwhile, kept up his chanting of *'O Saviour Lord, save us and take us across',* pausing only to turn around and rouse the others in the room. 'Sugara dear! Turn your thoughts towards Allah, will you?' After a while, 'Rukman my child, let the hymns of Lord Ram flow.' Naseem, though, was much too restless to pay any heed. The slightest sound from outside and she would leap out of her bed. Any voices near the door and she was out in a flash, standing beside Boote Shah or Aziz to pick up the latest.

It must have been around ten at night. Aziz, Boote Shah and their compatriots, weapons in hand, were maintaining their vigil in the courtyard when they heard a voice outside their door, 'Some kind of noise coming from the east … Did you pick up something too, Karimdeena? Or am I just imagining stuff?'

Aziz and Boote Shah rushed out to join them, cupping their palms around their ears to get a better sense. Was it just the buzzing of a bee in the night sky or were they really hearing something?

'Let's go upstairs and try to listen carefully,' one suggested. They were back in the courtyard and soon clambering up the stairs to the roof to take a look. 'What's going on?' Naseem asked Aziz and followed him up the stairs without waiting for a response.

'It's nothing,' Aziz snapped. 'Go back inside the house and stay put, will you?' Naseem continued right behind him.

From their vantage point on the roof, muffled sounds could clearly be heard rising from the east. Hearts thumping in their chests, they looked at each other.

'Look that way, Bhaaji,' Naseem placed her hand on Boote Shah's shoulder and asked him to follow the direction of her finger. 'There, behind the peepul tree. Can't you see that flicker of light?'

Everyone turned their attention towards the peepul. 'You are right. There does appear to be a light there,' Boote Shah murmured.

'Of course, it's there, Boote Shah,' Karimdeen declared. 'Can't you see that flickering light move?'

'There's two of them, Bhaaji,' Naseem interjected. 'They look like flaming mashaals to me. Look, there's a third one on the other side too.'

'Absolutely! That's what they are. Mashaals,' Aziz concurred. The sounds in the distance were becoming more distinct as he spoke.

'The horde is coming towards us. Let's move!' Boota exclaimed.

'Aziz!' Karimdeen said anxiously as they returned to the courtyard. 'The two of you should stay here and make sure the folks inside stay safe. We'll go and find out what we can,' he said and hastened towards the street with his friends.

Naseem was going to step into the room when Aziz grabbed her arm and whispered, 'Don't create a panic when you go in, okay?'

'Okay,' she responded as she went in.

Boote Shah held on to his staff while Aziz tended to his makeshift battle axe as they waited.

'Bhaaji,' Aziz panted, 'let's ask our folks to leave this room and go to the storeroom at the back. Our trunks and other stuff is also lying there.'

'What's the rush? Let them rest,' Boote Shah replied with the assurance of one who doesn't see any imminent danger. Aziz was still pondering his response when they heard someone outside their gate shout the warning, 'The horde is headed this way! Beware! It's a huge mob! Let's all get out to guard the Khatri houses. Be ready to die if you have to. But make sure the Khatri area is not touched.'

Naseem came out running, drawing a sharp rebuke from Boote Shah. 'Where do you think you are going like this? Go and sit inside like you've been told.' Naseem beat a hasty retreat, with Boote Shah calling after her, 'Tell everyone to head towards the storeroom at the back.' Seeing the logic behind Aziz's plan, he called out to her again, 'And open the window at the rear of the store room. Just in case we have to use it to escape the horde.'

'Okay Bhaaji,' Naseem felt a numbness creeping up her legs as she went indoors.

The menacing noise of the mob, punctuated by intermittent sounds of gunfire, was now drawing closer.

'Wait here for a bit,' Boote Shah told Aziz, 'I am going upstairs to take another look.'

'Keep your head below the parapet,' Aziz called after him. 'I can hear gunfire.'

The moment he saw Boote Shah hurrying down the steps, he knew that the final alarm bell had rung.

'It's a huge mob, Aziz,' Boote Shah muttered.

'Don't you worry, Bhaaji. Let them come this way and we'll deal with them,' Aziz mustered all his bravado to cloak his own anxiety.

'The mob's almost here, folks. Beware!' came the warning from an unknown voice in the street. 'Boote Shah! Make sure the gate is bolted from inside,' another voice advised. 'Rest assured the whole village is ready to protect you. With Allah's mercy, not a hair on your heads will be harmed.'

Aziz hurried to close the gate that had been ajar all evening.

Barely ten minutes had passed when they heard a growing commotion. The thud of footsteps. People yelling. Gunshots. A pandemonium had suddenly erupted across the village. The darkness of the night added to the chaos. Nobody was sure what was going on. But some voices could now be heard saying that the horde had reached the village and was going about its vile enterprise of ransacking Khatri houses and setting them on fire.

The two men stood behind the door, ears straining to pick up any update from the street. The vigil was in vain and they heard nothing.

A gun went off nearby, five or six bullets fired in quick succession. Aziz told Boote Shah to wait by the door while he went inside to check things out. Naseem was standing at the entrance while the others had made their way to the storeroom. Sugara was also lying on a cot in the storeroom, barely conscious as the Baba held her hand to gauge her pulse.

'Are you waiting here to get yourself dishonoured?' Aziz snapped at Naseem. 'Go inside and wait with the others.'

Aziz joined his companion to guard the gate.

The noise coming from the direction of the Khatri neighbourhood had increased. The sound of axes crashing into doors and breaking them down was becoming intolerable. Both were convinced that the blows were directed at the sturdy gate of Baba Bhana's haveli, or perhaps of Gurudwara Gulab Singh itself.

17

THE UPROAR IN the street had grown to a crescendo. Bullets going off somewhere close by only made matters worse. The battleground, it seemed, had arrived right outside the Chaudhry's house where his men were taking a stand against the intruders.

Boote Shah, Aziz and Naseem stood with their ears pressed against the gate as they tried to fathom the scene unfolding outside the house.

After a while, the noise subsided by a few decibels and they could hear the Chaudhry pleading, 'Please believe me when I say that there are no Khatris in my house. There's just our two girls and my daughter-in-law. Why would I be hiding kafirs in my house? To invite my own death?'

'In that case, swear by the Quran,' ordered a gruff voice.

The Chaudhry swore by the Quran that there was no Hindu or Sikh in his house, but some of the assailants remained sceptical. 'Listen, you bloody Chaudhry! If we find a single kafir in your house, I'll put a bullet from this gun straight through your head. Got it, you bastard?'

'Subedar sahib! You can search my house if you want. If you find a single imposter inside, may I face eternal damnation,' the Chaudhry again implored them in an abject tone.

The Chaudhry's second vow was even more potent than his first one and it seemed to have the desired effect. As the army man's footsteps receded, the three miserable souls hiding behind the gate heaved a sigh of relief. The imminent danger had ebbed away.

Another thirty or forty minutes had elapsed. The ruckus had largely receded, barring the occasional thud of heavy boots in the street or the intermittent noise of axe crashing against a reluctant door. Inside the house, the blanched faces of the occupants were getting back some of their colour. One of them, though, seemed to be completely unaffected by the ordeal. Baba Bhana sat serenely, eyes shut as he sang the verses of 'O *Saviour Lord, save us and take us across...*' He was in the middle of the fifth verse when someone was heard knocking on the gate as he called in a hushed tone, 'Babaji! Babaji!'

Recognizing the Chaudhry's voice, Aziz rushed to open the gate.

The Chaudhry was accompanied by three or four men as he entered the courtyard, his face a picture of fear and dismay. Aziz closed the gate and bolted it shut.

Skipping the customary greetings as he entered the storeroom, he started to speak in a voice that appeared to collapse under the burden of regret. 'Babaji! We made all those tall promises to you but we find ourselves utterly helpless. I don't even know who to blame. It was a bunch of youngsters from our own village who spilled the beans. The only way now to save your lives is to get you out of here as quickly as possible. That mob is thirsty for your blood and could be heading back this way any minute. Hurry up! Get up and leave through this window. I've positioned a few of our boys outside to help. They will take you to safety as soon as they see an opportunity. But move quickly, for God's sake. There isn't a moment to lose.'

His words unleashed a flurry of activity. Naseem and Rukman set about trying to sort their baggage. Sugara was already in a bad shape. The Chaudhry's frantic message had pushed her to the edge. Her breathing became laboured and the Baba could see that her pulse was slipping.

The Chaudhry and his companions had no idea that Aziz and Naseem were prepared to leave their mother on the deathbed and accompany the Baba and his family. He tried once again to prevail upon the siblings to stay back even though he knew it was a lost cause. 'Naseem, my child! I don't think it's right to leave your mother in this condition. I suggest that you…'

With tears streaming down her face, Naseem replied quietly, 'Chachaji! Our mother is now in Allah's safe hands and in yours too.'

And that was that. The Chaudhry knew that it was pointless to pursue the subject any more. The Baba tried his bit too, but both brother and sister remained implacable in their resolve.

Once again, the street outside was reverberating with the echo of gunshots and the irregular beat of footsteps. Aziz and Rukman had barely managed to pick up a couple of pouches, thinking that they would carry as much as they could manage. Voices could be heard just outside; fists banging on the gate, demanding it be opened. The occupants of the little storeroom picked up what they could and headed for the window. Before leaving, Naseem, Aziz and Boote Shah bowed before the barely conscious Sugara and touched her feet. The Baba also extended a trembling hand to caress her forehead. With that briefest of goodbyes, they were in the fields behind the Chaudhry's house.

A mild drizzle had started and the cool March breeze was gathering strength as they huddled in the open. The Baba, who could barely see in the best of times was blind as a bat in the darkness. He froze where he stood, staying motionless until Boote Shah reached out and grasped one arm while Naseem took the other one. Aziz was looking after Rukman, who appeared paralysed by the scale of the unfolding calamity. She latched herself to Aziz's arm and followed his directions.

Naseem, meanwhile, had undergone something of a metamorphosis. Inside the house, the atmosphere of fear had reduced her to a lifeless zombie. But as soon as they stepped out of the window, she donned a different mantle—alert, confident and ready to confront any challenge. Gone was the diffidence, the enervating uncertainty of the last few days; this was a new Naseem, one who had found her true purpose. She must make sure that the Baba and his family reach a safe destination and if losing her own life was part of the deal, she would consider it a real bargain.

The rear side of the Chaudhry's house opened into a large, open field that gently sloped towards the river. The Chaudhry's farms and his well stood a short distance from the river bank. As ever, the Soan continued to flow gently into the night.

It must have been around eleven, or maybe a bit later than that. As their eyes got used to the dark, they peered into the distance. A spiderweb of clouds, dark and light, was covering the sky. A sliver of moonlight fought its way through a gap in the clouds, only to disappear once the breeze had nudged them closer to each other. That sliver, though, was enough to reveal the shimmering Soan as it curved its way around the Chaudhry's lands.

'Bhaaji! I don't see anyone at all. Do you?' Naseem asked Boota after allowing her eyes to sweep over the horizon.

Boota had barely opened his mouth to respond when a lantern appeared to the left of the field, and they heard a whispered call, 'Boote Shah! This way! Go down to the Soan and walk along its bank towards the well.'

They followed the instructions and started to walk towards the river without uttering a word. They were carrying just the small pouches with which they had jumped out of the window.

They had barely walked a couple of hundred yards when they heard the sound of incessant hammering on the Chaudhry's gate. Doors and windows were being broken and the voices coming from the direction of the house made it clear that the Chaudhry was being punished for providing refuge to the Baba and his family.

Craning their heads every couple of minutes to look pensively towards the house, they sighed and continued their unsteady march into the night.

As they approached the Chaudhry's well, they paused to take in the scene unfolding at the abode they had just left. The noise had risen to a crescendo and it was now accompanied by a bright yellow flame that was rapidly making its way into the sky. It had to be Chaudhry Fazal Karim's house, they mused. Couldn't be any other!

As they approached the grove adjoining the well, they saw a group of nine or ten young men standing beneath a cluster of jujube trees. They were armed with sturdy staffs as they waited impatiently for the Baba and his group to arrive.

'Boote Shah!' the Chaudhry's son Fatta stepped forward and spoke. 'You'll have to walk faster than that if you value your lives. The subedar and his mob know everything. It's our own lads who have stabbed us in the back. They have also learned that we planned your escape through the window at the rear of our house. That's why they got so angry and set our place on fire. But that's not so important. A house can always be rebuilt. Before that, we must find a way to get you to safety because their men have fanned out in all directions to hunt you down.'

His stark words sent a shiver down their spines. Boote Shah and Aziz wore a worried look on their faces. But not the Baba, nor Naseem. Both appeared unperturbed by the turn of events.

The Baba had been quietly chanting his favourite verses. He interrupted his own rhythm for a moment to ask Fatta, 'And what happened to the ones hiding in the gurudwara?'

Fatta's response left them all in a state of abject dismay. 'What can I tell you about those poor souls, Babaji! Our boys did their best to save them but these scoundrels were hell bent on wreaking havoc. Two of our men fell to their bullets and the others had to flee to save their own lives. You can't fight bullets with courage alone, can you?

'You remember the seven or eight young girls in the gurudwara? Gurmukh Singh Sahni from Dheri village prepared a potent brew of opium and fed it to all of them. By the time the mob arrived, some had already met their Master while the others were taking their last few breaths. The men were literally butchered to death inside the gurudwara. Not one of them survived.'

They reeled under the impact of Fatta's sombre account, forcing their reluctant legs to follow the boys into a spacious cowshed that stood just beyond the grove. Eight or nine cows were tied to one side and a largish cot was parked adjacent to the mud wall on the other side. They sat on the edge of the cot, the Baba perching himself on one corner and continuing with his barely audible recitation of '*O Saviour Lord, save us and take us across…*'

Fatta gave a long look towards Naseem, mouth ajar as he observed her ethereal composure. This was just not real, he told himself. Finally turning towards her, he counselled, 'Seema, my sister! If you had insisted that Aziz accompany Babaji, I would have understood. But you should have thought about your own responsibility towards your mother. The poor lady is counting her final moments and you…'

'Fatta my brother! Please don't stop me from going because I'm not going to change my mind,' Naseem interrupted him gently. 'You know fully well that Bapuji stood by the promises he made to my father even after my father died. We have also made a similar promise. We are not going to be separated from Bapuji for the rest of his life. As far as my mother is concerned, I know that she is at the end of her life. By the time you guys get back home, she may already have left us forever. Your family has already done so much for us and I am sure you will cover her with a proper shroud and place her in Allah's mercy. I will pray that I meet her again on Judgement Day, God willing. And if not...' Naseem's voice choked as she spoke. Fatta looked away to hide his own emotion and never raised the subject again.

18

CHAKRI AND DHERI were two small villages that lay on opposite banks of the Soan. It was close to midnight and the Khatri quarter of Chakri was still smouldering when the occupants of the cowshed saw flames light up the sky above Dheri.

Every few minutes, one of the young men escorting the five refugees would step out of the cowshed and return with fresh information. Each new report was more depressing than the last. There was no need to hear anything about Chakri, Dheri or Kohli villages. Their eyes told them the whole story. But a similar tragedy was also unfolding in villages further away. 'Two hundred and fifty Khatris have been killed in Gheelan ... all Khatri homes in Sihala have been looted and burned ... the Sikhs of Jhada put up a brave fight but eventually all of them were killed and their women have been abducted ... the entire Khatri population of Maira has been decimated ... there isn't a Hindu or Sikh left alive from Dhudhambar and all the way to Talagang...'

Each blood-curdling report had the effect of delaying the onward journey of the five travellers as they absorbed the new information. At the same time, each minute lost meant an invitation to even bigger problems. The Chaudhry's son Fatta, very much the leader of the twelve young men, decided that waiting any longer would be pointless. It was better to start moving.

But which route was safer? A small discussion ensued, and the first option was to get on the road to Rawalpindi even though it was a more arduous route. The hilly terrain and dense woods along the way, it was felt, could provide some protection if the situation became dangerous. The other option was to leave immediately and somehow reach Dulla village by dawn. The village had a police station and a small government inn. Besides, they had heard that a sizeable number of Hindus and Sikhs fleeing from neighbouring villages had gathered in Dulla and the army was making arrangements to evacuate them to safety.

It was a little after twelve-thirty that they emerged from the cowshed and started to move towards the Soan. They had barely taken a few steps when they saw two men coming towards them from the direction of the village. Apprehending that they might be hostile, the group braced itself. The duo came closer, and they saw that it was none other than Chaudhry Fazal Karim, accompanied by a worker from his farm. The worker was carrying two trunks, one in each hand. The Chaudhry himself was carrying a bundle of chapatis wrapped in a piece of cloth.

'Here you go, Babaji. I've packed your cash, jewellery, clothes and a few other things into the large trunk. Including some of your precious silks,' the Chaudhry spoke before turning towards Naseem. 'This smaller trunk is yours, isn't it? I told my fellow to bring it along. I didn't have the time to open it but I gather it must be some clothes of yours that will come in handy.' Handing the food to Fatta, he said, 'I've packed some parathas and jaggery for the journey. Who knows when you will find something to eat!'

Looking again at Fatta, he spoke sternly, 'Listen young man! Take good care of this trunk, will you. It's got a fortune of at least twenty-five thousand rupees inside.'

Paying heed to the warning, Fatta picked up the big trunk himself and gave the smaller one to one of his compatriots.

The young men were getting impatient over the delay while the Baba and the Chaudhry had their arms wrapped around each other in a tight embrace. Neither wanted to let go until the Chaudhry took a step back and said, 'Take care! May Allah be with you. And if the Lord is merciful, He will make sure that we meet again.' Eyes moist with emotion, he turned to bid farewell to the other members of the family.

The group thought that the Chaudhry would walk with them for some distance but he surprised them by saying he had to take their leave immediately. 'I hate to go back but I must. Unfortunately, it also falls upon me to break the sad news to Naseem.' Looking at her, he continued, 'My dear girl! Your mother has reached Allah's home. It would be good if you came with me for her last rites. The final decision is yours.'

The siblings let out an agonized sigh. Their duty towards their departed mother brought a momentary pause but there was a larger purpose that beckoned. The tears accumulating in Naseem's eyes coalesced into two large drops and fell at her feet. She put her arms around the Chaudhry and sobbed, clutching him as though she was at her mother's bosom bidding her final farewell.

'Chachaji! Please carry this embrace to my mother and...' she found herself unable to complete her sentence.

The Chaudhry remained silent. The Baba stood next to Naseem and continued to recite 'O Saviour Lord, save us and take us across.'

Without uttering a word, he placed his arm around Naseem's shoulders and pulled her to his chest.

As the group got ready to move, the Baba again turned towards his childhood friend and said, 'Chaudhry! The Lord alone can bless you for the way you've played with your own life to save us. Those devils have even set your lovely home on fire and you are here…'

'Babaji', the Chaudhry again threw his arms around the old man. 'What's the big deal about the house. If Allah desires, we'll build it once again. At least I have the satisfaction that I could retrieve some of your valuables from the house before it burned down completely.' He looked at the trunk Fatta was carrying on his head as he spoke.

Each of the five members again stepped forth to give the Chaudhry a warm embrace as the group finally embarked on its uncertain journey.

19

OVER HALF THE night had passed. The thick cover of clouds meant that the trek had begun in pitch-dark conditions. A light drizzle had resumed and there was a distinct nip in the air.

The group of five refugees and their dozen-strong posse of guardians left Chakri and took the road towards Talagang. One of the boys was assigned the responsibility of staying ahead of the group to make sure it was safe, while another maintained a similar vigil behind them, eyes and ears open for anything unusual that might be a cause for alarm. They knew the mobs could be spotted from the light of their flaming mashaals, and every few minutes they would stop to reassure everyone that it was safe to continue.

The Baba was clearly struggling to keep pace. His poor eyesight meant that he kept stumbling on the uneven ground. And the biting cold had seeped into his legs to make every step an ordeal.

Naseem had handed her pouch to one of the boys and was walking alongside the Baba, his hand resting on her shoulder. Aziz had taken up the other side to prop him up and propel him forward.

They had walked about a mile and a half when Fatta noticed that the Baba's condition was not getting any better. He handed the large trunk to one of the other boys, turned around to sweep the old man off his feet and carry him on his shoulders.

The caravan picked up pace, walking silently to make sure they didn't attract any unwanted attention.

They walked another mile or so when the young fellow at the rear of their group asked them to pause. He thought he had seen a flash of light some distance behind them. A wave of alarm swept through their band. Could it be the same mob that had ransacked Chakri, Dheri and Kohli villages and was now heading in their direction?

A few large boulders could be seen dotting the landscape a short distance from the road. They decided it was best to leave the road and hide behind the boulders until the danger had passed.

The boulders closest to them were at an angle that afforded them a clear view of the road while allowing them to stay out of sight. As the subdued voices and sounds of the footsteps drew closer, they guessed that there were at least twenty or twenty-five members in the approaching party. Coming up the winding road, it looked like a formless shadow that was slowly lurching in their direction. They certainly didn't have the bearings of a mob. For one thing, no one in the party was carrying a mashaal. Nor were they making the kind of racket that is typical of a mob going on a rampage. Their voices were subdued as they trudged slowly towards the boulders.

Once the new party could be seen clearly, there was no longer any doubt that they, too, were refugees fleeing their homes in search of safety. They had come parallel to one of the boulders when a male voice could be heard reassuring a lady, 'Don't you worry, Maasi, if anyone even *looks* disrespectfully at you, he will have to face our wrath.' A timorous voice replied, 'I could have sworn that there was a group ahead of us. God knows where they have disappeared?'

'Well! You don't have to be scared of us,' said one of Fatta's boys as they emerged from their hideout. Their sudden appearance created a frenzy in the new group, many of whom were women. Fatta had to quickly step forward and pacify them by explaining that they were all in the same boat.

The new group was much larger than their own. It had maybe ten or eleven women and young girls, another ten children, five or six men and about a dozen well-armed Muslim men who had formed a protective cordon around them.

Very soon, it was seen that some members of the two groups knew each other while others had common acquaintances. The new group was coming from Sihala and their Muslim protectors, like the ones from Chakri, had sworn to take them to safety even if it meant risking their own lives.

The two groups merged and started to move together. Having fellow travellers on the trek made the journey a little bit easier. There was also the feeling that the more dangerous section of the march lay behind them. And between their groups, they now had the protective umbrella of about twenty-five strapping young men that could hold their own against a mob.

The clouds made the night sky darker than usual. The expanded caravan moved silently along the road, its escorts vigilant as ever. The scout in front made sure that the path ahead was clear, while the one at the rear kept a watchful eye behind them. Others monitored the flanks with the same alertness.

The Baba was finding himself increasingly uncomfortable on Fatta's back. He could see that Fatta was tiring and his feet stumbling every now and then on the potholes and bumps in the road. His mind went back to that evening about two and a half months back. On a similarly dark night, Fatta had picked him up from his place and carried him on his back all the way to the Lohri celebration. Oh, the way they had swung him around with such unbridled joy! The laughter, the cheering and the claps resonated in his ears. What a difference between that ride and this, like the difference between life and death itself!

The Baba ordered Fatta to set him down and silently swore that this was the last time that he would allow another human being to carry him. Several members of the group offered to take turns in carrying him, but he stood firm. He placed his hand on Naseem's shoulder and resumed the journey as he had begun—faltering occasionally but determined to carry on.

The new group was hampered by the fact that it had a relatively larger number of women and children who kept falling behind and needed constant encouragement from a couple of the young men. 'Come on! Be brave! Yes, that's the way!' they chirped.

It didn't take long before the caravan split into two groups, the men walking on one side while the women formed their own group, exchanging mutual tales of woe. Naseem found herself in the middle, providing support to the Baba even as she tried to pay attention to the chatter of a young lady who looked quite incongruous in formal wedding clothes. The girl was saying, 'It was the wedding of my maternal uncle's son. We were a group of about twenty—eight or nine women, five men and a few kids—who had gone from Kamdhiala to Sihala for the wedding. But a mob of Muslims attacked the village in the middle of the night. A lot of my relatives from my mother's side of the family were killed. Their houses were looted and set on fire. We would have been killed too, but for the kindness of some of Sihala's Muslim families who gambled on their own lives to take us to safety.'

'Our real worry was the gold and jewellery we had on,' the young lady continued. 'You know how it is with us Khatris. Weddings are the time to show off all our precious stuff. Even those who don't have much feel compelled to borrow from others to deck up for a wedding. I think between our group, we must be wearing at least three to four hundred tolas of gold, just to give you an idea.'

Similar conversations were taking place between other members of the caravan as clusters of two or three walked abreast. The topics were the same—the sheer horror that they had witnessed, the brutal murder of so many friends, neighbours and relatives, the wanton looting and arson, the vicious dishonour and abduction of women— each element was described in graphic detail. And then there were the questions about an uncertain future. Where were they heading? Where would they end up? Would they be able to hang onto their meagre savings to start a new life, somehow, somewhere?

The defenders of the two groups had also blended into each other, giving the impression of a fairly sizeable posse that was now escorting the refugees.

The road was winding along an undulating terrain, every new turn revealing huge boulders interspersed with caves that burrowed deep into the belly of the earth. Coming out of a dip in the road, they could see a substantial mountain rise high into the dark sky. It must have been about a mile and a half away and as they got closer to its base, they could see the distinctive karira and phulahi trees make appearances with each flash of lightning.

The women and the smaller children were close to exhaustion and it was felt that the Sarnihali cave situated to the right of the mountain would be the ideal place to rest for a while. The cave was known to extend for miles into the mountain and had several fresh-water springs for sustenance. It also had an abundance of nooks and crannies and if a fellow chose to hide in one of these, it would be hard to find him even in the middle of a bright day. On a dark night like this, he would be well-nigh invisible.

The mountain was less than half a mile away when the drizzle picked up pace. The clouds descended low into the hills and cast a dark shadow around them. The raindrops became fatter and the drizzle itself grew into a proper rain that was starting to drench the travellers.

The weary feet quickened their pace. Even the ones who were pleading complete exhaustion could be seen attempting to make a dash for the safety of the cave. But they were handicapped by the fact that most of the refugees were carrying a bag, a package or a pouch that prevented them from making rapid progress. The young escorts relieved them of the burden and the group was soon running helter-skelter in the direction of the cave.

The rain again slowed to a light drizzle but their clothes were wet and the chill of the night air had their teeth chattering. The women and children were in bad shape and the Baba wasn't much better.

A voice from their midst suddenly froze everyone in their tracks. 'Can you see those guys walking along the ridge ahead? Who could they be?'

All eyes turned towards the ridge as they tried to follow the direction of his arm. The dark shadow of the mountain made it hard to be sure. Could their eyes be playing tricks with them? They waited impatiently for a flash of lightning to clear the picture.

It didn't take long before the hillside was lit up by another flash. It confirmed the alarm sounded by their observant companion. A long and somewhat ragged line of men could be seen snaking its way down the hill towards them.

Another voice announced, 'It looks like a huge mob of bandits.'

A collective shudder went through the bedraggled group. The young escorts tried their best to reassure them but to no avail. The sinking spirits of the refugees were also bringing down the morale of their defenders. No doubt, the teams of escorts from the two villages had set out with the clear intention of taking their wards to safety. But there is a big difference between the desire to save someone's life and laying down one's life for that cause. Rare is the man who is ready to do the latter. They also knew that while the bandits were out to target the Hindus and Sikhs, their loathing for the Muslim protectors was of an entirely different order of magnitude. The gold and jewellery-laden women from Sihala were on the verge of hysteria and the men were at their wits' end as they tried to control their shrieking.

Another flash of lightning left no room for doubt. They were up against a massive horde and they could see that each one of them was armed with an axe, a spear or a staff and a few of them could also be seen bearing rifles.

If the lightning revealed the presence of the bandits to us, the reverse must also be true, they surmised. They must have seen us too. The only escape now lay in reaching the Sarnihali cave, even though this, too, felt like a bit of a delusion to some. Deep in their hearts, they knew that if the bandits had already seen them, they would chase them down to the ends of the earth. But there was no other option and they started to run towards the entrance of the cave. Maybe this was the last straw for the drowning souls.

Breathless and panting, they somehow managed to reach the entrance of the cave. Naseem didn't pay too much heed to the others. She grabbed the couple of packages that Aziz was carrying, took hold of the Baba's arm and pulled him into a passage in the cave. She could see that the Baba was on the verge of collapse after the strenuous trek.

His forehead was warm and he appeared to be running a fever. Her first priority was to get him into a sheltered place where he could get some rest.

Shivering with cold, stumbling in the dark, legs quivering with each step into the unknown, the Baba followed Naseem without demur. He paused just once, to delve into the folds of his dhoti and take the dagger out from its sheath. Handing it over to Naseem, he gasped, 'Keep this carefully, my child. Take its help if you feel that your honour is in danger. If you have to kill the enemy, do it. And if you have to kill yourself to save your honour, don't hesitate. But don't allow them to take you away alive.' Naseem took the dagger and nodded in assent.

Naseem led him around several bends in the cave until she reached a place where she could feel the soft grass under her feet. She could also hear the gentle gurgling of waters from a spring.

This was the place where the Baba could rest for a while to recoup his strength, Naseem reasoned. Feeling around in the dark with her hands, she identified a patch where he could be comfortable. She opened one of the packages that she had taken from Aziz and without paying any attention to what might be precious or formal, she spread out the clothes to fashion a bed for him.

She helped the Baba lie down on the makeshift bed. The items in the other bundle included a light, double-sided duvet that she used to keep him warm. She knew that his clothes were damp but there was little she could do about it. She sensed that he was still shivering from the cold. Resisting her instinct to check on the fate of her other companions, she knelt down beside him and started massaging his feet and legs to keep him warm and to keep his blood circulation going.

Her own hands were getting numb in the cold, and every minute or two she'd pause to stick her palms under her armpits or to blow her own breath on them to keep them warm. She wanted to dash out of the cave and see if she could help any of their companions but for now, keeping the Baba going was more important. She bit her lip and stayed put.

The first aid that Naseem administered to the Baba played a critical role in keeping him alive that night. She heaved a sigh of relief when she heard the Baba resume his silent chant of 'O Saviour Lord, *save us and take us across...*' His voice trembled as he uttered the words, but it was enough for Naseem to raise her hands to the Lord in a gesture of gratitude.

She was still busy nursing the Baba when she heard a rising clamour outside the cave. Seeing that the Baba was restful, she left his side and hurried towards the entrance.

20

NASEEM LEFT HER sanctuary beside the spring and started to walk in the direction of the voices. It wasn't easy to find her way around in the pitch-dark environs of the cave. The sounds coming from outside were her only guide. She could clearly make out the screams of the women and children, and the bellows of the bandits as they showered abuse on the hapless victims.

She paused for a brief moment, sensing the dangers lurking just outside the cave. But the Baba's dagger gave her a sense of confidence. Reaching into her salwar, she took the dagger out of its sheath and continued on her path.

She paused again, regretting her foolishness. How could she abandon the Baba in that condition and just walk away from him? She took a few steps back, unsure of the direction of her next step. 'Oh God! Save me please! Help me!' The cries for help strengthened her resolve and she started to walk in their direction.

She was in a daze, knowing that she was walking straight into danger, mindful and yet unable to stop herself. With each step forward, she was crying, 'Oye Aziz ... O Rukman bhabi... Bhaaji ... Bhaaji ... where are you?'

Her shouts were meaningless. She found herself stumbling, bumping against the rocks as she made her way out of the cave. Her body was shaking like a leaf in a storm, her mind at a complete loss. On the one hand, she was mortified that she had left the Baba on his own and on the other, she was worried sick about the fate of her family. She ran like a maniac, oblivious of the risk that she could stumble into some unknown crevice, never to be found again.

Somewhere in the distance, she could see a pair of mashaals move rapidly in her direction. Naseem's eyes followed the patches being lit up by their flames. She saw big, fearsome looking characters using their spears, swords, axes to gore or hack down anyone they encountered in their path. She saw an elderly woman cowering in a corner, clutching three small children close to her bosom. A young girl hid behind her, trying to make herself invisible in the shadows. They were spotted by a sword-wielding man and in the flash of an eye, the older woman and children had been reduced to a pile of shapeless corpses. The girl was picked up by a pair of muscular arms and carried off into the darkness.

Naseem found a wedge-shaped boulder that allowed her to watch the unfolding carnage without fear of being spotted by the marauders. The sound of running feet. Huddled bodies illuminated by a passing mashaal. The flash of metal. Cries of terror. A sudden deathly silence. Young women being hauled away on brawny shoulders, legs flailing helplessly. Screams falling on deaf ears. Trunks, baggage, bundles and other loot piled up for distribution. Corpses of men and women kicked around and searched. Earrings and necklaces ripped off the lifeless bodies. Pockets turned inside out and emptied. Clothes torn off to find cash and jewellery tucked away in the folds. A whoop of joy as a man's waistcoat or a woman's salwar yielded an unexpected treasure. Bundles of currency. Gold coins twinkling in the moonlight.

The swords and spears were used with such violence that the victim was usually dead in the first blow. A scream, a moan and then silence. The group following the first lot kept its eye on the bodies. A twitch or whimper and they would return to stab the victim and make sure that he was dead. It was like they had sworn that there would be no survivors from the pathways leading into the cave.

Naseem felt her body go numb with horror as she witnessed the slaughter of the innocent souls. Her head was spinning and her eyelids heavy as she allowed her body to lean against the boulder. She closed her eyes and sank to her knees.

She had no idea how long she stayed in that condition. She tried to move her body, but it refused to pay heed to her commands. When she willed her eyes to open, she could see the early light of pre-dawn filtering into the entrance of the cave. In the distance, she could see a pile of clothes burning in a dark plume of smoke. It wasn't clear if someone had deliberately set them on fire or the fire was the result of a carelessly abandoned mashaal. Patches of grass had taken a reddish hue from large pools of blood. In other places, it had blended into the previous night's rain to form ugly maroon puddles. Naked bodies lay strewn around the uneven tracks, limbs left battered by the violence. There was no sign of any of the marauders. They had completed their gruesome mission and vanished into the night.

Naseem closed her eyes again. She was still in a daze, unsure if she had actually seen what she thought she had. Or maybe it was just an ugly nightmare that would go away. Was she alive? Or was it her spirit that was now roaming the area?

When she opened her eyes again, the fire from the pile of clothes had subsided. The soft glow of dawn had become a little brighter.

She rose to her feet and started to walk towards the glow. She was still in a stupor. She felt that her brain had ceased to work, unable to comprehend or reason. Her legs carried her out of the cave on their own volition. Encountering the crisp morning breeze as she stepped into the open, she found herself regaining her senses.

She walked for a short while up the rocky track leading away from the cave. It was still fairly cloudy and the sun hadn't yet made its appearance. But there was enough light to make out the boulders lying in the direction of the road.

From a distance, she could hear the sound of raised voices. An argument, it seemed. 'My brothers! You are Muslims, and so are we. In the name of Allah and his Prophet, we beg you to let these poor wretches live. They've already seen their homes being destroyed. What do you get by taking their lives? You'll be better off taking all their belongings. Carry away whatever they have.'

In response, a voice could be heard cursing, 'Who says you are Muslims? You are kafirs. Nothing but kafirs helping other kafirs. Now get lost or we'll make sure not one of you sees another day.' Three or four men took a step forward and trained their guns on the group confronting them.

Naseem couldn't believe her ears. She was livid that her brave young escorts were walking into a trap that had been laid out for them by the marauders. They were trying to negotiate with the leaders of the mob to spare the lives of their wards, oblivious about the massacre that had already been carried out near the caves.

The marauders had played a clever hand. A large part of their horde had taken a different route to hide in the vicinity of the cave and set upon their hapless victims as soon as they arrived. Their sanctuary, in effect, had become a death trap. A smaller group from the horde, meanwhile, had come down the road from the hills to engage the escorts in meaningless discussions and keep them away from the cave while their compatriots went about the slaughter.

A long, painful sigh escaped Naseem's lips. She wanted to do something to warn her escorts and was trying to figure out the best way to do this when the squabble between the two sides escalated. Most of the escorts decided that it would be suicidal to take a stand against the opposing force. They could see that the marauders were not only armed with rifles, pistols and other weapons, but also had a few members sporting distinct army attire. Naseem had also seen their heavy army boots and long woollen coats and arrived at the same conclusion.

The ranks of the protectors depleted quickly and in minutes, only four or five were left standing to face a group of some forty or fifty. They made short work of the brave-hearts, shouting 'Ya Allah, Ya Ali!' and disappeared into the forest.

Who were these men who had died at the hands of the marauders? Naseem couldn't see their faces but she surmised with a shudder that they must be from her own family or from the group that had come with them from Chakri. She thought of making the trek up to the road to make sure. But that would take a while. More important to go and find the Baba, she reasoned, as she hurried back towards the cave.

Walking back, she realized that she was still holding the dagger that the Baba had given her to protect her honour. Now that the marauders had all left, she felt safe enough to return it to its sheath and tuck it into her salwar. Her feet picked up pace and she was soon running to the entrance of the cave.

As she entered the cave, her mind started to process everything she had seen. Where was Rukman bhabi? And Boote Shah? And where had Aziz disappeared? She hadn't seen any of them. Had they managed to follow her and find a safe hiding place in the caves? Or had they also perished at the hands of those devils?

The sun had risen and broken free of the clouds. Its light allowed Naseem to see everything more clearly and as she looked at the carnage surrounding her, a dense fog once again started to cast its shadow on her mind. She heard herself wail and cry out the names of each member of her family as her feet flew over the bumpy tracks in the cave. She found herself skirting around bodies, leaping over them, looking for any clues that might reveal the presence of her loved ones. But her cries merely bounced off the heartless rocks, returning to her as multiple echoes reverberating through her skull.

She kept shouting names as she ran, peering closely at every corpse on the way to see if it were a familiar face. Finding none, she decided to concentrate on finding the one whom she had left resting in a safe place. 'Bapuji! Bapuji! Where are you, Bapuji?' She screamed at the top of her voice but to no avail. She ran wherever she thought she might find that small spring, stopping every few steps to see if she could hear its gurgling waters. But there was no sound at all. Nothing.

Every step took her deeper into a state of despair. There was no sign of Aziz, nor of Boote Shah and Rukman. And now, she couldn't even find her beloved Bapuji. Which way should she turn? Who could she ask? The cave appeared to extend till infinity. She might keep walking for ever and still not find its end.

Her throat was hoarse from all the shouting and her legs could no longer carry her. Her frail body was collapsing under the cumulative effect of lack of sleep and utter fatigue from the night's exertions. She wasn't sure how she stumbled. Maybe she accidently tripped over a body or bumped her foot against a stone. But she was unconscious the moment she hit the ground with a thud.

21

'*O SAVIOUR LORD, save us and take us across…*' Naseem heard the mellow notes from a voice doused in spiritual fervour. Her eyes opened a tiny crack to get her bearings. Another second or two and they were wide open as she discovered that her head was comfortably nestled in the Baba's lap.

Like the touch of a feather, the Baba's hand was caressing Naseem's forehead. He breathed a sigh of gratitude as he saw her regain consciousness and felt her head stir in his lap. 'Seema! My child! Are you alright?'

She gazed for an eternity into the old man's loving eyes without lifting her head. Clasping his hands into her own palms, she raised herself and asked, 'Bapuji! It is really you … you…'

'I am right here with you, my child,' he replied.

Naseem's face had a worried look as she stifled a yawn. A question was forming in her eyes and without waiting for it to reach her lips, the Baba replied, 'My child, soon after you left me here, I started to hear the shouts of the marauders and the helpless cries of the victims. I was deeply troubled. There was a massacre taking place so close to me and there was nothing I could do to help anyone. Given the state of my eyes, it was too dark for me to contemplate getting up and moving. So I forced myself to stay put where I was and slowly counted the moments for you to return. Hearing whatever I did, I had this sinking feeling that this was the end of my family. Seema! I've always believed in the destiny that our Lord has chalked out for us, and I've made it a point of not seeking anything beyond that. But for the first time in my life today, I knelt before the Master and pleaded to him, "My Lord! If it was Your will that I should lose everything we had built over the generations, I gratefully accept Your command. But please do not snatch my daughter from me, I beseech You". I prostrated myself on this ground and rubbed my forehead in the soil as I made my submissions. I even prayed to Him, "My Lord! If my daughter's journey in this world has indeed come to an end, give me the opportunity to see her one last time, allow me to shed some tears on her corpse. I'll try to be content with that."'

Looking up towards the heavens, he called, 'Thank you, my Lord! Thank you, a million times! You've listened to my appeal. You've returned my eyes, my walking stick, my support to me…' His eyes welled up with tears that were soon running down his craggy face. This was the first time that she had seen him express his emotions so openly. Soon, she was also sobbing in his lap as she threw her arms around the Baba and clutched him in a child's embrace.

The Baba was left speechless by his own emotions as he cradled Naseem in his hands. Her head nestled against his chest, his fingers gently stroking her head until she had regained her composure.

'Bapuji!' she asked like one who had suddenly remembered something important. 'Let me go once again and check, just in case…'

'It's pointless, my child. Come, sit beside me,' the Baba read her mind and interjected.

'Why do you say that, Bapuji?' she asked, anxiety writ large on her face.

'My child!' the Baba's voice trembled as he spoke. 'We have to show fortitude in the face of this calamity. I am afraid they have all been called by the Lord...'

'All of them?' Naseem queried.

'Yes, my child.'

'Bhaaji too?'

'He was killed by the marauders' bullets.'

'And Aziz?'

'He met his end while fighting them.'

'And Rukman bhabi?'

'I am not sure about her, but I fear that like the other women, she was also captured alive and taken away.'

'And how do you know all this, Bapuji?'

'Once there was a little light, I stepped out to look for you. I saw their bodies near the mouth of the cave. The unfortunate Chaudhry's son Fatta also died along with them. I returned to the cave to look for you and that's when I saw you lying unconscious. It took all my strength to bring you here to safety.'

Naseem felt her body go stone cold as she heard the grim account. There were no tears to shed, no words to be spoken. Her eyes were fixed in the distance, like marbles that had frozen in their place.

After some minutes of silence, she felt an irresistible urge build up inside her. She sprang to her feet and announced, 'Bapuji! I want to go and see them one last time.'

The Baba also took hold of his walking stick, got up and caught his arm. 'Wait, my daughter. Please don't go off again without me. Those who had to leave this world have already gone. Promise me that you won't leave my side as long as I am alive.'

Naseem quietly nodded in assent and took his arm. Walking carefully over the rough surface, they made their way towards the mouth of the cave.

The marauders had achieved their nefarious goals and moved on. They had left behind piles of corpses and pools of blood. Everything owned by the unfortunate refugees had been looted and the younger women had been carted off as spoils. They had left the scene of the massacre with the confidence that they weren't leaving behind a single survivor. It was sheer providence that Naseem had found the Baba a sanctuary where he could escape the savagery of the bandits.

The sun was up and there was a fair amount of light inside the cave as they walked towards its entrance, heading for the place that had allowed Naseem to witness the barbarity unleashed by the bandits.

Their eyes first fell on a heap of four bodies—a woman, two children and a middle-aged man who might have been her husband. The woman and man were lying on top of the young ones; it was evident that they had tried in vain to absorb the blows and save their children from the swords of the assailants. Their bodies were so badly hacked that Naseem was forced to turn her face away. She covered her eyes with her palm to avoid looking at the mutilated corpse of the woman whose neck, nose and ears showed the violence she had suffered as the bandits had impatiently ripped away the jewellery from her dying body.

Moving forward, they continued to encounter bodies strewn across the pathways that led into other sections of the cave. The older women seemed to have met the same fate as the one they had seen earlier. The poor souls who had thought they would save their precious gold and jewellery by wearing it on their person or hiding it in their clothes had suffered the worst fate. The gashes on their faces and bodies and the way their clothes were shredded stood mute testimony to the savagery with which their ornaments were taken. As she walked through the scene of the bloodbath, Naseem couldn't help observing that the corpses represented all the men, the older women, and the children in their caravan. There was no trace of any of the younger women, including the five or six who had fled straight from the wedding in their village. Nor could she see any sign of the woman who had walked alongside her the previous night, recounting the horrors that had taken place in her village. Moving a step ahead of the Baba as she held his arm, Naseem forced herself to look carefully at the faces of all the female victims but failed to spot Rukman among them. She reluctantly acknowledged that the Baba must be right in his assessment that the younger women had all been abducted by the bandits.

They moved in grim silence, looking at the carnage around them as they finally emerged out of the cave. The clouds had parted and the sun was rising towards its zenith. The rocky terrain outside the cave was also littered with corpses. Naseem asked the Baba to rest near the boulder that had provided her shelter during the pre-dawn hours and allowed her to see the bloodbath as it unfolded. Telling the Baba that she would be back soon, she moved ahead to take a look. Her eyes first fell on the body of Chaudhry Fazal Karim's son Fatta. Two of his compatriots also lay by his side. Poor souls. They had come to provide protection to the Baba and his family and had given up their own lives in their mission.

Naseem looked at each of them with the kind of gratitude and reverence one reserves for a saint or a spiritual guru. She was unable to control the flow of tears pouring to the hallowed soil where they had fallen. Her mind replayed the same line over and over again, 'Ah! Why did we have to include these young men with us and bring such a fate upon them? We knew that our family was the one in trouble. We had to deal with that. Why did these poor fellows have to lose their lives?' She braced herself and kept moving.

She didn't have to go far before locating the two persons that she had set out to find. The bodies of Boote Shah and Aziz lay close to each other, riddled with bullets and pierced by the sharp steel of spears. Looking at them, Naseem thought that maybe they had chosen to stay by each other's side even when they left this world.

She fell on their bodies and sobbed. 'My brothers! O my dear brothers!' she cried as she embraced the lifeless body of one and then the other. The anguish in her voice beseeched the divine spirits to come just this one time and wake her sleeping brothers from their slumber. But none appeared to rouse the ones who had already left for their eternal journey.

She took a while to gather her senses, her own clothes marked with the blood of her brothers as she lifted herself to her feet. Remembering that she had left the Baba alone, she retraced her steps back towards him. The incessant flow of tears made it hard to see the ground ahead as she walked.

As soon as she reached the Baba, her valiant efforts to steady herself melted. Her tormented cries echoed across the rocky landscape as she sought solace in his embrace. She wanted to tell him what her eyes had seen but she couldn't find the words. Deep, anguished sobs that came from the pits of her stomach were the only vocabulary left with to share her feelings.

The Baba's demeanour helped her calm down and she gazed at his face with awe. It bore not the slightest trace of pain or anger. His countenance appeared untouched by the sheer loss they had experienced. His voice was clear, and his tone was steady as he recited, 'O Saviour Lord, save us and take us across...'

He paused for a second and drew in his breath as he responded to Naseem's grief-stricken sobs. 'This is the will of the Lord, my child.

Fortitude, that's what we need. None among us can change His will. None.'

His measured words, his belief in the immutable destiny, however, had an unexpected impact on Naseem. The intensity of her sobs increased, as did the flow of tears from her eyes. Beside herself with grief, she collapsed into his lap and clutched at his clothes.

The Baba caressed her head and stroked her back as he tried to soothe her frayed nerves. Her sobs gradually quietened, and her breathing returned to a more even rhythm.

Naseem's eyes were closed as her mind soaked in the healing effect of the Baba's chanting and her body started to relax in response to his gentle ministrations. She felt herself move into a state of deep detachment. The impact of all that she had seen and experienced over the last few hours was being erased, a slate being wiped clean of all the misspelt words and flawed images. Looking at the Baba's serene countenance, Naseem started to experience the true spirit behind the words, 'O Saviour Lord, save us and take us across...' She felt herself transported into a tranquillity that she had seldom experienced. Each word coming from the Baba's lips was like a balm on her tortured soul, a nectar that was coursing through her veins to nurse her back to health. Her body felt lighter, her soul set free to soar above her troubles and discover a different sense of being.

The Baba's hand stopped moving as he sensed that Naseem was now breathing deeply and had fallen asleep. He knew that Naseem was exhausted in mind and body and desperately needed the rest to rejuvenate her. He gazed at her the way a mother would gaze at a baby that she is nursing. His hands were now still but his lips were still moving with 'O Saviour Lord, save us and take us across...'

22

THE CLOUDS HAD dispersed and the sun was ablaze in all its glory. Naseem was still sleeping in the Baba's lap. His legs had stayed motionless for an eternity and he could feel the pins and needles in his feet. But he stayed still, willing himself to avoid any movement that might disturb the sleeping girl.

When Naseem finally opened her eyes, the Baba gave her the doting gaze of a loving mother and said, 'Get up, my child. This is no time to sleep. The ones who have left this world have been spared our trials and tribulations. But we have to set our mind to getting out of this place and reaching a safe destination.'

Naseem's eyes opened wide as she looked at the Baba. She thought that his words weren't entering her mind through her ears. They were piercing her skin and reaching straight into the depths of her heart. Her soul, which had been traversing through valleys of great tranquillity, was summoned to return immediately to its moorings. The nightmarish scenes of the previous night began appearing before her eyes.

Naseem could hear a cacophony build inside her, each new voice exploding with the violence of a cannon. 'My dear brother Aziz is dead ... my older brother has also been killed ... Rukman bhabi has been abducted … Bapu's precious trunk, the one worth some twenty or twenty-five thousand rupees according to the Chaudhry, has been stolen … my own little trunk has also vanished…'

'Please don't cry, my child,' Naseem felt the Baba's trembling hand stroke her head. 'What are you crying for, silly girl … No one in this world of ours belongs to anyone forever. The amount of time we are allotted with each other is already destined. That's how this life is. We journey together for a while and then we go our separate ways. This world of ours … it's like an inn on a roadside, my child. You meet, and you part. So put an end to this business of crying and bow your head before the Lord in submission. Submit to the Lord…'

'Submit to the Lord!' Naseem's mind focused on that simple phrase. The Baba was still speaking but she didn't hear anything else. Submit to the Lord. Those words seemed to rejuvenate something within her, giving her renewed energy and purpose.

A little while later, the Baba's hand was leaning on Naseem's shoulder for support and they were walking together. The Baba was matching his pace with Naseem's and was saying something as they walked. But she was no longer paying attention. 'Submit to the Lord.' Those words were getting embossed loud and clear on her heart as she walked, her mind concentrating on the message and shutting out all distractions.

Her head was lowered as she walked. She was paying obeisance, not to some shrine made of bricks and mortar, but to one that was located in a distant spiritual realm. It wasn't so long ago that a carefree old fakir passing by her home had shown her its location.

> The Creator resides within you
> Submit to the Lord, whatever you do…

She remembered the verses of the fakir as they echoed in the depths of her being. Somewhere along the way, they made their way to her lips and she was gently humming them as she walked.

After being shaken by the turmoil and tragedy of the recent past, Naseem felt her mind again being transported into a serene space. She had finally found a sense of stillness, a calm that had resolutely eluded her over the last few days. The fakir's melodious verses were cleansing her heart; she sensed a dark cloud leave her body and float into the sky, carrying with it all the intense grief of losing loved ones and the profound fear of what the morrow might bring.

As she walked in the cave with the Baba, she felt a new lightness in her being. The weight of sorrow and fear had lifted, the sobs and sighs were replaced with a sense of anticipation. The despair in her eyes was replaced with a new resolve, the faltering steps had discovered a fresh wellspring of energy. When she lifted her head to look at the Baba, their eyes locked and their lips appeared to move in unison as they sang:

> Let Allah o Allah be your song
> And leave those sighs so painful and long
> The Creator resides within you
> Submit to the Lord, whatever you do...

Swaying gently to the rhythm of the melody, they made their way carefully through the cave. The pools of blood, the corpses spread-eagled across their path could neither halt their steps nor still their voices. They had transcended the reality of the cave even as it reeked of violence and death. They were in a realm of their own, floating away in a flying chariot that was carrying them into the skies.

Naseem found herself repeating the last lines of the fakir's song:

Will pull you down, this sorrow of yours
And drown you in its deathly wave
Like a boat so frail, these eyes of yours
Filled to the brim, pose danger grave
Let Allah o Allah be your song
And leave those sighs so painful and long.

As she finished the verses, a wave of self-belief ran through her body. Gone was the feeling of being frail or vulnerable. She felt that she had the power to take on the whole world and to change it if she had to.

The ways of the Lord are truly mysterious. How can one explain the transformation of a soul by the touch of a song? The helpless cries of yesterday turning into today's soothing melody? Surely there must be a strong, invisible force that enabled Mansour to chant 'Ana al-Haq' even as he was hanging from a noose. Or think of Bhai Matidas who was sawn into two halves and calmly sang, *'I find this saw ever so sweet'* as he died. What is this unseen, unfathomable power that the human mind just can't comprehend?

It appeared that both the Baba and Naseem had been touched by the rays of that unique sun which endows its chosen ones with such powers. How else could the heart-rending cries of this sensitive young girl abruptly have transformed into a soulful melody?

The song ended and the Baba found himself being hurled back into the reality confronting them. He gazed at Naseem for a while, reflecting on the speed with which his expansive world had shrunk. His universe was now limited to this eighteen-year-old girl, no more and no less. All his hopes and aspirations were encompassed within her slender frame.

In the flow of the fakir's song, Naseem too had lost track of her journey. As the song finished, she looked around and saw that they were standing amidst the very same corpses over which she had cried not so long ago. She sank to the ground beside their lifeless bodies, unable to move until the Baba grasped her arm and pulled her back to her feet. As she stood up, Naseem found the dark clouds of grief and despair again beginning to rise within her. The dam of tears had burst its banks and was flowing freely down her face.

How to leave this place? Which way to go? Even as they pondered over these questions, there was a more pressing matter before them. What should they do about the corpses? They couldn't just leave them there in the open. This much was sure.

After some deliberation, they decided that it would be best to reach the road and try to seek the help of a passing army truck. The surge in communal violence had created hectic military activity in the area, with army trucks going back and forth as they tried to ferry survivors to the safety of refugee camps that had sprung up in places like Chakwal. They were also collecting dead bodies from massacre sites like this one so that they could be granted their last rites.

They knew that going to the road carried its own hazards. They would be sitting ducks if another mob passed that way before an army truck. But there seemed no other option. Besides, they had reached a state of mind where they were no longer afraid of confronting Death. They had lived in its shadow and witnessed it at close quarters.

Before heading for the road, they decided to go to the cave and pick up a few clothes and other essentials for the journey. They had barely walked a few minutes and were near the entrance of the cave when the Baba signalled for her to stop. He had spotted a couple of scrawny dogs chewing into a body that already looked badly mutilated.

'Seema! My child, if we leave this place now, we can be sure that these dogs are going to mangle all the bodies,' the Baba observed.

'What do you suggest we do, Bapuji?'

'I suggest,' the Baba looked around and paused briefly before replying, 'that you look around and see if we can find an axe or some other weapon that they might have left behind.'

Naseem set off without asking why the Baba wanted some kind of weapon at a time like this. She didn't have to go far before she spotted a broken spear, a couple of axes and a dagger. She collected everything and took it across to the Baba, who was sitting on a rock besides the bodies of Boote Shah and Aziz. Placing the weapons at his feet, she mentioned that she also had the dagger that the Baba had given her.

'These axes should serve the purpose,' the Baba said as he took one in his hand and gave the other one to Naseem.

It didn't need much effort to dig a pit. The area was full of natural hollows and trenches. The Baba selected a largish hollow that was close by and turned to Naseem to outline his plan.

They abandoned their intent of going to the road for help and got to work on their arduous project, lifting the bodies by the arms and legs and heaving them into the hollow.

It was tough work and it needed a hardened soul to carry out. And who was doing it? A seventy-year-old man and a wispy eighteen-year-old girl. God alone knows where they found the mental and physical strength to perform the task. Without a thought to their weary bodies, they searched the caves for the corpses and paused only after they were sure that they had carried every single one of them to their final resting place.

It took four or five hours to finish their grim project, leaving them psychologically drained and physically exhausted. They were also hungry and thirsty and their clothes were soaked in the blood of the bodies that they had carried. They stopped to rest besides a small stream and washed the blood off their hands and feet.

'Let's begin, Bapuji,' Naseem urged as she rose to her feet. She picked up an axe and started hacking at the dense shrubs that were scattered around the stream. The Baba also got up and joined her with his axe. After an hour or two of strenuous effort, they had managed to put together a sizeable pile of branches, twigs and leaves. The next step was to reach into the pile, pick up whatever they could carry in their arms and spread it over the bodies in the hollow. They continued until they were sure that all the bodies were properly covered with leaves and branches and not a single naked limb could be seen from any direction. The Baba looked at Naseem's hands and took a deep breath as he saw the patches of raw skin and blisters caused from wielding the axe.

'You must be tired, my child?' he asked with all the affection of a loving father.

'I am absolutely exhausted, Bapuji,' she replied without hesitation.

'But it's going to be dark soon, my dear,' he continued tenderly. 'I wish we had the time to rest. I feel it would be prudent if we can somehow manage to reach Dhurnaali during the night. There is a road from there that goes to Khaurh and we might find an army lorry on that route.'

'Then let's move, Bapuji,' she responded as she rose to her feet. The Baba felt a trifle embarrassed at being forced to push her but there was no option.

They went back into the cave to retrieve the couple of bundles that had their remaining possessions. When they emerged back into the open, the sun had also completed a long and weary day and left their environs submerged in a sea of inky darkness.

The path they had chosen to Dhurnaali was a gruelling one, rough and irregular. It rolled through high rocks and dense undergrowth, the track no more than an indistinct shadow on which the two of them treaded uncertainly. It was becoming darker with every step, making their journey even more tortuous as they proceeded.

The Baba knew these winding tracks like the lines on his calloused palm. Over the years, he had walked every inch of this land and knew the area intimately. But his poor eyesight was proving to be a real handicap and he was forced to rely on Naseem. 'As we emerge from the cave, there is a narrow track on the left,' he had told Naseem. 'That's the one we have to follow. Any departure from the track and we may get lost forever in this desolate jungle. It takes no time to lose your bearings once you make that mistake. We have to cling to this track until we cross the Soan and reach a peepul tree so large that it resembles a banyan. That peepul will tell us that we have crossed into Dhurnaali.'

They were carrying a bundle each as they walked. The Baba had slung his package behind his back, while Naseem had perched hers on her head. Neither appeared mindful of the fact that their clothes were encrusted in blood that had dried a while back.

Naseem had to stay alert and vigilant as they made their way along the track. Her left hand was on her head to keep the bundle in place, while the right palm kept a firm grip on the Baba's hand as it rested on her shoulder. She was afraid that a single misstep could see the Baba stumbling on the rough surface. But the bigger worry was that she might lose sight of the track in the dark and lead them into disaster.

The Baba had his walking stick in his right hand while the left hand didn't dare leave Naseem's shoulder as they gingerly made their way along the track. He was humming some verses that helped break the intense silence of the night as they walked:

> *Recite the name of Lord Ram and keep your mind at peace,*
> *He will solve your troubles, our Lord Ram Chandra...*

The jungle extended for miles in each direction, a gloomy and menacing presence as they walked. Naseem had joined the Baba in his chanting and the line 'He will solve your troubles, our Lord Ram Chandra' seemed to banish her fears each time she got anxious about getting lost in the forest.

A puff of cool breeze suddenly wafted across Naseem's face. She could hear a gentle sound coming from the distance. It must be an angel, she thought, sitting in the middle of the forest and strumming his tambourine to produce music so exceptional that it had to be divine.

'Bapuji,' she interrupted his chant of 'He will solve your troubles…' as she spoke. 'What's this sound we hear?'

'It's the Soan, my child,' he replied.

Naseem's spirits rose as she got his confirmation. Her steps quickened and her mind sang, 'My Soan … my childhood companion … my friend … my Soan.'

A few minutes later, Naseem was on the banks of the river. She had set aside the bundle that she'd been carrying on her head and was flapping her legs in its cool waters. The Baba had also placed his bundle on the ground and was leaning back against a rock to rest. He closed his eyes but his lips continued to chant the verses.

Naseem was like a five-year-old child who had discovered the joys of the river for the very first time. She was splashing its water with her hands and feet while her mind was having its own conversation with the river. 'Hello, dear waters of my Soan! Did you pass through our Chakri before coming to this place? Did you touch the soil of our village on your way? I'll never forget you, my ever so sweet and gentle Soan. Will I ever get the chance to laze on your banks? Will I join the other girls and swim in your waters again? Ah! My dear dear…'

Her train of thought came to an abrupt halt as she felt a hand rest on her shoulder. It was like someone had suddenly shut her up in the middle of a conversation. The Baba was looking at her with a tired smile as he said, 'Silly girl! Abandon these foolish thoughts for now and get up, my child. We still have quite a way to go.'

Naseem shook herself to bring her mind back to reality. Getting up and placing the bundle back on her head, she asked, 'Where are we heading now, Bapuji?'

The Baba also picked up his bundle and slung it over his shoulder before turning towards her. 'Why don't you ask these waters, my child … Find out if they will tell you their destination.'

'But Bapuji,' Naseem took a deep breath and mumbled, 'will we never come back to our motherland?'

The Baba recoiled from her question. His lips wanted to say 'No' or at the very least, he wanted to convey the same message through a shake of his head. But that single word took an entirely different shape as it emerged from his mouth, his hoarse throat producing an out-of-tune version:

> Let Allah o Allah be your song
> And leave those sighs so painful and long…

The verse made Naseem forget her painful question. She gathered her salwar and pulled it up to her knees, took the Baba's hand and carefully led him across the shallow waters of the river. As they reached the other bank, the gentle gurgling of the waters blended into the divine notes of the tambourine that she had heard earlier. The Soan appeared to be humming 'Allah o Allah' and the music uplifted her soul once again.

They had walked less than a mile from the river when Naseem spied the grey outline of what appeared to be a huge mound. Looking more carefully as they approached it, she discerned that this was the giant peepul tree that the Baba had mentioned. The roots of the tree were spread like tentacles across a vast area, each one taking a menacing form in the pitch-dark night and producing an eerie sound as the wind rustled through the leaves.

The two weary travellers were walking through this unnatural landscape without a clear idea of their destination. Seen from a distance, they looked like two frail shadows trudging forward into the night, their shoulders bent under the weight of their memories. Their eyes carried the grim picture of the horrors they had witnessed over the last twenty-four hours, their lips pursed as they reflected on the loss of their motherland.

The Baba's walking stick was striking an uneven rhythm on the rocky terrain. His lips parted to let out a painful sigh before settling into a quavering voice that resonated through the night:

'O Saviour Lord, save us and take us across...'

Afterword

Navdeep Suri

Aᴸᵀᴱᴿ THE UNEXPECTED accolades surrounding the publication of *Khooni Vaisakhi: A Poem from the Jallianwala Bagh Massacre, 1919* (Harper Perennial, 2019), I started to think about my next translation project. I was committed to taking up other literary works of my grandfather Nanak Singh, but the choice wasn't easy. As the Father of the Punjabi novel, our Bauji had left behind a vast treasure chest of thirty-eight novels, along with several collections of short stories, plays and even an autobiography. Which one to choose?

A serious discussion ensued within the family. How about *Ik Mian Do Talwaran* (1960), the Sahitya Akademi award-winning novel about the Ghadar movement and the life of freedom fighter Kartar Singh Sarabha? Or, why not *Chitta Lahu* (1932), the novel that many critics regard his absolute masterpiece? Somewhere during these debates at our home in Amritsar, the conversation veered towards his Partition novels. Bauji had written four within the span of just over four years, between 1947 and 1950. Of these, *Khoon de*

227

Sohile (1948) and its sequel *Agg di Khed* (1948) are widely regarded as a contemporaneous account of the Partition, while *Manjhdhaar* (1949) and *Chittarkar* (1950) take up the post-Partition trauma of the refugees.

Even as these deliberations were underway, the Government of India announced ambitious plans to celebrate the seventy-fifth anniversary of India's independence. It would be a grand carnival of India's accomplishments over the seven and a half decades since that famous tryst with destiny on 15 August 1947, we were told. But what about the Partition, which was the flipside of the same independence? What about the price paid by Punjab and Bengal—the millions who were forced to flee their ancestral homes, the hundreds of thousands who were killed in the most senseless sectarian frenzy the world had ever seen? On the eve of Independence Day in 2021, the government announced that 14 August would henceforth be commemorated as the 'Partition Horrors Remembrance Day'. But the intent behind this belated move isn't clear at this point. Would it serve to inflame communal passions once again? Or would it also carry a message of healing, as my grandfather attempted through his novels…

It had to be those two—*Khoon de Sohile* and *Agg di Khed*—if only to provide some additional context and texture to the seventy-fifth anniversary. I'd read both books as a teenager but didn't recall too much of the storyline. Reading them now from the perspective of a translator provided fresh insights into the mind of my own grandfather—an opportunity to appreciate Bauji's unwavering commitment to humanity, his abiding respect for other faiths even as he remained a devout Sikh, his loathing of communal and sectarian elements and his courage and honesty in telling the story as he saw it.

In an essay written in his autobiography *Meri Duniya* (1949, updated subsequently), he laments that his idea of a united India was rudely shattered by the Partition. To use his own words, 'My readers would bear witness that each time I pick up the pen, my words reflect my deepest desire to see a united, independent India. The plots in my novels may have varied but their purpose was unambiguous—to foster unity between Hindus, Muslims and Sikhs and to warn against the perils of falling prey to communal forces...

'Through my writings over the years, I had conjured in my own mind this image of an independent nation where the unity and amity amongst its peoples were its two brightest jewels—an image that became ever more vivid as we marched towards independence. I could never imagine that a crazed bloodlust would hit our nation with the force of a tornado, its gusts carrying away everything that I held sacred and shattering the image of Mother India that I had nursed with such fervour.'

He writes of the mind-numbing savagery that he witnessed on the streets of Amritsar and his own helplessness in doing anything to provide comfort, barring the one occasion when 'he could somehow save a group of Muslim women from the raging flames at a mosque in Chowk Paragdas and get them safely on a truck that was heading for Pakistan.'

And he acknowledges that the havoc wrought by the Partition left him in a state of acute depression. He spent the days brooding, unable to sleep or eat. His family got especially worried when he started to lose weight and finally persuaded him to see a doctor from Guru Ramdas Hospital. The doctor administered a plethora of Western medicines and vitamins, along with a set of twelve expensive injections. But to no avail. He wanted to write, to find an outlet for the darkness building within him but neither his mind nor his body were up to the challenge. His family struggled with ways to entertain him, getting him books to read and even taking him to the cinema hall. Nothing worked. Listless and morose, he drifted from one day to the next until his exasperated wife, our much-loved Bhabiji, told him that maybe he should try to find some solace in the Sikh scriptures. He agreed and reluctantly started to turn the pages of the holy Guru Granth Sahib. I was therefore not surprised to learn that the novel's title Khoon de Sohile comes from a verse of the Guru Granth Sahib: 'Khoon ke sohile gaviai Nanak rat ka kungu pae ve laalo.' It is believed that Guru Nanak composed these lines after having witnessed the devastation caused by the first Mughal emperor Babur's invasions of north India between 1519 and 1526. The four hymns written by Guru Nanak are collectively called 'Babur Vani'. The lines can be translated as: 'The paeans of blood are sung, O Nanak, and blood is sprinkled in place of saffron...' The reference to saffron is poignant because it was sprinkled on clothes at the time of weddings as a celebratory tradition.

Coming back to our Bauji's story: the first few days were hard, and he struggled to concentrate. But he soon found himself drawn into the hymns and began to appreciate the true meaning of the verses. He felt lighter as he immersed himself deeper into the text, rediscovering a spiritual dimension that he had cherished in his younger days. He would wait for the family to go to sleep, for the clatter of bullets, of exploding bombs and of shrieking victims in the streets around him to subside. And he would quietly tiptoe up to the rooftop to close his eyes and meditate. To his own surprise, he still retained the ability to disconnect from the immediate, to feel his untethered soul soar into the unknown. He found that he could once again experience that unique feeling of bliss, that ecstasy which comes from the stillness of mind.

With that stillness, he also quickly regained his health. That familiar itch to pick up the pen and write was back. His mind was buzzing but he needed some solitude. His family acquiesced as he packed his bag and took a bus for the sleepy little hill town of Dharamshala on 1 August 1948. This had been something of an annual ritual for him over the last fifteen years or so, going up to Dharamshala for a month or two in summer and returning each year with a fresh novel. He describes Dharamshala as one of the less attractive hill stations of the north, not quite comparable with the charms of Dalhousie, Kullu-Manali or Kashmir. But the upper floor of a small house in a predominantly Muslim area of the McLeod Ganj suburb of Dharamshala, the hospitality of its owner Munshi Abdullah and the company of a bunch of adorable kids from the neighbourhood had combined to make it especially salubrious for his pursuits. Over the years, he had developed a strong affection for Dharamshala.

As he left for Dharamshala that morning, he recalled his previous visit in July 1947 when the situation in Punjab was going from bad to worse. Taking advantage of a short lull in violence, he set aside the warnings from friends and family to board the familiar bus. His mind was humming with everything that he had seen and heard over the past few months, and he desperately yearned for the quiet of the hills so that he could put pen to paper. The warnings, however, proved accurate and he was forced to pack his bags early and return to Amritsar barely a fortnight before the convulsions of Partition were unleashed in full measure. He writes in *Meri Duniya* that among his modest baggage as he clambered aboard the bus from Dharamshala was the semi-finished manuscript of this novel. Going by the timelines gleaned from his autobiography, I would assume that he completed the novel in Amritsar during the ensuing weeks. It's lengthy foreword, drenched in his own anguish over the Partition, was written in February 1948.

While working on this translation, I had several conversations about the book with my father, each one revealing something new about our own family. He reminded me of our old home at 489, Green Avenue—the one that he had built in 1968 after we moved from the cramped quarters of Gali Punjab Singh in the walled city. Do you remember the mango tree near the gate in the front yard? I do, I responded. It had those small juicy mangoes from Illumdin's orchard near Bauji's home in Preet Nagar. 'Yes, but there's a story behind the seedling from which that tree grew,' he said, smiling. 'Your mother and I shared that particular mango and lovingly placed its pit in the spot where you now see that huge tree. We were inspired by the story of the mango tree and it's link with the eternal love of Naseem and Yusuf in *Khoon de Sohile* and *Agg di Khed!*' Really? As kids, we had seen that tree grow from a little sapling but never knew the story behind it. And now, even as I am immersed in Yusuf and Naseem's world again while translating *Agg di Khed* (to be published next year), it seems fitting that my wife insists that we do the same in the home that we are building in a newer suburb in Amritsar. With a mango from the same tree to carry forward the legacy!

My father and I also spoke at length about the Partition. He was fifteen at the time and had some fairly lucid memories as a teenager growing up in Amritsar during that period. Three of his recollections stand out. He had a vivid recall of the time Bauji came home with blood-soaked clothes after he had rescued a couple of Muslim girls from being butchered by a Sikh mob. My father also spoke of the day he had accompanied his older brother and one of his more adventurous cousins to Maanawala railway station on the outskirts of Amritsar. This was the preferred stop for relief trains to pick up Muslim refugees as they sped towards Lahore. A train that had been waylaid by rampaging mobs on its way from Delhi was standing at the platform and my father remembered the horror of seeing scores of dead bodies spilling out of the doors and windows of the carriages.

In one of our conversations, I probed him further. Yes, there were people he knew who had joined in the arson and looting of Muslim shops and homes. Some of them were from our own neighbourhood and later, after some hesitancy, he revealed that one of them was close to us. It was chilling to know how far the hatred had seeped in and that someone from our own circles had indulged in savagery of this kind! But had he or any of his brothers been tempted to pick up a knife or sword and join other youngsters of his age to attack Muslims? No, he responded firmly. Bauji's unequivocal position had perhaps provided them with some inoculation against the pestilence. They also knew that any drift towards that direction would invoke Bauji's wrath.

Translating this book was also a learning of a different kind. Having grown up in Amritsar during the 1960s and 1970s, we had little appreciation of the close social engagement amongst communities in the Pothohar region in undivided India. We came of age amidst the Indo-Pak wars of 1965 and 1971 and the reality of Pakistan-backed Khalistani terrorism in Punjab in the 1980s, peppered every now and then with some elder's lurid stories of the massacre of friends and relatives by the murderous Muslims. Amritsar itself had been largely depopulated of Muslims during the Partition, the desolate masjids of the walled city standing as mute witness to its once thriving Muslim community. For the average Amritsari during those days, contact with Muslims was limited to the occasional visits by Kashmiri or Afghan businessmen who continued to maintain their traditional links with traders in Amritsar. The 'othering' of our erstwhile neighbours was complete.

Lahore, for long regarded as Amritsar's larger and more influential twin was still a mere forty miles away. But a city that my parents could visit in the late 1950s and early 60s to see cricket matches was now a distant mirage. I have friends in Amritsar who have travelled the globe but haven't contemplated a visit to Lahore, inhibited by cumbersome visa regulations as much as by some lingering antipathy. And if Lahore is distant, the rural areas around Rawalpindi where this book is situated might as well be from another planet.

Translating this book provided me a window into those areas, into the texture of life in a part of rural Punjab that now lies on the other side, a glimpse into its sights and sounds, into its colours and contours. It also brought home the message that Bauji was trying to convey through his characters. The machinations of the Muslim League were evident, and the violence inflicted on the hapless Hindu and Sikh communities of the Pothohar was real and he portrays it in all its gory detail. But the bonds between the communities were equally real and the raw courage of some of the Muslim protagonists while trying to save their Hindu and Sikh neighbours is palpable.

In trying to deal with the trauma of Partition, the book provides a message of healing that is as relevant today as it was seventy-five years ago.

Amritsar
20 January 2022

Nanak Singh (1897–1971) is widely regarded as the father of the Punjabi novel. With little formal education beyond the fourth grade, he wrote an astounding fifty-nine books, which included thirty-eight novels and an assortment of plays, short stories, poems, essays and even a set of translations. He received the Sahitya Akademi Award in 1962 for *Ik Mian Do Talwaraan*. His novel *Pavitra Paapi* was made into a film in 1968, while *Chitta Lahu* was translated into the Russian by Natasha Tolstoy.

Navdeep Suri is a former diplomat who has served in India's diplomatic missions in Washington, D.C., and London. He was India's ambassador to Egypt and UAE, High Commissioner to Australia and Consul General in Johannesburg. Navdeep has been striving to preserve the legacy of his grandfather Nanak Singh and to bring his works to a wider audience. He has translated into English the classic 1930s Punjabi novels *Pavitra Paapi* (*The Watchmaker*) and *Adh Khidya Phul* (*A Life Incomplete*). His translation of Nanak Singh's lost poem *Khooni Vaisakhi* was published in 2019 and continues to be in the news and media mentions.

THE SEQUEL TO *HYMNS IN BLOOD*

A GAME OF FIRE
by Nanak Singh
translated by Navdeep Suri

1947. Amritsar. In a shelter near the Golden Temple complex, Hindu and Sikh refugees come together to find solace from the terror and bloodbath they have escaped. Satnam Singh, the leader of the local Ittihad Sabha, directs his group of volunteers to provide meals and protection to a new group of people who have just arrived. Among the newcomers, he is struck by the extraordinary sea of calm that surrounds an erudite-looking old man, with a long flowing beard, and his companion, a young woman with determination written on her face.

Meanwhile, Satnam's old friends are swept up in the winds of change and want to seek revenge by starting a chain of communal violence. *A Game of Fire* takes the story of the Partition forward from *Hymns in Blood* by following Satnam as he makes new friends and moves between deep despair and steadfastness. He wants to hold on to the values of humanity and brotherhood he believes in but faces a new challenge in every step. Against the backdrop of emerging fissures in a new country and its communities, *Agg di Khed* paints the picture of a changing city that remains as relevant today as it did when it was first published in 1948.

A compelling portrait of Punjab in the 1920s. Originally published in Punjabi in 1940, *Adh Kidhiya Phool* is an intense meditation on the choices people make and the consequences these may have. The author's engagement with social issues like superstition and blind faith, religious bigotry, casteism and the emancipation of women seems as fresh and relevant today as it did when he wrote this book. Fluently translated by Navdeep Suri, *A Life Incomplete* introduces a stalwart of Punjabi literature to a new readership.

ALSO BY NANAK SINGH

Jallianwala Bagh. 13 April 1919. Twenty-two-year-old Nanak Singh joins the mass of peaceful protestors agitating against the Rowlatt Act. What then turns out to be one of the worst atrocities perpetrated by the British Raj, and a turning point in India's independence movement, also becomes a life-changing experience for Nanak Singh. After going through the traumatic experience, he proceeds to write *Khooni Vaisakhi*, a scathing critique of the British Raj. The poem was banned soon after its publication in May 1920. After sixty long years, it was rediscovered and has been translated into English for the first time by the author's grandson, Navdeep Suri. *Khooni Vaisakhi* is not only a poignant piece of protest literature but also a resurrected witness to how Sikhs, Hindus and Muslims came together to stand up to oppression in one of India's darkest moments.